The Unwrapping of T..........

'Absolutely fucking glorious' Rachael Lucas, author of *The Telephone Box Library*

'I guarantee you won't have read a Christmas story like *The Unwrapping of Theodora Quirke* before – but that's what makes it marvellous. It's clever and inventive, ballsy and beautiful, never saccharine but always startling in its revelations about life, love and loss. A remarkable, funny, truly redemptive read. I flippin' loved it!' Miranda Dickinson, author of *The Day We Meet Again*

'A cracking Christmas story full of warmth, wisdom and deliciously sweary Northern characters' Alex Brown, author of *The Great Christmas Knit Off*

'Deliciously told and witty, dripping with darkly festive wisdom' Helen Lederer, comedian and founder of Comedy Women in Print (CWIP)

'Caroline delivers Christmas magic with a gut punch, conjuring up the truly spectacular from a decidedly broken and ugly world. It might change your view of Christmas forever' Amanda Brooke, author of *The Widows' Club*

'Beautifully written, full of Northern humour (and soul), somehow both magical and down-to-earth, *The Unwrapping Of Theodora Quirke* is a cracker' Keris Stainton, author of *The Bad Mothers' Book Club*

'A sparkly festive tale with all the wit, warmth and irreverence that its Liverpool setting is famed for' Debbie Johnson, author of *Maybe One Day*

'A cracker of a Christmas rollercoaster! I loved it' Luke Cutforth

99 Reasons Why:

'Caroline Smailes and Will Self are arch-experimentalists' *The Observer*

'Witty and touching' *The Guardian*

'A new digital novel will overturn centuries of literary tradition by allowing readers to choose how they would like a story to end…' *The Independent*

'In a radical departure from literary tradition, author Caroline Smailes' latest work *99 Reasons Why* has a choice of eleven possible endings' *The Telegraph*

Like Bees to Honey:

'*Like Bees to Honey* is a didactic story that deals with an array of important issues including family, trust, grief, love, religion and faith – a thought-provoking, intense book that treats the topics of life and death with a serious pen, yet includes a tongue-in-cheek-tone that keeps it from falling into depressing depths' *The Sunday Times of Malta*

'… an up-and-coming author' *The Times*

'... a sparkler in the shape of a fiction book' *The Times of Malta*

'Haunting, heartfelt and beautiful' Chris Cleave, author of *The Other Hand/Little Bee*

'This book contains many hilarious scenes between Nina and the spirits! Jesus makes his entrance with a passion for Cisk beer, ruby red toenails and a desire to ask questions about Paul O'Grady. But to get the feeling of the book, one has to read it all' *The Malta Independent*

Black Boxes:

'... vivid descriptions of the body as a battleground and pleasure-zone reminded me of Angela Carter and Jeanette Winterson' *Big Issue North* No.756 19-25 January 2009

'*Black Boxes* is the best novel I have read all year. I laughed, I cried and I cried some more. And came away a changed person' *American Chronicle*

'The character's [Pip's] account of being picked on in class is likely to strike a chord with many readers' *Liverpool Daily Post*

In Search of Adam:

'There is little in the way of relief in this harrowing first novel, but Smailes' sensitivity towards her subjects – and the poetry of her writing – carry the story' *Financial Times*

'A unique, exciting and unforgettable read' Ray Robinson, author of *Electricity*

'*In Search of Adam* by Caroline Smailes – an absolutely wonderful and original book by a talented author who is north west-based' *The Guardian*

'Staccato prose that crackles with experience' Danny Rhodes, author of *Asboville*

'Original, authentic and technically brilliant, Caroline Smailes' *In Search of Adam* is a debut of remarkable quality and devastating power' Nicholas Royle, author of *Antwerp*

'An engrossing and touching read from a new talent' *The Big Issue in the North*

'*In Search of Adam* by Caroline Smailes, a stunning insight into the disturbed mind of a girl living in the North-East. It has re-defined what writing can do for the reader – it can change the way you look at people' Terry Deary, author of *Horrible Histories*, *The Sunderland Echo*

'I think [a novel] should impart emotional energy. Not every good novel will do this, but most will. *In Search of Adam* is one of them. By the end of the first chapter, I was saddened and uncomfortable. The book has an emotional engine that Smailes guns mercilessly. The story succeeds as a study of disconnection, contamination, and the loss of momentum in a young life' *Spike Magazine*

The Drowning of Arthur Braxton:

'Magical, weird, wonderful, dark unique Northern brilliance' Matt Haig

'... there was so much about this book to love; the decrepit seaside setting, the terrible weather (the way the storms and rain inhabit both the background and foreground of the novel), the gritty realism, the magic, the freshness, the strangeness, and the way the story and the characters haunted me afterwards. I felt safe throughout this novel – I knew I was in good hands; with each change of voice and structure I remained confident in Smailes' ability to lead things to a satisfying conclusion. And that's exactly what she did' Carys Bray, author of *A Song for Issy Bradley*

'This thoroughly modern retelling is everything a fairy tale should be: strange, beautiful and wholly unexpected' Tanya Byrne author of *Heart-Shape Bruise*

'This beautifully told and sometimes disturbing tale will intrigue as it reaches its dramatic conclusion' *Bella Magazine*

'... I'd recommend you request *The Drowning of Arthur Braxton* by Caroline Smailes, one of the most unusual and talented writers around (for more info, visit her website). This is a reimagining of three Greek myths and a compelling and harrowing modern fairy tale' Stuart Evers

The Finding of Martha Lost:

'A magical tale about the power of family, fables and railway stations. Shot through with wisdom, wit and melancholy, Wallace demonstrates what skill it takes to write a truly charming novel' Sarah Perry, author of *The Essex Serpent*

'A cracking read' Cathy Rentzenbrink

'Phenomenal... *The Finding of Martha Lost* spoke to my soul, I loved it so much' Carrie Hope Fletcher

'This magical book had me bewitched within a few paragraphs. Martha is an irresistible character, who brings light and laughter into the lives of every person she meets – and will do to yours too! If you love the films Amelie or Hugo, you will adore this magical modern fairy tale' *Essentials Magazine*

One of *Marie Claire*'s must-reads of April 2016 *Marie Claire*

A charming tale. One of the most gripping new reads of March' *The Stylist*

'A charming, quirky tale that I really took to' *Woman & Home*

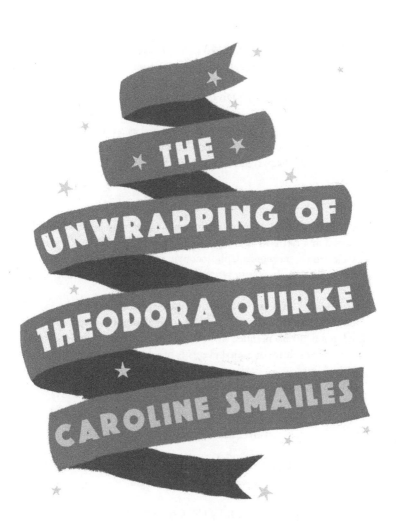

THE UNWRAPPING OF THEODORA QUIRKE

CAROLINE SMAILES

Red Door

Published by RedDoor
www.reddoorpress.co.uk

© 2020 Caroline Smailes

The right of Caroline Smailes to be identified as author of this Work
has been asserted by him in accordance with sections 77 and 78 of
the Copyright, Designs and Patents Act 1988

ISBN 978-1-913062-51-4

All rights reserved. No part of this publication may be reproduced,
stored in a retrieval system, copied in any form or by any means,
electronic, mechanical, photocopying, recording or otherwise
transmitted without written permission from the author

This is a work of fiction. Names, characters, businesses, places, events
and incidents are either the products of the author's imagination or
used in a fictitious manner. Any resemblance to actual persons, living
or dead, or actual events is purely coincidental

A CIP catalogue record for this book is available from the British
Library

Cover design: Anna Morrison

Typesetting: Jen Parker, Fuzzy Flamingo
www.fuzzyflamingo.co.uk

Printed in the UK by CPI Group (UK), Croydon

Għall-qalb ta' qalbi, Poppy, din l-istorja għalik
For the heart of my heart, Poppy, this story is for you

Then the Grinch thought of something he hadn't before!
What if Christmas, he thought, doesn't come from a store.
What if Christmas... perhaps... means a little bit more!

Dr. Seuss, How the Grinch Stole Christmas!

PART ONE

THEO (THEODORA QUIRKE)

'What the actual fuck?' I say. 'But. What? How? You're—'

The door to Dante House clicks shut behind me but I don't step forward.

'I mean…' I pause. I know it's rude to stare and point at the fat man sitting on the floor outside where I live, but I can't quite get my head around what I'm seeing.

Long beard. Clearly old. Fluffy red coat with a white fur trim. Matching hat. Broad buckled belt. Black boots.

'I mean,' I say. I wiggle all my fingers at him like an excited kid. Can't help myself. 'You're actually Santa Claus?'

The bloke shakes his head as he wobbles to his feet. What the hell? Why would I even say that? I've not believed in Santa since—

He tuts, then he sighs. 'Bloody brilliant. I've been sent to rescue an imbecile who believes in *him*,' he says, eyes staring up at the sky, and then I'm sure he whispers, 'Commercial wanker.'

'I'm nineteen, I don't believe in Santa,' I say. 'Haven't since I was…'

I've no more words. I'm nodding like a loon. Totally contradicting what I've just said. I reckon my mouth might be hanging open.

'Definitely *not* Santa Claus. I prefer to be called St Nick,' he says. He's not smiling and there isn't a glimmer of irony in his tone.

'Or you could just be a weird fat bloke, in a Santa suit, trying to pick up the young, vulnerable folk from Dante

House,' I whisper. I mean I'm saying that but then I'm smiling still. He's definitely Santa. I'm looking at Santa. I'm talking to the actual Santa Claus.

Dante House is a dumping ground for all the kids whom the care system failed. We never found our happily ever after, and this is our last bit of government help – independent living in an allegedly safe environment – before we're thrown out into the big bad world. I was supposed to leave after my A-Level results in August, but seeing as I never took them and I lied about going back to college, I'm still here.

Of course, it's not actually a house, rather a purpose-built block of flats. Three storeys, bars on our windows to stop jumpers. It was *sold* to me as somewhere with nine self-contained flats and a 'community feel'. It's actually nine shitty bedsits with a shared bathroom on each floor. My cooker's been broken since I moved in, I'm scared shitless being in this part of town when it's dark, and I've only met one of my neighbours in my nine months of being here; Sally – she lives on the ground floor like me.

But now it's Christmas Eve, I'm going to be late for work and Santa's visiting Dante House of all places.

I hear the bloke laugh. It's more a wicked laugh than a ho ho ho and his belly's solid fat, probably from drinking loads of beer down The Swan, so it doesn't seem to wobble like jelly. This is so screwed up.

'True, very true, I've turned up at Dante House *of all places* but I've never been in *The Swan*,' he says.

What the fuck? Did I say that out loud?

'But please don't call me Santa Claus. I'm definitely not *him*. I'm St Nicholas. Patron Saint of Liverpool. Folk tend to believe in me or in him, rarely in us both,' he says. He bends down to the floor to pick up an umbrella.

I look to the sky. I can't remember ever seeing as many twinkling stars. A too complicated dot-to-dot in the pitch black. It feels weird though. Like it's unfamiliar and new and not quite right. No rain either. Not even a hint of it. I take another look at the bloke and his umbrella.

I mean, on closer inspection, he's not exactly like the image of Santa Claus you'd see in one of them Christmas films like *Santa Claus the Movie* or on the front of a box of charity Christmas cards from Asda. There's nothing actually fluffy or cute about him. He's more like how Santa would look just before he goes into rehab for alcohol addiction, and possibly after several months of him living on the streets. He's very hairy, like untamed and possibly unwashed, and not at all jolly. His coat's less fluffy, more crusty. And added to that, I've just walked out of Dante House and, by the state of the empty tins of beer and half-eaten bag of chips on the floor, he's been squatting outside for some time now.

For fuck's sake, Theo, I tell myself. You're ridiculous. Grow up. There's no such thing as Santa Claus.

'I was a bishop who lived during the fourth century A.D. in the city of Myra,' he says. He swirls his still-closed umbrella to the left.

Great, he's a nutter.

'Santa Claus is a fictional character who is based largely on the stories of me.' Now he's twirling his umbrella to the right.

'But—'

'The Victorians liked me. What with their storytelling and all,' he says.

'You're off your head,' I say. It's a mumble really. I'm pissed off with myself, not him.

I look around to see if anyone else is near. We get every kind of loon in this arse end of town and there's supposed to be a warden and CCTV twenty-four seven, but there's something proper weird about the air tonight. I can't quite figure out what it is. It's like time and the air's stopped spinning, and the only sounds I can hear are being made by me and *definitely not* Santa *fucking* Claus. Only a few minutes with the bloke and I already sound like I've caught his mad, but still something's definitely off. Something I can't quite figure out.

Dante House is on a busy main road, but not one car's gone past since I came out. No dogs barking, no drum and bass from the top floor, no babies squawking, no TVs blaring, no birds tweeting. Nothing. And, if that's not weird enough, I'm still not scared of the fat bloke standing in front of me, even though every crime drama on TV would have me killed off in the next five minutes.

'You don't even look that old,' I say. 'You know... to be Santa.'

'Santa Claus was created for commercial reasons, whereas I'm all about peace, goodwill and a sprinkle of hope.'

'Really?' I say. I can't help that my face crinkles up. He doesn't look like the embodiment of hope and joy.

I need to make a move. I either try and get past him or retreat back into Dante House and wait until he's gone. I fumble in my bag for my keys. Best I go into my flat, phone the warden and then let work know I'll be a little late. Stacey, the boss from hell, will probably give me a formal warning, or something, but she can't sack me tonight. Only those without family are willing to work the Christmas Eve nightshift.

'Of course it depends on where you're from,' he continues, and I listen because that's the polite thing to do. 'In the Netherlands and Belgium I'm called Sinterklaas.'

'So you're Santa Claus,' I say. He sighs.

'Why do people do that? The words don't sound anything

6

alike,' he says. 'I blame the Europeans, spreading my name to foreign lands and then those bloody Americans went and—'

'What you going on about?' I ask.

Why am I still talking to this odd-looking man? Why am I not back in my flat and making them phone calls I really need to be making? I've still not turned back to the door, but my keys are poised and ready.

'The Americans. Europeans landed there with tales of their Sinterklaas, a shortened form of Sint Nikolaas, an elderly man with white hair and a beard. Me.' He points his umbrella at his face. His beard's grey and scraggy. I'm not convinced. He's not the Patron Saint of anyone.

'They'd talk about the candy and cookies I placed in nice children's shoes in conjunction with my feast day on December 6th. Yes?'

I nod, but I don't really follow. I reckon I stopped listening properly when he first said Sinterklass.

'Then came illustrations of a fat man with sacks stacked full of toys. Comic strips were created of that jolly tubby gent, films were made, consumerism exploded and voilà.' He jiggles his solid fat belly, then shimmies forward in a weird Beyoncé style dance. I shake my head. 'That's how that imposter was born. I am definitely *not* him. I do quite like being a Patron Saint of New York.'

'You said Liverpool—'

'And Ghent, Prokhod, Quebec, Le Souich, Corfu, Verona, Sveti Nikole, Siggiewi, Nieuwveen, San Nicolas, Liptovsky Mikulás, Alicante, Lutsk, to name but a few. So many glorious places to visit and explore. But being the reigning Principal of the Christmas World carries much responsibility.'

He's doing my head in. I've got to get to work, an overnighter at the local old people's home. Mainly wiping arses and hearing stories of lost love and relatives that have done one since the home stole all their inheritances. I don't have time for this fat bloke's bullshit.

'How do I know *you're* not the imposter?' I ask, sounding like a right mardy cow. 'You don't exactly look like the Patron Saint of the Christmas World. Or whatever.'

'And how should I look?' he asks. 'Your society and its bloody need for everyone to look perfect. Obviously, I came about first, and *he*'s a mere inferior imitation,' he says. He shakes his head. 'I'm not that charlatan.'

'Aren't you sponsored by Coca-Cola?'

'Are you an *actual* imbecile?' he replies. He moves forward and prods me with his umbrella.

'Whoa,' I say, my hands up and taking a step backwards to the door. 'Whoever you are, you need to stay away from me. It's Christmas Eve. Shouldn't you be delivering presents?'

'On Christmas Eve?' he asks, his voice raised. 'Why?'

I don't speak, my hands still up in front of me. My keyring dangling around a finger.

'Oh, you think the miracles happen tonight,' he says. 'How disappointing. You really do believe in *him* and not in me.' His face is angry looking. I shrug my shoulders. 'My magic emerges as December 5th turns to December 6th.'

I look at the floor and whisper, 'For fuck's sake. I stopped believing in your bullshit the first Christmas I got nowt and everyone else at school got PlayStation 3s. Why am I even listening to you?' I've had enough of this. 'Haven't you got someplace else to be? I know I have.'

'Not before I save you,' he says. He smiles, his teeth are crooked and he looks like he could be the love child of the two bad men in *Home Alone*.

'I don't need *saving*, and if I did I wouldn't need the likes of you—'

'But I'm still a little bit confused about your gender. Do you want to be a man?' he asks.

What the actual fuck?

'Nope, sorry,' I say, shaking my head and putting my key into the lock.

'Let me check. What's your name?' he asks.

'Theo,' I say.

'A girl named Theo,' he says and I nod. 'Maybe that's what confused them.'

'It's short for Theodora.'

'Yes, I know. Well this is going to be slightly unorthodox,' he says. 'But it is what it is. We'll make the best of it.'

'Were you after some male company?' I ask, turning the key. 'There's this man who hangs out on Gambier Terrace. Heard he's cheap and—'

'Are you sure you aren't transitioning? I'm totally chilled about transgender—'

'No transitioning plans for now.' I open the door, turning to him for one final look.

'Well this is *very* unorthodox, Theodora Quirke,' he says, as he stretches out his arm towards me and opens up his palm.

'What the—'

I look to his unfolded hand. His fingers are plump sausages, but resting on his palm is a lock and a piece of paper.

Scribbled on the paper are the words:

SAVE THEO – SPITFIRE AND ORAL

THEO (THEODORA QUIRKE)

'What the fuck? How did… How?' I say.

I know I should be asking a million questions about how he knows my surname and running away because he possibly wants oral, but I can't take my eyes off the lock resting on his palm.

It's identical to the lock we'd attached to the railings near the Mersey, down by Albert Docks. That was three years ago now. We'd bought that lock from Home Bargains in town after college. Gabriel had a red sharpie in his coat pocket and he'd written our names on it. I'd drawn the heart. I'd attached the lock and Gabriel had captured the moment on his phone. A guy had played guitar, just beside the Billy Fury statue, and Gabriel had asked me if I wanted to dance. I'd said no. The thought of tripping or being watched or being laughed at, or being anything other than perfect for strangers, had stopped me. I hate that about myself, all those missed moments for fear of what strangers might think of me. Gabriel had wanted to throw the lock's key into the Mersey. I didn't. I'd grabbed it from him. I'd put it in my pocket.

'For our grandchildren,' I'd said.

That moment's still clear as a bell in my head. Gabriel brushed his long, curly fringe off his face, then he flicked his chin with his middle finger. He did that sometimes. He flicked his finger onto his chin when he was thinking.

'We should have five kids,' he'd said.

'And then I'll tell all *their* kids about how our names are locked together forever overlooking our Mersey,' I'd said.

Back then I'd thought Gabriel and me would grow old together. Sometimes, I reckon when people are actually living, they almost forget to live. Not me, others. I remember the lock; I remember every precious thing about that moment. It was a small moment that felt huge, because it was. It was the first time Gabriel promised me a future. Gabe, kids, grandkids. Family.

I let out a breath; I see it swirl. I used to love doing that when I was a kid but now mainly I do it as if I'm forcing out a thought I no longer want in my head.

I lift the lock from St Nick's outstretched palm. Our names are unaltered by the attacking weather from the last few years. I reach up and undo my necklace, releasing the key from my silver chain. I try my key and the lock springs open.

'How did you—' I start to ask.

I realise that I'm crying. This has been happening a lot recently. I could be walking in town or on a bus and suddenly someone will turn to me and ask if I'm okay. It'll take me a minute or two to realise that tears are streaming from my eyes. Someone on the internet said it's the final stage of grief. Acceptance. That it's okay to feel sad and to feel lonely. That as long as I'm still feeling, then I'm on the right tracks.

'Shit,' I whisper. 'I miss him,' I say. I wipe my snot onto the sleeve of my coat. 'Sometimes, when I'm alone, when it's really quiet, I think I hear Gabe. He's telling me to eat or that I need to go back to college, and sometimes he's telling me that everything will be okay. But I don't believe him. Not anymore. I don't think he's got any right to talk to me any longer. Last night I was sure that I heard him say, "I love you".' I rub at my eyes with the heel of my palm; mascara spreads onto my hand.

'And how did that make you feel?' he asks.

'Sad,' I say. 'And now I'm going to look shit for work.

Again.' There's so much more I can add but I don't want to be spilling my guts to some weirdo camped outside Dante House.

'How did you get my lock?' I ask.

'Magic,' he says. 'Do you believe in magic, Theodora Quirke?'

I shake my head, too scared to admit that I do. 'And my name's Theo.' How does he know my surname though?

'I prefer Theodora,' he says.

'But—'

'How about Christmas magic?' he asks. 'Do you believe in that?' I shake my head again. 'Seeing Gabriel again. Seeing him one last time. That's what you desire the most, is it not?'

I don't nod straight away. I think about Gabriel, about what I'd say if we could have one last time together. When he first died, I'd spend hours and hours writing down everything I wanted to say, but that was ten months ago. Now I don't write about him but I still think about him every day. I don't stop myself anymore. I don't tell myself that I shouldn't, I don't pretend that he never existed. Thinking about Gabriel has stopped hurting in my belly.

'And that is what I do,' St Nick continues. 'That is what St Nicholas does...' A pause. 'I perform miracles. I fulfil the wishes of those who have hearts that are pure.'

I don't mean to, but I can't help but laugh. The bloke's as mad as a bucket of frogs on acid. He stares at me. I'm not sure if he looks angry or confused. I can't let myself believe any of this shit. Gabriel was my hope. Gabriel was my promise of everything I'd never had. I won't, I can't let my head go there again.

'You're sounding like those dodgy words written inside a card. Or on those plaques of encouragement that sell by the bus load,' I say, the words rushing out to fill the awkward silence.

'People like to believe there's hope, Theodora Quirke,' he says.

'Am I mental? I mean, have I properly lost my shit and made up a Santa Claus, who looks like crap, to have a chat with?'

'Hollywood made up stories about me being *him*, made me into a hero for little kids and got who I *really* am all confused in the process. What am I supposed to do? Break hearts and destroy traditions?' He pauses. 'St Nicholas exists, *Santa Claus* has been fabricated for commercialism,' he says. 'Most go through life without a Christmas miracle. Like I said—'

'You fulfil the wishes of those who have hearts that are pure. So I have a pure heart?'

'There was another female, many years ago. She lost everything in a fire. Her heart was a similar shape to yours.' He pauses, his fingers lifting and seeming to trace the shape of a heart in the air between us. 'But yes, Theodora, your heart is the purest I have seen since then,' he says. 'But…'

'My life has been one big but,' I say.

Gabriel would have laughed at that. St Nick sighs. He looks sad.

'Don't you find people are always nicer nearer Christmas?' I say. I pull my puffer jacket tighter around me. It's suddenly colder. Too cold to be standing still outside. 'It's like Christmas offers a glimpse into how they could be.' I pause. He doesn't fill in the silence, instead he stares at me. His eyes are tiny, but now that I'm looking at him a little closer. Now that I'm looking beyond the fact that he smells like he's been sleeping rough for the last two weeks, I think they might be full of kindness. 'People who are lonely and full of pain, they pretend everything's okay…'

'Tell me, Theodora,' he says. 'What's making you so very fatigued of life?'

'I don't think I am,' I say. I shake my head. 'I work hard, I exist, earn a crap wage but I don't need much. I've a roof over my head.' I point at the shitty building behind me. 'Considering everything, I'm okay. Honest.'

'You're tired of pretending,' he says. 'You're exhausted.'

'Am I?' I ask. I don't know if I am. 'Maybe.'

I mean I'm okay, like I said – *all things considered*. If I'm honest, I've seen a shift in me over the last few weeks. Yes, I'm crying a lot, but I'm also finding tiny bits of joy in my everyday shit. There's Moira, the eighty-three-year-old woman at work who keeps flirting with eighteen-year-old Tom. Moira's convinced she's eighteen too and the poor lad doesn't know what to do with himself every time she pinches his arse or winks. There's my neighbour Sally, who leaves me cookies outside my door every Sunday, with little notes about how well I'm doing. There's Bernie the bus driver, who always offers me a sherbet lemon. Says he saves them just for me. So many characters I meet every day who remind me about this now.

'I have been sent to save you,' St Nick says, breaking my thoughts. 'Or at least I think I have.'

'You what?' I say. 'I don't need you or anyone—'

'All the letters were mixed up, but I've tried my best to figure it out.' He waves his piece of paper in the air. '*Save Theo – Spitfire and oral.*'

'I'm not giving you oral,' I say. I take the piece of paper from him and step back.

'God, no,' St Nick says. He's shaking his head and then waving his hands out in front of him. He's clearly horrified that I think that's what he means.

'Bet you could spell loads of names from this.' I stare at the words. I shrug my shoulders. 'Look – Lottie. Sarah. Fiona,' I say, pointing at the different letters. 'Honestly, mate, you've got the wrong person. And "Spitfire and oral" sounds dodgy as fuck,' I say.

'But you're one of mine,' he says, then he must see my face change because he adds, 'God, no, no, no. Not like that! It's not as mad as it seems. Trust me.'

I shake my head. There isn't any way in holy hell I'm trusting some fat, homeless bloke who's dressed as Santa and hanging out where unloved kids live.

'There is a slight problem,' he says, snatching back the piece of paper, 'but we'll deal with that later. For now, I've a job to do.'

I turn and push open the door. I'll go back inside and then look out of my window and wait until he's gone. I'm already late. Bus will be gone by now. I'll phone Stacey when I'm inside. Tell her about the weirdo. She might even send a taxi for me, if it means she doesn't have to work the Christmas Eve shift.

'It was nice meeting you, *St* Nick,' I say, but I don't stop or turn to face him.

'Theodora Quirke. Wait,' he shouts and I turn around.

Light snow is falling. I swear it wasn't even close to snowing a minute ago but now it's falling onto him; a streetlight nearby is making him glow and shimmer like a juicy strawberry. I hold out my palm and watch as flakes land, then dissolve instantly.

'And I suppose this is Christmas magic she'll understand?' he says, looking up at the sky.

Who the fuck's he talking to?

A Mrs Claus lookalike wobbles along the opposite side of the road; she's unsteady on her high heels. Her candy cane stockings and her red mini dress look super cute. She shouldn't be out here though. It's dark. It's not safe. Dante House is shoved on the edge of an industrial park. Only one bus stop near and she's going the wrong way to reach it.

'Where you going?' I shout.

She sees us and waves. 'Merry fucking Christmas, Theodora,' she slurs. 'Alright, St Nick.' I watch as she vomits all over her shoes.

'You know her?' I ask St Nick but when I look back to where she should be, she's not there anymore.

'Will you come with me?' he says, ignoring my question and instead stretching his arms out in front of him. The tip of his closed umbrella wiggles near me.

'I've got work,' I say and I turn back to the open door. 'I'm late already and I don't want to be sacked. Stacey, my boss, is—'

'Can't it wait?' he says.

'Not really. It's Christmas Eve and I'm the only one without family commitments.'

I look back at the path down to the main road. The snow's starting to stick to the pavement. Snow wasn't forecast so I doubt the gritters have been out. The pavements and roads could be covered by morning. What if I'm snowed into the old folk's home for days? Stacey would love that. Free labour. Bet she'd still take board and food out of my wages. Bet she'd—

'But have you ever watched *A Christmas Carol*?' he asks.

'At least a million times,' I say. This bloke is off his head. Is he after an invite in to my flat to watch a festive film and nibble on a mince pie? I step inside.

'Excellent. Then I can but assume that you're tempted to see what I think I've been sent to show you…'

'Do you really think you're Santa Claus?' I ask, turning around again and half expecting him to be flashing his dick at me. 'I mean, surely you must know that—'

'For bugger's sake, Theodora Quirke. How many times?' he says. He looks up to the sky, thick snow landing on his face. 'Definitely *not* Santa Claus. I'm Nikolaos of Myra; in your language I'm more commonly known as St Nicholas. But clearly my being a fictitious figure is the only explanation that makes sense to you.' He looks at me, the snow hugging his beard and hair, making his cheeks rosy, and somehow making him look more like the real deal than I want to admit.

He winks.

And that's when something changes. I can't help but walk towards him. I hear the front door click behind me. It's like the most powerful magnet in the world's pulling me to the fat, smelly weirdo. I reach him and I let my fingers dance along the fabric of his whopping red coat. It's fluffy, it's soft; it's wonderful. Large flakes of snow continue landing and don't dissolve into the thick fabric. There are stains of varying sizes and colours. I'm not convinced they're all food. The coat is very red, I'm sure there's a name for that red, if I was an artist, I'd know the exact shade.

'Carmine,' he says and then I'm smiling.

You can read my mind, can't you? I think. My eyes watch his face, and St Nick smiles.

What the hell's going on? I've lost all control of myself.

He moves one hand to his huge coat pocket and I stop stroking his arm. It's all a bit weird really, and yet it feels natural and truthful. I look at his face again. He's all snow and crooked smile and tiny blue eyes. There's no pity though; if anything he somehow looks both excited and a little bit pissed off that he's got to deal with me.

'Where to?' I ask. I smile, it's weak but he seems to latch onto it and he throws me a huge crooked smile back. 'I might have to text Stacey at work on the way. Tell her I'll be a bit late.'

'I must show you scenes from your—' he says.

17

'How do I know you're not a serial killer?'

'You don't,' he says, his face entirely deadpan.

'Brilliant disguise for a serial killer,' I say. 'You must get loads of kids wanting to sit on your knee and tell you secrets.'

'You young folk don't trust anyone, do you?'

'Internet generation; everyone's dodgy until they prove they're not,' I say.

'You know, Theodora Quirke—'

'It's Theo.'

'You know, Theodora Quirke, maybe tonight, maybe just this once, maybe you should just trust in Christmas magic and let me guide you,' he says.

'I'm pretty sure that's exactly what you'd say if you were a serial killer.'

'There's no joke in this,' he says. 'He must think that I'm your last hope.'

'He?' I ask.

St Nick stretches out his arm, his palm is open and before I've time to overthink or switch on my Snapmap, I'm holding hands with him and he's smiling like he's a master criminal.

'Did I mention that I'm a saint?'

'Yeah, it came up,' I say.

MY STORY – BY DOTTIE SMITH

(Founder of Spitfire Saint Nicholas Umbrella Collective)

I'd been out for a few beers. One of the mums from Noah's new school had arranged it. We'd moved into the area a couple of months earlier, just before my little boy Noah started in reception. I didn't know any of the other mums at school, just a hello nod at pick up and drop off, so Neil, my husband, thought it'd be good for me. A chance to make mum friends.

We'd arranged to meet in the local pub. It was all going to be pretty low-key and harmless. Neil had laughed. He'd said I should watch how much I drink, so as not to be telling all my secrets to strangers. Of course, I drank more than I should have drunk. Nerves probably. I ended up in a toilet cubicle, showing one of the mum's my boob tattoo. She showed me one she'd had done on her arse cheek. We were bonding.

It was one of the best nights out I'd had since my daughter, Betty, had been born. There'd been five of us mums in the pub and we'd laughed. Properly laughed. We'd all hugged when the landlord chucked us out. We'd had a soppy group huddle and said we'd make having a mums' night out together a monthly thing. I'd staggered out of the pub car park feeling happy. I was excited for Noah and for Betty. I was making friends. There'd be playdates, there'd be friends to have home for tea, there'd be sleepovers to arrange too.

I can't even remember the names of them mums now. Funny that.

I heard the screaming when I turned the corner into our street. One of the neighbours was hysterical. She was standing in the

19

middle of the road shrieking. There was fire. The air was eerie. Hot like the summer, but full of chaos. At first, I thought it was her house that was on fire, then she clocked me and she ran. I'd never seen no one run like that. I remember looking to see what was chasing her. Nothing. That's when I felt fear in my belly. Before my head realised. It was like a punch and then I knew that it wasn't her family that was on fire. I couldn't move. She tried to hug me but I pushed her away.

'I tried,' she screamed. She was sobbing. 'There was too much smoke.'

'Where's Noah? Betty?' I shouted. 'Neil.'

No one answered. I ran. I was sober then.

Someone had put a ladder up against the front of the house. No one was climbing it. I ran straight to it. I had heels on and I wasn't steady on my feet, but I started climbing the ladder to the front bedroom. My eyes were streaming with tears. I don't know if it was because my body had already figured out what was coming, or that my eyes couldn't be coping with the heat and smoke. The glass to my bedroom window was all smashed but I started climbing in. The glass was cutting into me. I didn't care. I couldn't breathe. The heat. The smoke. The pain was in my head and it was in my belly.

Someone pulled me back. My new blouse was all rips and blood. I don't know how I got back down that ladder.

MY STORY – BY DOTTIE SMITH

(Founder of Spitfire Saint Nicholas Umbrella Collective)

Next day, the local paper said I was a 'devastated mum'. Paper said, 'Dottie Smith, devastated mum, 26, escaped the blaze. The bodies of her daughter Betty, 2, her 4-year-old son Noah and her husband Neil, 28, were found huddled together in an upstairs bedroom.'

My neighbour, the one that ran to me screaming. She'd tried to help. Even though my house had been all flames, she'd opened my front door and tried to go in. Brave that. I can't remember her name now. I'd been out getting pissed. She was the one who'd tried to get upstairs to help rescue my family. There'd been too much smoke though. It was a fully developed fire; it was hot and 'challenging'. Folk said it was 'incomprehensible', that such a vicious fire would rip through that home.

Fire services, paramedic crews and police arrived too late. Everything was taken from me before they got there.

You know, I used to have a career. Before that I worked as a SEN teacher, mainly with children with sensory impairments. Working around my kids and juggling childcare was a struggle sometimes. That's what I used to say – 'a struggle' or on better days just 'a juggle'. I didn't have no clue what a struggle really was.

After the fire, I moved into temporary accommodation. I only had the clothes I was wearing. Strangers and new friends were kind though. They rallied around. Donations to help towards three coffins, charity, second-hand shoes for me, toothpaste, gentleness. I can't be faulting their kindness. I just wanted to be alone though. I wanted to die too.

Time stopped the day Neil, Noah and Betty died. I can't bear to think 'bout how scared they must have been in them last moments. It helps that they huddled together. Neil would have been doing his best to protect them. I can't picture their faces beyond that time. It's funny that, isn't it? How when folk die, they become frozen in a specific time and at an exact age. Like Han Solo in carbonite, but different.

I survived. I continued living. I was a shuffling zombie most of the time, but folk weren't into judging. No stable home, no returning to work, no seeking out a replacement family, but there was a support network that was full of patience and kindness back then. There was a timetable of people visiting, staying the night, bringing food. I was on a whole heap of benefits, I had a doctor who cared and a therapist who asked the right questions.

People would commend me on how I continued with life and I'd shrug my shoulders. The word 'hero' was bandied 'bout. 'Courage' too. I don't think me surviving was a conscious decision or anything like that. I had a support network, I was rarely alone, and somehow amongst all the despair and pain, there was always a glimmer of something.

I guess seeing hope is a choice.

MY STORY – BY DOTTIE SMITH

(Founder of Spitfire Saint Nicholas Umbrella Collective)

It was on the morning of December 6th, 1990. Three years after Noah, Betty and Neil died, when Saint Nicholas came into my life.

I was living in a bedsit, in the same village. I don't know why I stayed local. Maybe because I wanted to be close to their graves. Maybe because my support network hadn't wavered in all that time. Anyway, my doorbell rang and when I opened the door there was a large cardboard box on my welcome mat. There was no note and no one around who might have delivered it. I left the box and ran to my window.

Looking outside, I saw a man. He turned at that exact moment and he looked up at me. None of this is sounding weird yet, is it? Anyway, the man, who I'd never seen before, carried a weird looking umbrella, even though it wasn't raining. I can't remember anything 'bout his face or body shape, just the umbrella. I watched as he waved his umbrella in the air, and then he disappeared. Just like that. Poof.

That's the point in my storytelling where most people roll their eyes, and, before you do, I'm very aware that normal folk don't tend to wave an umbrella and simply disappear into thin air. I'm the first to acknowledge that what I'm saying's off its head.

Back then I'd not heard of no one called Nikolaos of Myra or Nicholas the Wonderworker. Back then I didn't know the foggiest difference between Saint Nicholas, Santa Claus and Father Christmas. I wasn't religious and I wasn't on the best of terms with God. I had a ban on all things festive. Those near knew how much I dreaded anything to do with Christmas.

23

Obviously, I kept a lookout for the man. I reckoned he was doing a magic trick. I thought he might have ducked behind a car or he might have jumped into a garden. I stayed at my window, looking up and down the street for an hour or so. I was desperate for a wee but I refused to move. I remember a fizzing in my belly. Like the nerves you get waiting for the results of a test you've studied really hard for and kinda know you've done well.

My doorbell rang again. I didn't want to go leaving my window but I hurried to see who was there. Again, there was no one and nothing there except that cardboard box. So I picked up the box and took it inside with me. Of course I went to have a look out of the window. And yes, he was there again! The same man with the same weird umbrella. He smiled, waved his umbrella and then vanished again.

At this stage, I won't lie, I thought my grief might have pushed me over the edge. I thought I was seeing things and was wondering who to call for help. But still I sat down on my bed and I ripped open the cardboard box.

To say what was inside was unexpected would be understating.

Inside were memories. Precious memories of Neil, Noah and Betty. There were photographs, negatives, framed prints, videos, drawings, letters and even Betty's favourite cuddly rabbit. The photographs were from when Neil and I met, our wedding day, baby scan photos, holidays, there were even some photos I'd never seen. Photos that were still film in a camera when my life was burned.

Everything in that box had been inside my home when all the contents, and everything I loved, burned. Everything had been destroyed.

It was the most precious and wonderful gift. It was miraculous, unbelievable and inexplicable. And for all of them reasons, no one believed me. And for all of them reasons people became suspicious of me.

Of course, first thing I did was phoning people in my support network. I was crying down the phone, not quite able to get words out between my sobbing. Friends dropped whatever it was they were doing. They rushed around to see me. Someone informed that local reporter who'd labelled me a 'devastated mum'. They all came. They all huddled into my little bedsit. They all delved into my cardboard box of memories.

Together, they asked the same question: How could I have possibly been given a box of items that were destroyed in a fire that killed my husband and my beautiful babies?

Together, they reached the same devastating and fucking ridiculous conclusion: I must have stored them memories before starting the fire and murdering my own family.

I stayed put for another year, but in the end I moved away from that village and them so-called friends of mine. In the end, all their hate got to being too much. Letters through my door, threats from strangers I met on the street, articles written 'bout me in the local paper, former friends refusing to speak. My support network didn't exist no more.

And you'd think I'd be pissed off 'bout that, wouldn't you? But I'm not.

Saint Nicholas changed my life that day. He saved me. He gave me a new focus. He gave me back my hope.

THEO (THEODORA QUIRKE)

We're standing in a room. It might be in an abandoned building, maybe even somewhere derelict. It's dark, it's cold and it stinks of wee. I turn around; St Nick's wearing boxer shorts, no top on, his belly hanging over his too-tight waistband. His umbrella's on the floor beside him and he's biting a large pork pie.

'Where are your pants?' I say. 'What happened to the snow?'

Is this how my life ends? My naked body found in some weird, abandoned—

'And where the fuck are we?' I say. I wait for him to chew and swallow. Tiny chunks of pork pie fall into his scraggy beard.

'You know who I am now, no need to wear the costume. Just need to bring the parasol,' he says. He kicks his umbrella as if that's enough explanation for the fact that he was fully dressed and we were someplace else a blink ago.

My eyes scan the room, adjusting to the lack of light. 'You didn't wear the *costume* for very long,' I say.

'Have you any idea how hot it gets wearing it?' he says. His mouth's full of pork pie so the words escape between chews and swallows.

'So this is how you normally dress?' I say, looking at his naked belly again. There's no anger in my voice. I'm mainly a mix of curiosity and what-the-actual-fuckness.

'I'm at my computer all day,' he says. Like that justifies him walking around in public in his too-tight boxies.

'Is that smell you?' I ask. He sniffs under his armpits. I turn away, my eyes searching around the room while I say, 'Someone needs to tell Hollywood that you stink. I'd love to see them remaking *Miracle on 34th Street* and focusing on your whiff.' I laugh, but before he can reply I hear crying. I twist on the spot and as I do they seem to come into focus. Like it's suddenly the start of a show and the spotlight hits the main characters on stage.

In a corner, just below the broken window, on a small mattress, possibly from a cot, there's a girl, perhaps a teenager, clutching a toddler, an orange streetlight from outside shines in and lights their faces.

'Are you okay?' I ask. I take small steps towards them.

'They can't hear you,' St Nick says. The crying is constant, like a rattling car engine beginning. Not like a pain cry, probably a tired, a cold, a hungry cry. All I know is that I'm hit with an overwhelming need to comfort them.

'Can I help you?' I say. I take another step closer. I don't rush, I don't hurry to them; I'm aware that two people suddenly appearing in a room might scare them. Also, I'm with a fat, smelly man who's only wearing too-tight boxer shorts and eating a pork pie; we possibly scream out 'stranger danger'.

The toddler stops crying and looks straight at me; she's wearing a red jumper with a reindeer on it.

I don't know why, but I ask, 'Is it still Christmas Eve?'

'First week in December,' St Nick says.

'So we've travelled back in time a couple of weeks?' I say, all calm and everyday chilled, as if that's a perfectly sane and normal question to be asking. St Nick doesn't reply. He's behind me. I don't turn to look at him. I'm smiling at the toddler. She holds up an outstretched hand, folding her fingers in and out as if she's waving. In her other hand she clutches a green, plastic dinosaur. It's a brontosaurus.

'Hey, hey,' I say. I wave back to her. I smile, she smiles too. She's beautiful.

'December this year?' I ask, my eyes still on the little girl.

'I wouldn't say that,' St Nick says.

'What are you doing, Theodora?' the teen with the little girl asks.

'Theodora?' I spin back to face St Nick.

'Yes,' he says. He doesn't look at me. He's watching them too.

'Like me,' I say.

I undo my puffer jacket and place it on the floor. My work clothes are gone and I'm wearing leggings and Gabriel's old Nirvana T-shirt, with one of his hoodies zipped up over it. I've never worn these clothes before. What the fuck's happening to me? No time to figure that out. Not really. I sit cross-legged on the floor, just a little way from them.

'Who are you?' I ask. Neither of them answers.

'Mummy's going to keep you safe,' the teen says to the toddler.

'Mummy?' I say to St Nick, but I keep looking at them. 'She looks younger than me.'

'Seventeen,' he says. 'The police are looking for her. They say she's kidnapped her own child.'

'Theodora, that little girl, is in foster care?' I say. The ache in my throat lets me know that I'm about a sentence away from tears.

I know this story; I used to ask to hear it when I was younger. I don't take my eyes off the mother. I've never seen a photograph of her. There were none in my file. I think I might look like her; she's smaller than me, thinner than me too. Her hair's blonde and looks like it's been untouched since it was backcombed a week ago. Her eyes, such a bright blue, are the saddest eyes I've ever seen. They're darting around the room and she jumps at the smallest noise. I don't think she's well. I wish I could capture this moment, no matter how sad and broken it really is. I wish I had my phone, that I could take a photo, that I could record her voice. I don't want to forget her face; I want to remember her words to her child. I know her, I don't know her, I want to know her. We could be sisters, twins even, yet this child is my mum.

'You both understand what it feels like to lose the thing that you love more than yourself,' St Nick says.

I have no words to respond. I don't dare to speak.

I watch her pulling her baby in close to her, rocking, humming *Jingle Bells*. The toddler's eyes are on me, bright blue, just like her mummy's; wide and alert. She's relaxed, chewing on her dinosaur. She's not frightened. She feels safe with her mummy; it'll be years before she feels truly safe again. Gabriel's arms will give the best hugs. His mum's, Francesca's, too. I let out the breath I've been holding.

'Theodora is eighteen months old; she's been in foster care since she was nine months old. Her mum, Katie, is in an abusive relationship with Theodora's dad. I don't really know what that means, other than she won't give up her man for little Theodora.' I gulp the words over the lump of emotion that's stuck in my throat.

'She can't give him up,' St Nick says. 'She has no one else. She has no one to turn to, no one to protect her from him. She's been waiting, hoping he'll change.'

'She was told I was going to be adopted,' I say.

'Today,' he says. 'She has visited you every week, three times a week. Those visits kept her going. They kept her hoping. She wanted to see you every day, but they limited visitation. They worried she was too attached to you; too reliant on you.'

'She loved me?'

'Look at her. You were her world,' he says. 'Today, at the start of the visit, authorities told her that you were going to be put up for adoption,' he says. He pauses. We watch as Katie kisses little Theodora's head and pulls her in closer. 'She couldn't bear handing you back; the thought of letting you go unbearable. She never thought the foster care would be forever. She loves her little girl.'

'So she ran away with Theodora?' I ask. I'm blinking like windscreen wipers, desperate to get rid of my tears. Desperate to see my mum.

'Police are calling it kidnap,' he says. 'They'll find you both here tomorrow; she'll be arrested and bailed. This will be the last time she sees Theodora. She had no idea she was on my list for a Christmas miracle.'

'You knew my mum?' I say.

'Shit. Didn't mean to tell you that yet,' St Nick says. He shakes his head in an exaggerated manner, his hands out trying to rub away the words.

'But you knew her?' I say.

'I remember all of my children,' he says. 'Even though I failed to save her, I've never forgotten her... or you.'

'And that's why you answered the call? When you thought I needed saving?' I ask. 'That's how you knew my name?' St Nick doesn't reply. He might have nodded a couple of times, but I'm not taking my eyes off my mum.

'He attacks her,' I say.

'Baseball bat. She's furious when she goes back to his flat. She lashes out, screaming at him to help get you back. He wanted her to forget about you,' he says.

'But she couldn't?' I ask.

'She told him she was leaving him, that you were more important. The thought of losing you finally kicked some sense into her. She loved you more than anything else, but then he beat her badly. That was when she realised there was no hope of getting you back. She was trapped. She could never escape him, and she would never let him near you. She would never risk him laying a finger on you. That was when she decided—'

'Fucking Ghost of Christmas Past,' I say. 'Why are you doing this to me? Are you trying to push me over the edge like her?'

I nod at my mum, but instantly wish I could take back that nod. How desperate must she have been to think death would be better than a life without me?

'I don't remember Dickens being this fucking depressing,' I say.

THEO (THEODORA QUIRKE)

I don't move from my cross-legged spot on the floor. I watch my mum, pulling me closer and rocking as she sings. She's singing *Little Donkey* now; I still know all the words to that one.

Little Theodora moves her green plastic dinosaur from hand-to-hand. My mum's kissing my head again and again, tears falling down onto my wispy strands of blonde hair. Little Theodora hasn't cried since I noticed her. Now she twists out of the embrace and looks up into her mum's eyes. She drops her little dinosaur as her tiny chubby fingers reach out to touch her mum's hair. I wish I could remember what it felt like to be held by my mum.

'I used to spend hours in the library searching for famous people called Theodora,' I say. 'I reckoned finding out about other Theodoras would help me understand who I was. To understand my mum a bit more.'

I'm barely holding myself together.

'All those hours of pointless research. I was so desperate for a snippet of information about my mum and why she might have chosen my name. And this here,' I throw my arms out, 'tells me more than I'd ever hoped to know.'

'Is that a positive?' he asks and I nod. I'm calm, weirdly calm, like my body's been told this isn't the time to freak out. Later though, fuck knows what kind of state I'm going to be in.

'Maybe Mum had high hopes for me, maybe she thought that if she gave me a strong name, then somehow I'd inherit a strong personality,' I say.

'She meant well,' he says. I turn to look at him. He's finished his pork pie and lumps are resting in the jet black hairs on his chest. Maybe he dyes them. He's now sitting on a portable camping chair and pouring himself a cup of something from a flask. He's watching little Theodora and her mum.

'The number of times I've watched *The Muppet Christmas Carol*,' I say.

'In my opinion that's the best version of *that man's* novella,' St Nick says. 'Puppets acting out *his* masterpiece.' He laughs, spurting liquid all down his belly and almost falling from his flimsy chair.

'Not once did I think about where a ghost would take me,' I say.

St Nick wriggles around and I reckon the chair's material's going to split apart and he's going to fall on his arse.

'Most don't,' St Nick says. 'And don't get me started on that *childlike Ghost* from Christmas Past, it's—'

'I was born into a shitty dysfunctional family. I didn't even know love until Gabe,' I say. My calm's clearly done one; the anger is sudden. All of these emotions. It's too much for my head.

'Doesn't look that way to me,' he says, nodding at my mum, his words comforting.

'How do I make this better, Theodora?' she says. My eyes are back on her. 'I want to make this better.' Her voice is strong; she's searching inside herself for a solution. I can see the absolute, unquestionable love that she has for little me.

'She's got no one,' I say. 'Like me.'

'You have Gabriel's mother. Francesca, isn't it? She—' he starts to say.

'I have no one,' I repeat. I won't talk about Francesca.

'You are similar, but you're not the same as your mum,' St

Nick says. 'She was dealt a bad card, but she isn't a bad girl,' he says. 'She wanted to be your mum, but she was reliant on him. She had no one to ask for help. She had no money, no home and no education.'

'What about her parents?' I ask, still not taking my eyes from her.

'Chucked her out when they found out she was pregnant,' he says. 'They'll cry at her funeral, but they never ask to see you.'

'I don't go to the funeral?' I say. He's sitting next to me now. I look for the camping chair but it's gone. The flask's nowhere to be seen either. 'Can you show me the funeral?'

'No, Theodora,' he says. 'I'm showing you this so that you'll know you've experienced love other than from Gabriel and Francesca.'

'It's too late though, I can't ever know her and—' I start to say but then, 'Was he sorry?'

'Your father?' he asks. I nod.

'He never showed remorse,' he says. 'The day after he attacked her, your mum took her own life. She thought she had nothing,' St Nick says. 'But she was wrong. There is always hope, Theodora Quirke.'

'He's dead now too,' I say and St Nick nods.

'Drugs. He died in prison,' he says.

I sigh. 'My parents were screwed up,' I say, but in that moment I look at my mum, holding me tight and covering me in love, and I'm hit with a wave of guilt for saying those words aloud.

I wish I could hold her. I've spent years dreaming about the conversations and confrontations I could have with my parents. It was all about me saying 'LOOK AT ME' and pointing out how I'd survived against the odds and despite them. In my imaginary world, I'd planned on showing my mum Gabriel and our five kids, on talking about how I'd survived the care system, about how I didn't need a crap mother or a father to have a perfect life.

But now everything's so very different. I've spent the last ten months clinging to life. And, right now, I've no desire to shout in her face. Right now it's taking all of my strength not to crawl across the floor and into her arms. I want to tell her that she made the wrong decision, but that I forgive her and that I understand. Because I do. In this moment, I really do. I want to tell her that it's okay, that humans make mistakes, that it's okay to screw up so badly that you can't imagine anyone ever forgiving you. I want to tell her that she's enough, and I want to thank her for giving me life. I realise; my mother sacrificed her life for me. I want to say that I'm sorry; I'm so fucking sorry.

I want the pain to stop but I've never really wanted to end my life. There's a difference, there's a vague line of distinction. I look at my mum and I know that soon she'll think about killing herself. She won't feel the glimmer of hope that she's given to me today.

What would I say to her now? Would I tell her that I met the most amazing boy ever? Would I tell her that I fell in love? Would I tell her that Gabriel dies, that he leaves me just like she left me? Because, looking at her, I realise that I don't want her life to be wasted. She gave up living for me yet I'm sitting here, hanging out with a mental bloke in his boxies, until he lets me return to a life where I don't trust anyone to get close to me.

I've forgotten to value all that I've had and all that I could still find. Yes, recently I've been able to find joy in little things but I'm not living. I stopped living at Gabe's funeral. I think I might have stopped being truly grateful too. For my mum, for Gabriel, even for Francesca.

'If only she'd asked for help to get away from your dad. If only she'd held on to hope. It was in the system, Theodora. It was all part of her Christmas miracle. Your mum stopped believing in the goodness of others,' he says.

'The adoption didn't happen,' I say. I know that it didn't; I've lived the story.

'It's easy for others to preach. When you're drowning in pain, where life feels unworkable, the last thing you want is to open up to others and to seek help,' St Nick says. 'She'd been feeling worthless and unloved for months. Each day, without you, those feelings were building inside and she believed that she deserved your dad's abuse. She believed that she was unlovable and a failure.'

'Am I like her?' I say.

'Only a little,' St Nick replies. 'Your heart is fragile and your mind is weary, but we're talking. I think I might have the beginning of a plan for you to do great things. To be someone remarkable. That's the difference…'

'The same but different,' I say, watching my mum. She holds me so very close.

'I was going to help,' St Nick says. His voice is full of regret. 'She gave up on herself, not on you. She was protecting you. I feel it's important that you grasp that, Theodora Quirke,' he says and I nod. 'When she decided to change, she was beaten down. She stopped believing that there would be an up away from her despair,' he says.

'You're asking me to be more than I currently am, aren't you?'

'I'm saying I understand. It's only been ten months. But yes, Theodora Quirke, be more for you, for Gabriel and for your mum,' he says. 'I'm asking you to honour their lives and your own.'

'Are there paradox issues with me seeing myself? Am I going to explode or something? There was this episode of *Doctor Who* where—'

'Well that's the most ridiculous question I've ever heard,' St Nick says.

'Am I actually dead?' I whisper.

'No, you are very much alive,' he says.

'This is so fucked up,' I whisper.

'It's fine to be a little fucked up. We all are, to a certain extent. Yet some are masters at pretending they're not,' St Nick says. 'I'm here to save you.'

'From what though?' I ask and St Nick shrugs his shoulders.

'If I'm being entirely honest... I've no idea,' he says. 'But the note...'

'I'm not sure if I should be scared or grateful that someone thought you were my best shot at being saved,' I say.

St Nick slaps me on the back and my entire body wobbles. He laughs. In that moment, little Theodora looks over at us. She waves a hand at me and I wave back. Our mum has her eyes closed.

'She can see and hear us,' I say.

'Your eyes are open for the first time. You're letting me in to that wonderful heart of yours,' St Nick says.

'I wish my mum could kiss my cheek and make everything feel better,' I say. My fingers reach up to stroke my face. I watch as my mum twists little Theodora around to look her in the eyes.

'Never forget how much Mummy loves you,' she says. She bends and kisses little Theodora on the cheek. A flutter of air dances over my fingers.

'Thank you,' I whisper, as I turn to look at St Nick. And in this moment I know that every ounce of my being believes in magic and I believe in Nikolaos of Myra.

'There are things that I can't change,' he says, looking over at my mum.

'But you're able to remind me of what I've forgotten,' I say and he nods.

'I've been in your life since the beginning. You just didn't realise,' St Nick says.

'Maybe this is how you save me. By making me realise that I want to help people.'

'I hope so,' St Nick says. 'That would be quite the result.'

'I want to be a better person for Gabriel and for my mum,' I say.

'And for you,' he says and I nod. 'Shall we go?' He picks up his umbrella and places his hand on my shoulder.

I nod, mouthing 'goodbye' to my mum and my little self.

SPITFIRE SAINT NICHOLAS UMBRELLA COLLECTIVE ☑

COMMUNITY

Hello friends! DOTTIE SMITH, founder of the SpitfireSNUC, here. Welcome to our rebranded Facebook page. I thought I'd tackle some questions and answers to help you understand why I founded the group. Leave a comment below if there's anything that's still not clear. Thanks for visiting!

IS IT TRUE THAT SAINT NICHOLAS PERFORMED MIRACLES?

Over the years, stories that centred on Saint Nicholas have been fabricated and exaggerated. Yet true stories remain and I'm keen to keep his origins and essence alive. Of the reported reminiscences it is the story of how Saint Nicholas returned a burned child back to full health that first linked him to children. Then came the tale of how he prevented a poor merchant from having to force his three daughters into prostitution. The poor merchant was unable to afford dowry for his three daughters when Saint Nicholas threw three bags of money into the merchant's garden. Of course over the years the retelling has altered to the bags being stockings and those stockings being deposited down the merchant's chimney, which is where the origin for that Father Christmas tradition began.

Also aside from the many miracles Saint Nicholas is said to have performed at sea, it is reported that he crumbled prison walls to prevent condemned, innocent prisoners from death, that he multiplied a shipment of grain to prevent famine and that he resurrected three students, who had been butchered to death, from the dead. I believe each of these tales to be truthful.

I have identified many other miracles and acts of kindness that can be traced back to Saint Nicholas. They all occurred on or around December 6th and will all be reported here, on this Facebook wall.

DO PEOPLE STILL CELEBRATE THE FEAST OF ST NICHOLAS?

The feast of Saint Nicholas is on December 6th. Even in modern times, this day brings much celebrating in Eastern Europe and Germanic countries. Italy also observes and parties. But I have founded the first ever Facebook group to state that Saint Nicholas is still living amongst us. This is also probably the first Facebook group to mark the celebration of Saint Nicholas and all that he has offered the world over hundreds of years, without him once asking for gratitude and thanks.

WHAT IS THE SIGNIFICANCE OF DECEMBER 6th TO YOUR GROUP?

On December 6th each year, people remember the death of Saint Nicholas of Myra. Nikolaos of Myra was said to have died on December 6th in 346, others claim the date to be between A.D. 326 and A.D. 341. Thus no date of his death can be confirmed.

I (and all the other members of this group) believe he didn't die. I believe he is immortal and continues to work amongst us.

He was a Greek bishop and I am committed to celebrating his life and his legacy. He is said to have performed miracles and to have given secret gifts. Known as Nicholas the Wonderworker for his miracles, the claim that he is linked with Santa Claus is rejected by those, like me, who know of St Nicholas' true purpose.

WHERE IS MYRA?

Formerly a Greek town, Myra is now known as Kale and is situated in the west bay of Antalya, Turkey. St Nicholas' tomb in Myra remains a popular place of pilgrimage. Perhaps this is where I need to add – where Saint Nicholas lived there was no snow, no reindeers and no elves.

THEO (THEODORA QUIRKE)

OK, so we're in the middle of a school playground. There are huddles of children scattered around the vast concrete space. There are voices at every level of sound, from a whisper to a squeal. I can hear them all. It's like all the noise has been concertinaed together and now someone's squeezing out the individual sounds to set the scene.

I spin on the spot, trying to get my bearings. I recognise this place. It's my old high school. Some boys are playing football with a tennis ball. They race across the concrete, sliding about in their school shoes. No trainers allowed. There's another boy, over on the right, opening a plastic Tupperware box and he's showing his friends something inside. A gasp and a collective, 'Oooh,' from two of his friends. There are girls standing in small huddles, sheltering each other from the wind. Girls walking over to boys. There are boys chasing girls, there are girls chasing boys, there are girls chasing girls. It's chaotic and noisy and very much real.

I'm trying to figure out how we're standing outside in what looks to be cold but there's no shift in temperature for me. I've lost my puffer jacket and seem to have lost the hoodie too. The leggings and Gabriel's old Nirvana T-shirt shouldn't be keeping me this warm. I've no idea of the year, the time, the season. It's all familiar, what with me only having officially left the sixth form a few months ago, but there's something different that I can't quite grasp. It's present but past.

As I spin for another good look, I see St Nick. He's sitting a little way away, on a patch of grass near a group of boys.

The grass must be wet. He's smoking what looks like a long joint and he's smiling. A tub of Original Pringles next to him and a red boombox playing *Everything's Gonna Be Alright*. He's wearing grey trackies and a white vest top covers his belly. He mustn't feel the cold either. He twirls his closed umbrella like a baton in time to the music. I can't help but feel grateful. Clearly, he's made an effort to wear clothes so that I won't think he's a paedophile, or possibly so that children won't scream 'stranger danger' at him. Although no one's looking at us so clearly we're invisible. I want to linger and figure out why we're here, but I run over to him instead and crouch down.

'Nice vest,' I say, nodding at his clothes. He smiles and then winks.

'I've never been one for fashion,' he says. 'I consider myself more of a trendsetter than a follower.' I laugh.

He lifts the joint to his lips again. The reggae music stops then *Jingle Bells* blares out. Too loud. Sounds like a kids' choir and makes him look ridiculous.

'I'm not in control of this,' St Nick says. Joint balancing between his lips, he turns the buttons rapidly and that just makes the music louder. I've no idea what he's going on about but it's all very noisy and real.

As I look around, I have a vague recollection that it's December, and that it's close to Christmas. No snow, not that much rain, almost too mild for winter.

'Will I get a cold if I sit out here without a coat?' I say.

'Nope,' St Nick says. He inhales a long drag on his special cigarette. He exhales the smoke into my face and the smell is distinctly herbal.

'Want some ganja?' he shouts over the music. He offers it to me.

I shake my head as I sit down. He plays this game by his own rules. 'So…' I say. 'You going to tell me why we're here?'

He points his joint at something. I follow his direction as *Jingle Bells* stops. The entire playground seems to quieten, and that's when I see her. She isn't too far away from where we're sitting. That's why this all seems familiar.

It's her first day at a new school. She's been moved to this new area, to a new foster family. It's the start of December, not long before the Christmas break; it's year seven and friendship groups were established weeks before. She knows no one and no one's bothered with her. She's sitting at a picnic bench, ignoring the wetness seeping through her coat and skirt; she's not really bothered that she's on her own. She thinks she prefers it that way, but she's wrong. It's just that she knows no difference. I watch as a boy walks over to her.

'I know what happens next,' I say. I stand and run across to them. I'm close enough to hear him speak.

'What football team do you support?' he says. She looks up to see him standing in front of her. Brown curls and blue eyes, his cheeks are pinked from running around the playground. He's all smiles and confidence. I look at his eyes and I smile too. He's a cheeky kid, with no worries and the self-assurance of someone much older.

She doesn't reply straight away. She's trying to figure out what to say. She wants to say Liverpool but she thinks supporting Everton might be cooler. 'Never been to a match,' she says. She's cross with herself the minute she says those words.

'You can still support a team without going to the match,' he says.

She shakes her head. 'What's the point of that?' she asks and she hates that she does. She knows she should try to keep her opinions to herself if she wants to make friends. She's amazed that he laughs and then sits down next to her.

'Gabe,' he says. He holds out a hand to shake. It's a formal gesture that feels too grand and too old when I'm watching them, but that's Gabriel. I used to joke that his spirit animal was a Victorian butler.

'Theo,' she says, taking his hand and letting the shake happen. It was her first day of being just Theo. She'd spent all of the day before writing out her name on a piece of paper. She never wanted to be Theodora again.

'A girl called Theo. Awesome,' he says.

I know that her hands are sweaty, his are too, and the shake's a little too floppy. After the handshake, they wipe their palms on their blazers and she giggles. The sound makes me smile. This memory isn't causing me pain. I'm not watching and wishing I could go back to that time and change anything about it or stop it from happening. I'm looking in on a moment and feeling grateful.

'First day of me being just Theo,' I say to no one, but St Nick's appeared next to me, because he's magic and clearly a little bit of a freak. I smell his sweat and the new herbal essence from his joint, and then I feel his hand on my shoulder. He squeezes and it's a little too much like a pinch, but I recognise he's doing that to let me know it's all okay.

'I prefer you being Theodora,' St Nick says. 'That was your first Christmas miracle.' He points his umbrella towards younger me and Gabriel.

'What?' I ask.

'It's December 6th,' he says, as if that offers explanation.

'You did that?' I say, looking at the instant connection between me and Gabriel.

'I've always felt a responsibility for you, Theodora Quirke.

THEO (THEODORA QUIRKE)

My hands grip each other and I haven't taken my eyes off Gabriel and Theo. They're chatting away like they've always been friends. They maintain eye contact and they laugh. I know that the laughter's genuine and comes from their bellies. Seeing the instant connection reminds and comforts me that I've not somehow made up the narrative of how I met Gabe to try and make me feel better about myself.

Since his death, or maybe more since what happened after the funeral, I've worried that I daydreamed our connection. That worry's gone now though. There's magic in that very first contact. Pure St Nicholas magic. We're all smiles and there's none of the awkward boy-meets-girl bollocks that so many have when they're trying to impress the other person.

That's the thing about Gabriel and me. I never felt like I had to impress him. I never felt like I needed to be perfect around him. It was like, from this very first moment, and in all the years of our friendship, he trusted in me to get it right. I mean, he trusted in me to be the best possible version of me that I could be. Of course he worried that I'd fall off the rails and he'd not be able to save me. I imagine that burden was shit and overwhelming at times, but he never showed it. Not once did I look in his eyes and see doubt. He genuinely believed that everything would be okay in the end.

I pretty much had a million issues with being abandoned and not having roots. I was wild, untamed and opinionated. I was reckless, outspoken and completely lost for a lot of the time he knew me. Yet he just seemed to recognise that I

47

was a contradiction – that I wanted to be different yet that I longed to belong. Fear of rejection and never quite feeling good enough often led me into ridiculous situations. And that's when Gabriel would step forward. His love for me boundless, his friendship unconditional. He proved that time and time again. I pushed and he pulled me closer. I jumped and he'd wait until I needed him. He understood that I was a ball of inconsistency; he understood beyond his years and experience.

Fuck, I miss him.

I wanted to belong, but belonging terrified me. I wanted to be loved, but loving terrified me. I fought him for years, and all he did was keep showing just how much he loved me. He proved himself time and again, and eventually I let him in. I let myself feel loved and I gave myself to him completely.

I glance away from them, my eyes full of tears. 'Now he's gone I'll never be able to tell him just how truly grateful I am to him,' I whisper. The tears escape. I'm crying again, but it's got nothing to do with sadness.

'He knows,' St Nick says. He puts his arm around my shoulder and pulls me in towards his sweaty armpit. I lean in, desperate for human comfort.

When was the last time I let someone hold me? I have to breathe through my mouth though. His sweat smells like the stinky cheese Francesca used to get for Christmas. Fuck, I miss her too.

'He showed me that I was capable of loving and worthy of love. His gifts to me,' I whisper.

'That's why I think my offer is perfect for you,' St Nick says.

'Offer?' I ask.

'Later,' he says, shaking a hand in the air to rub my questions away. 'You have so much to give, Theodora Quirke. I could suggest that it'd be an insult to Gabriel's memory, but...'

'But you think that's just an adult spouting bollocks again,' I say and St Nick nods.

'Francesca bought me a present that first Christmas. Gabriel went home from school and told her all about me. About two weeks later, on the last day of term, he came rushing up to me and pushed the gift into my chest. It was a small, square box, the wrapping paper covered in robins and a red ribbon was tied around it. Inside was a silver name necklace. I'd really become "Theo". There was a card too, saying how much she was looking forward to meeting me...'

I stop. The memory is full of happiness, but my stomach flips with an ache that drags.

'You miss her?' St Nick says and I nod. Every single day. In some ways the missing of her is worse than the missing of Gabriel. She's alive. That I can't just pop around and see her is knee-buckling, belly churning shittiness. We should be helping each other.

'I wore that necklace every day until Gabe's funeral.'

I shrug myself out of St Nick's sweaty embrace. The memory of Gabriel's wake still fresh, still unresolved. My eyes somehow feel itchy and raw. I'm tired. This discussion is raking up too much emotion.

'I don't think I can ever love again,' I say. 'I don't think I'll ever be strong enough to deal with more rejection or loss.'

'You're stronger than you realise, Theodora Quirke,' he says.

I stare at Theo and Gabe. That past is a better place than my conversation with St Nick. 'We arrange to meet at lunch,' I say, nodding over at my younger self and Gabriel. Tears make their way down my cheeks. 'Turns out we get the same bus home and into school.'

'Inseparable,' he says.

'As friends,' I say. 'Best friends.'

'A bright lad,' he says. 'An old soul.'

'We never ran out of words,' I say. My crying eyes refuse to shift from them. I'm smiling though. I can't help but smile. My life changed that day. 'We were best friends for almost four years before anything changed between us.'

'This one's only a short stop,' he says. 'Just a reminder. Time to go,' he says. I nod as St Nick places a hand on my shoulder.

And we are gone.

SPITFIRE SAINT NICHOLAS UMBRELLA COLLECTIVE ☑

COMMUNITY

Hello friends! DOTTIE SMITH, founder of the SpitfireSNUC, here again. I love how many of you are asking for practical ways to get involved! As always, I hope my answers make sense, but if they don't, leave a comment below. Thanks again, friends. Your kindness touched my heart.

WHY SHOULD I BE INTERESTED IN SAINT NICHOLAS?

Saint Nicholas embodies a spirit of bigheartedness, of kindness, of generosity and love. On the eve of December 6th and on December 6th, many people remember the spirit and meaning behind the giving of gifts. Widely celebrated in Europe, St Nicholas' feast day, keeps the tales of his virtuousness and open-handedness flourishing.

In Germany and Poland, boys wear bishop costumes and beg for offerings for those poorer and for themselves. In much of Europe, December 6th is still the main day for giving gifts and partying, with many beginning festivities on the eve of the day. The gifts are small, they are simple, and they are often handmade and full of love.

Why would you choose to reject such tradition and simplicity? You should be interested, because this is your path back to the true meaning of joyful Christmas gift giving and away from commercialism that so many companies are forcing upon you.

HOW CAN WE CELEBRATE THE FEAST OF SAINT NICHOLAS?

Some honour the tradition of leaving a shoe or sock outside their front door for Saint Nicholas on the eve of his feast day. They often only leave one of their pair, so as not to show greed. The gifts received are small: sweets, small toys, a few coins. They are gifts to be shared. This day is never about squirrelling and owning, it is about distributing, sharing, welcoming and being thankful. The day is about remembering the reported charitable acts and the true meaning of giving that has been lost within the commercial splurge of Christmas.

As well as small gifts left in shoes, Saint Nicholas has been reported to offer a select number of deserving individuals with large, life-changing rewards. This is what this group is all about. Some call them miracles, for there is little earthly explanation for how Saint Nicholas can achieve what he does. I call them rewards. I feel it is my role to help Saint Nicholas by drawing his attention to our worthy group members. That is the purpose of this group.

THEO (THEODORA QUIRKE)

We don't end up back outside Dante House, instead we're sitting under what appears to be a large wooden table. I think there are blankets and sheets hanging down from the table concealing us. The blankets and sheets are different colours and different textures. On the floor there is a multi-coloured array of cushions and pillows, and there are fairy lights wrapped around the table's legs. I'm sitting up, cross-legged, so the table must be quite tall. I shuffle about a bit, trying to get comfy by shoving a cushion under my arse. St Nick's lying down, his umbrella next to him, pulling pillows and cushions under him.

'How—' I start to ask but change to: 'Is this your grotto?'

'Imbecile,' St Nick says. He knows I'm joking though. 'Built us a blanket fort. Thought we could do with a rest before we travel again.'

He's wearing the same grey trackies and white vest, but he's added fluffy white slipper boots; possibly because we're inside now. I watch as he screws up his face and jiggles his body a bit, before letting out the biggest fart I've ever heard. It stinks so much I have to pop my head outside of the fort blanket to gulp in some fresh air. There's nothing useful out there; an empty room with white walls. I've no idea where we are or when this might be occurring on my timeline.

'There's something very wrong with your arse,' I say after putting my head back inside and getting a waft of his lingering eggy fart.

He laughs. 'Better out than in.'

I glare at him. He doesn't seem to know the rules about how to behave in social situations but there's something refreshing in his approach. Not his arse, in his inability to hide his true self. Seems to me that society wants openness, but only if we put a filter on it and only if we show the best bits.

'You know, Theodora Quirke, when I first met Charles Dickens, he—'

'You've met Dickens?' I say, but he bats my words away with his hand.

'He was very keen to hear about my line of work,' St Nick continues. 'I would like to think that my showing him moments that had altered him unleashed the nostalgic.' He rolls on to his side with cushions propping up his head.

'So you're basically saying that you're the Ghost of Christmas Past?' I say.

'I was thinner and only had a moustache then. It was majestic, twirled at the edges and made me look rather divine. I was less jaded by his society. Yet I must have touched on some of Charles' emotions and memories that he had long discarded, made him hungry for more.' He stops talking and looks me. 'Though I remain furious he didn't give me credit for that damn book of his. Tad rude.' A smile spreads across his face.

'Are there other ghosts still to come?' I ask and St Nick shakes his head. I can't help but wonder if Gabriel's considered a ghost and if that means St Nick won't be arranging for him to visit. I don't ask though.

'The fact I only revisited his past made Mr Dickens quite the angry elf,' St Nick says. 'No one knows your future, Theodora Quirke. That's not how it all works...' St Nick pauses.

'But?' I ask, still not able to say that word without a smile.

'I guess my fear is that you, my dear Theodora, also see the larger world as an unkind and unfortunate place. You had quite a negative opinion of your past. Not that I'm comparing you to Scrooge,' St Nick says. I can't help but laugh. He basically is. 'But by allowing you to see times that are real, when you were truly loved, or when you were happier, I'm preparing you to face your future with an optimistic and less cynical attitude. I have a suggestion to make soon. It'll be your greatest challenge yet, so I'm offering you these snippets before… Well, let's just say that we're unwrapping Theodora Quirke.'

He pauses and for a moment I wonder if he's about to fart again, but then he speaks.

'I'm proud of how you've embraced this so far,' St Nick says and that recognition sends warmth shooting through me. 'I'm preparing you for greatness, defiant Theodora. And let me tell you that Charles was very reluctant at first. His shrieks of "Show me no more", were heard all through the realms. You're quite remarkable in comparison.'

'You tell the best stories,' I say and St Nick nods again. I watch as he stays perfectly still. No itching his arse or shuffling around. It's like he leaves his body for a few seconds. Like there's a conversation going on just beyond what I can see or hear. Mad as fuck to watch.

'People change over time and when given space, throughout their many lives,' St Nick says, as he flicks back to being with me. 'But when the worst thing that a person can imagine occurs, it changes them instantly.'

'I don't really recognise myself anymore,' I say. 'Not when I compare this me to that girl who met Gabe for the first time.'

'Then we'll start from this very moment, and I'll help you. You're going to be someone entirely different again when I've finished with you,' he says. I smile.

'It's painful not to pretend, but it's tiring to pretend,' I say.

I read that somewhere, might have been on the wall in the toilets in The Raz on Seel Street. 'I don't want to get to the end of my life and conclude that it's been a pile of shit,' I say and St Nick nods. 'I don't belong anywhere,' I whisper.

'Then I'll give you a place to belong,' he says.

I rearrange the cushions and then lie on them, leaving a gap between me and St Nick. This should be weird, but it isn't. Faux fur and other super soft textiles surround me. I can't help but close my eyes. I couldn't remember feeling this very safe with anyone other than Gabe and Francesca. But I can now. Because, thanks to Nick, I remember being held by my mum.

'Super comfy grotto this,' I say, as I drift off to sleep.

MY STORY – BY DOTTIE SMITH

(Founder of Spitfire Saint Nicholas Umbrella Collective)

A new far away city and a new start turned out to be what I needed. I'm not saying I got over the deaths of Noah, Betty and Neil, but I was learning to function alongside my memories of them. I found some part-time work in a sweetshop and I made up a little story 'bout where I came from and what I'd been through. As far as my new boss and the customers knew, I was divorced, childless and not looking for love. Sometimes I looked at the kiddies in the shop a little too long, but it all fitted with my role of lonely spinster. I was old before my years, but none of that was any bother to me. I was just one more lost soul in a big city that didn't really give two hoots. I had my box of magic memories and this feeling in my gut that something more was coming.

Years passed, I stayed in the same routine, ended up manager of that shop, and even though I never talked 'bout the umbrella man, I had at least one dream 'bout him every single week, without fail, and, if I'm being entirely honest, from time to time he was naked and frisky. Them dreams fuelled the hope in my belly. Them dreams kept me going. My hope was my choice.

Then one day I read 'bout a bloke named Jack Warner. The sweetshop had branched out into selling magazines and newspapers. During one of them quiet times, just after the lunchtime school rush, I was having a nosey little read of one of the tabloids. The newspaper was reporting on how Jack Warner had been driving his car to work when he collided with a lorry. It was no one's fault, or anything like that. Newspaper said how the lorry driver was pronounced dead at the scene and how Jack was airlifted to hospital. He wasn't expected to get better, let alone be up and out of hospital within a week. The paper was calling it 'a miraculous recovery'. Jack's mother was quoted saying it was all down to her and the power of her praying.

Then, in the same article, Jack was quoted saying he was visited in hospital, on December 6th, by a strange bloke with a weird umbrella. Jack said the man waved his umbrella over him and that that was what cured him. Newspaper said there were no CCTV images to back up Jack's claim. One of the nurses interviewed said it was probably a 'drug-induced hallucination', but the fact remained that Jack Warner's injuries were near fatal and yet somehow he not only recovered, but he was healed completely within a week of a stranger with an umbrella visiting him. Newspaper said Jack Warner 'defied medical intervention'.

Of course, I was chuffed for Jack Warner, but what made me read that article at least ten times in a half hour was more than that. Some of them details jingled my bells. I mean they'd not be important details to others, but the miracle happening on December 6th and the mention of a man with an umbrella seemed like too much of a coincidence for my liking.

I wrote a letter to Jack, via the newspaper, and mentioned a few details 'bout the umbrella man. A few days later he telephoned me at work. We chatted briefly, probably for him to figure out if I was a nutter.

A few days later when I'd wangled a day off, I travelled to Brighton to meet him. I took my box of memories with me too. I liked him instantly.

After that initial meeting, that lasted all day and ended with us eating chips on Brighton pier, Jack and me were thick as thieves. There wasn't anything romantic to it, I mean not on my side anyway, but it's fair to say that his daily phone calls to my work brightened my day. Jack was the only person in my new life who knew the truth 'bout my Noah, Betty and Neil. Being able to talk 'bout them again meant everything to me. In many ways, it brought them back from the dead.

Jack and me figured there had to be more to this umbrella man and how both of our miracles had happened on December 6th. Jack got to doing some research and I scoured every newspaper that came into the sweetshop. He was the one who found out 'bout how Lucas Edwards got all that money for his operation and 'bout Birgitte Jesson's seven sacks of letters. The more we searched, the more we found out 'bout all these miracles happening on the same date, and the more we delved the more sightings we found of a weird bloke with an umbrella.

Later, we happened to come across details of the feast of Saint Nicholas being on December 6th. I can't even remember exactly how that came 'bout. After a bit more investigation, we found out 'bout the many miracles Saint Nicholas was said to have performed. We researched and researched and all them findings led back to the same place, Saint Nicholas, and they all seemed to be occurring on or around December 6th.

I guess when we put two and two together, we probably jumped to a conclusion others wouldn't have bothered with. But did any of that matter? We weren't hurting no folk. We were celebrating a bloke who embodied the spirit of bigheartedness, of kindness, of generosity and of love. He was all 'bout remembering the spirit of giving gifts, and I don't know 'bout your thoughts on Christmas, but the state of commercialism was getting me down.

And let's not forget that my Christmas spirit had gone up in flames. I wasn't 'bout to be popping up a Christmas tree in my living room and singing Christmas carols to my baubles.

And, from the research me and Jack were doing, Saint Nicholas wasn't 'bout anything like that either. Virtuousness, generosity and helping other folk were all things I wanted to be doing. It stopped me dwelling on all that was lost and made me consider all I could still give to the world. So, you see, it was Saint Nicholas who gave me back my focus and drive. I think I might even have been fancying his job.

MY STORY – BY DOTTIE SMITH

(Founder of Spitfire Saint Nicholas Umbrella Collective)

It was also around that time that blogging was starting to be popular and me and Jack were spending most weekends together. Not like that. Just friends.

We, Jack and me, decided to start a blog all 'bout what we'd found out. Called ourselves the Saint Nicholas Umbrella Collective back then. We mentioned the umbrella, thinking that any others who'd experienced the umbrella man would come looking. We reckoned that there'd be others just like us. I mean it was mainly just a hope, but still we put ourselves out there.

And they did find us, and they were spread all over the world. In the end, there were eight of us in total.

Birgitte Jesson we'd already contacted. Then Josette Borg was the first to find us online. She told us all 'bout them amazing details of how she got herself a miracle baby on December 6th delivered to her door. Then Laurence Rosseau and Sofia Beckerman got in touch. They told us all 'bout them emails Saint Nicholas had sent, introducing them to each other on December 6th and 'bout how they'd fallen in love as a result. Their story was a difficult one for me to hear. Sofia'd just had her first baby and them two seemed to have everything I'd lost. I don't feel like that now, but back then…

Anyway, Lucas Edwards and Christina Milano joined us later. Christina was cross as a bugger with Saint Nicholas for a while. Did you hear why? Saint Nicholas made her shag a ghost, which actually isn't as weird as it sounds.

What stumped us then was that it seemed we hadn't all seen the same person. When we were all describing him, his face wasn't always the same. Course we didn't have no photographs of him, but Laurence was pretty good at drawing and he sketched what we described. None of the drawings were the same. Not even close to each other.

Jack suggested it might be a group of blokes that went under the 'umbrella' name of being Saint Nicholas. Almost like the umbrella they carried was their calling card. We dismissed that theory because it just didn't sit true; there could only be one Saint Nicholas. And there was something 'bout our stories that connected them all together – as if it were the same bloke but he could take whatever form he wanted. I know I'm sounding crazy, but you've got to stick with this. Sometimes when all things point to a crazy explanation, there ain't nothing else to do but to go with it.

When all eight of us got to researching in our home countries, a whole host of possible other cases from back in time were found. George Washington's re-election, Nora Barnable's husband writing again, Emma Murray's life-changing millions, that missing Van Gogh painting turning up on David – Oh wait, I'm not supposed to say where it was found. Anyway, so many more instances all happening on the eve of December 6th or on that actual day. No doubt you'll have checked out our blog by now, so nothing I'm saying will come as a surprise.

I liked that there were only a few of us back then. We were all searching for the same answers, and not once did any of them accuse me of murdering Noah, Betty and Neil. I guess we'd all had experience of them folk with their eye rolls and accusing whispers. Each of us had been ridiculed and I wasn't the only one to have had my sanity questioned. Christina was even locked up on a psych ward for a bit.

With them seven strangers, I belonged someplace again. They believed me and, over time, they became my new family. Of course we were all dotted across the globe, but we wrote letters, emails, more recently Skype, WhatsApp and Facetime. A couple of years ago, I even started a public Facebook page for us. I never explained why the umbrella was in the title of my Facebook group name, but I figured that those who'd met Saint Nicholas would recognise it instantly.

By then the eight of us were meeting up once a year, always on and around December 6th. We'd give each other gifts, we'd play board games, we'd eat good food and we'd toast the man who'd brought us together. Our gifts tended to be small and simple, and they were always handmade with love. It's fair to say that I'm now a bit of an expert at papier-mâché.

All of us with our own baggage came together to celebrate Saint Nicholas on his feast day. We'd all travel to where one member lived. We'd take it in turns. The rest of the year was spent trying to track any more Saint Nicholas news, but often contact was an excuse to share a photo, a problem or a piece of good news. I watched their children grow. It didn't take away the pain of mine not being close, but it filled a gap when one of them called me Aunty Dottie. It's also fair to say that Jack was the best mate I'd ever had.

Saint Nicholas joined us all, but he wasn't some kind of driving force keeping us together. I loved each of them members, even Christina Milano, like they were my own blood.

Yes, we were happy, ticking along and feeling special to have been chosen by Saint Nicholas. Obviously, we were monitoring for sightings of Saint Nicholas, and of course we'd have quite liked to thank him for saving us and bringing us together. But I don't think we ever really thought that a possibility. I don't think we really questioned why stuff had happened or why we'd been chosen for a Christmas miracle. We were content and we were happy. More than that, probably, we were grateful. Jack used to say that sometimes the right response to gratitude was simply to keep your mouth shut.

Then along came them Spitfire arseholes and everything changed again.

THEO (THEODORA QUIRKE)

I wake to the air having a distinct smell of stale fart. I stretch out my arms and take in my surroundings. Still in the blanket fort, still got a hairy fat man lying next to me. This new reality is off its head. He smiles when I look at him, his teeth crooked and yellowing.

'You been watching me sleep?' I ask.

'It's what I do,' he says and he winks.

I can't help but laugh at him as I reach out and punch his arm. Not a hard punch or anything like that. His arms are naked, his vest removed and he's probably now only wearing his too-tight boxers under the red fleecy blanket, but I'm trying not to think about that. He wriggles about on the cushions, getting comfy again. He grunts with each movement. He's not a fit man. I wonder if he didn't move around when I was sleeping, so as not to wake me.

'You understand the pain of being alone, don't you?' I ask. Our eyes lock and he smiles. I fold my arms around my body, like I'm tying myself up and protecting me from what's coming next.

'Do you feel the best you've felt since Gabriel died?' St Nick asks.

I pause and I consider his question. Tiny shivers of excitement tickle when I breathe. I nod. I do.

'Very good. It's a prolonged process and not one that allows a sudden switch to your new identity.'

'What?' I ask, suddenly upright. I bang my head on the table. I swear that was taller before I slept.

'You've been with me a few months already, although I suspect it merely feels like hours.'

'Months?' I ask. 'Have I missed Christmas?' I ask. Like that even matters. Like anyone would give a fuck about me. Like Santa would even visit—

Stacey. Shit.

'My boss,' I say. 'I need to text her.' I scramble about the cushions and blankets, searching for my phone. 'I'll be sacked. That job was shit hard to get.'

St Nick laughs from his belly. 'Job's long gone,' he says.

'Fuck off,' I say.

'You don't need that job anymore,' he says. I'm about to scream at him when he holds up his palm. 'Listen.' There's this weird deep line between his eyes, like I've pissed him off and his tone's different. I nod, not looking him in the eyes, for him to continue.

'You're the sum of your past experiences; we all are. I feared that you'd rewritten the good moments in your life and given them a negative spin.' He pauses again but I don't look up.

I need to try not to react. I need to listen to what he's got to say. But he said months have passed? Months of my life have gone. How the fuck's that possible? I feel sick. My belly's whirling like a spin driver and I don't want to vomit on his cushions.

'You know, life is often *shit* but there have been and there will be extraordinary moments that make that *shit's* purpose understood,' St Nick says.

I gulp, then look up. 'Considering you look like a hairy nutter and smell like a drain, you're really very wise,' I say. 'You know, when Gabe was still here I was learning to trust and to ask for help. I was a work in process,' I say. I'm not sure why a nervous giggle emerges. I'm not finding this funny. 'I had to learn that I could turn to him, in my darker moments. I had to learn that it wasn't weak to ask for his help,' I say.

'And without him, you feel you'll never trust again and that you're entirely alone with no one to ask for help,' St Nick says and I nod. 'But that's not the case, defiant Theodora. I've been sent to save you and...'

I nod for him to continue.

'Well, I'm not really sure how this all works. It isn't really my area of expertise... I mean I'm not 100%, but I think I'm supposed to... I mean I might have to possibly show you that you can have a role in this life. You have a future.'

'A role?' I say.

'All in good time, but know it's a job offer that doesn't involve wiping old people's arses,' St Nick says. 'I've had to pull a few strings and some people,' he looks to the roof of our blanket fort, 'aren't that happy.'

'I'm not sure I—'

'You're a beautiful, magical, living, breathing child. You've been given life. A gift. And I think I can give you what you need. Many might even say that moments filled with the bleakest tragedy often host the most magnificent gifts.'

'Adults spouting bollocks,' I say and St Nick laughs. He's rolling from side-to-side, clearly scratching his back on the pillows below him. His face is a picture.

'Perhaps. But one day your life will be a complete painting. An extraordinarily beautiful painting full of your shit and good,' he says. 'Not literally. Not like that art Gilbert & George do with their bodily fluids.' His face twists into exaggerated disgust and he pinches his bulbous nose with his fingers.

I've no idea what he's talking about but still I'm smiling like I do.

'You'll never stop missing Gabriel,' St Nick says.

'I just wish I could see him again,' I say. 'One last time. Just to say goodbye.'

'That's a normal reaction. You'll still long for him and you'll still miss him with all that's within you, but that physical pain of grief does fade. Love and gratitude will replace that pain,' St Nick says.

'I want to believe you,' I say. 'But what about missing my mum. That's a new pain.'

'You'll learn to accept what can't be altered. That's all I can offer,' he says. 'I've known love. She died and I learned, over time, to live without her. Can't say I ever accepted her death though. I've spent lifetimes searching for her,' St Nick says. 'I don't want you to be like me. I mean it's bad enough I've been like this for centuries and the last thing they need...' He pauses to look up at the roof of the blanket fort. 'Is another one like me.'

'I don't understand how all of this works,' I say. I spread my hands out, as if to welcome an explanation for the madness.

'I'm not allowed to tell you about after death—'

'There's an afterlife? Is that where Gabriel—'

'Shit.' He shakes his hands out in front of him as if to rub out the words. 'Look, forget I said that. It's more that the concept of God ruling everyone is outdated. It's much more liberal up—' he says.

'But there's an afterlife?' I ask again. I rush the words out.

'No, who said anything about an afterlife?' He shakes his head in an exaggerated manner, his hands still rubbing out imaginary words.

'You've said it now.'

'I said "s'maftalif". It's... it's Turkish.'

'That's not a word,' I say. 'Something happens after death?

You can't take it back. But then why didn't Gabe come to me at the séance? That makes no—'

'Ah, yes, that was why I wasn't to mention—'

'So Gabe is somewhere? He hasn't just disappeared?' I ask. My heart's jumping and suddenly I'm formulating a plan for how, after a life well lived, probably helping others, I'll be reunited with him. I wonder if you can have babies in the afterlife?

'All in good time, Theodora Quirke,' he says, breaking my thoughts. He's sitting up now too, bending forward so as not to bang his head.

'But if I can get—'

'All. In. Good. Time,' he repeats, emphasising each word. I already recognise that I can't push him for more details. I can't risk pushing too hard and him too far from me. A pause. 'People die. They go somewhere—'

'Like where?' I ask.

'It's complicated. My reign is only within the Christmas World, so I'm not an expert on all things afterlife,' he says and then he pauses.

'So now you're declaring yourself King of the Christmas World? For fuck's sake.' I glare at him, he sighs.

'In very basic terms. You die and your essence goes to a realm. There are six of them. You can choose to live there for a bit or to be reborn,' he says.

'Is Gabe waiting for me in a realm?' I ask.

'I honestly don't know. I think he might have been the person who sent that muddled message to save you, but I'm not entirely sure. To be honest, I'm making most of this up as I go along,' St Nick says, as he leans forward then rolls onto his belly. I dodge an arm, then a leg.

'You're winging it?' I say and St Nick laughs.

'That's almost entirely unimportant in this moment. Just remember that life's a string of nows. Happiness passes through some of them. No past, no present, just now. Although I accept that my showing you moments from your past does contradict this thinking...'

I laugh this time.

'I don't want to let go of Gabe,' I say. 'I'm scared I'll forget him.'

'Live in this now. Your reaction to grief's how it should be, it's not a symptom of madness. You were in love, he died and now you're sad. Soon you'll not be as sad anymore, later you'll only be sad occasionally. One day you'll help someone else to understand,' St Nick says. He's talking about himself. He understands this pain.

'Just keep a clear head and an open mind. You'll need it with what I'm going to offer,' he says. He's on his belly with his giant boxer shorts covered arse in the air. He lets out another huge fart.

I cover my nose and mouth with my palms. 'What the hell have you been eating? Rotten mince pies?'

'More where that came from,' he says, with a hugely crooked smile on his face. Fluffy white slipper boots gone, he shuffles his belly about on his pillows, rolling from side-to-side until his feet are almost in my face. 'Right, defiant Theodora Quirke, it's time to go. You've given me a brilliant idea for our next visit. Touch my foot and we'll be on our way.'

I look down at his dirty sole. His feet smell of tuna in brine.

'Fuck off, I'm not going anywhere near your foot,' I say.

But I do.

SPITFIRE SAINT NICHOLAS UMBRELLA COLLECTIVE ☑

COMMUNITY

Hello friends! DOTTIE SMITH, founder of the SpitfireSNUC, here. You've been asking for more actual evidence of miracles and, as you know, I am devoted to bringing you details of all the wonderful acts, miracles and donations that Saint Nicholas has given the general public, all over the world, on and around December 6ᵗʰ. These gifts were often to seemingly normal, insignificant people, which begs the question **– do you need reminding of your worth in the world?**

On December 6ᵗʰ, 1983, Birgitte Jesson, a teacher from Copenhagen, Denmark, had reached the lowest point in her life. Suicidal and unable to find joy, the teacher had made plans to end her own life that day. At six in the morning, she heard a disturbance downstairs and approached, not caring if she lived or died. You can imagine her shock on seeing Saint Nicholas escaping through an open window.

You can also imagine her astonishment at finding seven large mail sacks, full of letters addressed to her. She sat and began reading each letter. There were thousands of them. The contents detailed how she had helped each individual over the years; former students, work colleagues, homeless people she'd stopped to talk to, people she'd served at a soup kitchen, people who'd read a book she'd recommended, someone who remembered a joke she'd told, strangers who'd looked at her and smiled, strangers she'd smiled at. For the rest of the day she read and realised that she wasn't worthless and unimportant. She saw the echoes of the kindness that trailed behind her. The following day she asked for help.

Birgitte is one of the eight original members of the Spitfire Saint Nicholas Umbrella Collective.

For details on how to join SpitfireSNUC to be eligible for a Saint Nicholas Christmas miracle, go to www. SpitfireSNUC.com/becomeamember

MY STORY – BY DOTTIE SMITH

(Founder of Spitfire Saint Nicholas Umbrella Collective)

What he'd written on the Facebook wall came through to my email. It was a Monday night and I phoned Jack straight away. I read him the message. Jack said to ignore the Facebook wall post and I said I couldn't as it'd be rude. Jack said to delete the post off the wall and forget 'bout it. I said I would. But I didn't. I'm not good at ignoring people. I mean if someone's taken time to leave a message, then I ain't too big for my boots to reply.

I'd not even heard of that company called Spitfire but one of their representatives was leaving a message on my group's Facebook wall and saying that he had a proposition he'd like to share. I did a quick internet search and read all 'bout how they were one of them new internet department stores. I'd used Amazon before, but Spitfire wasn't really on my radar. To be fair, I wasn't that big on all things internet but from what I could gather, they were like some copycat Amazon company, being much smaller and they'd only been trading for a year. They seemed to specialise in furniture, but had branched themselves out into other stuff like books, DVDs and clothes. Internet told me Spitfire had plans to launch an online toy department on the run up to Christmas. Anyway, they were interested in my Facebook group and I couldn't help but be curious as to why they were bothering with us.

I don't really know why I didn't do what Jack wanted me to do – curiosity killed the cat, didn't it? – but I sent the bloke from Spitfire a Facebook message. And then, and I mean within a minute or so, the bloke from Spitfire, Mr Belsnickel, replied and then I replied again and then he replied. It all happened in ten minutes.

I don't know if it was my need to always be liked by folk or my inability to say no, but I gave the bloke my work number and he said he'd call the next day.

All of that would have been hunky dory, if Jack wasn't also one of the admins on my Facebook page. Obviously, after I told him 'bout the wall post, he was watching to see what I did next.

He phoned as soon as he saw the messages between me and Mr Belsnickel, and it was the first time I'd heard Jack shout. He was fuming. He said he was confused and annoyed and that he wasn't sure who I was no more. Then he hung up.

THEO (THEODORA QUIRKE)

'The word "séance" comes from the French word for "seat",' St Nick says, as he puts his umbrella down beside his feet. We've arrived in this new place and before I've a chance to spin around, I know what I'm about to see.

I'm in my old foster mum's house. The house is empty. Just me and a crazy idea from the past that if I summoned Gabriel, then he'd find a way to communicate with me and let me know that he was okay. I think I had a notion that if he really loved me then he'd find a way to talk to me. Even when he was dead. At the time I'd not slept for a couple of nights and it was in the week after Gabriel's funeral. My head was fucked and I'd reached a new level of exhaustion; I wasn't being my best self.

Back then I'd not had much experience of contacting dead people, not that I've had any new experience since, but I'd used Google to help guide me. I'd typed in 'want to contact a dead relative' and 'want to communicate with a spirit' and been surprised at just how many websites there were offering services and anecdotal evidence. There was a local guy, Martin Savage, who sounded legit. I emailed him and he offered to come to my house if I paid him a hundred quid. I didn't have the money to pay. I thought about it. If I looked in the bottom of my wardrobe upstairs, there was a bag full of stuff – DVDs mainly and half bottles of perfume – that I was going to try and flog in town. I never did though, mainly because everything I owned was a gift from Gabriel or Francesca. It was all I had left of them.

Back then I was sure, thanks to the step-by-step procedures I'd written down from Google, that if there was a spirit world, then Gabriel would want to make contact with me and a séance would make it easier for him. I thought of it like I was making a phone call to heaven, opening up those phone lines for communication.

'What are you doing?' St Nick says. He's wearing an oversized black cape over a burgundy 1970s' crushed velvet suit. The jacket and pants look at least two sizes too small. I shake my head.

'It's a séance. I'm dressed up,' he says, twirling so that his cape floats out. I wait until he stops spinning.

'And you're doing what?' He points at the other me sitting at the kitchen table. I've got a lighter in one hand and a candle in the other.

'Thinking about Gabe,' I say.

I look over at myself. I'm a tiny little thing, all broken and sleep deprived. I'm a size eight now, back then I was probably a stone lighter. I'd taken a pair of scissors to my blonde hair, so it's all choppy and all fragmented. There are black circles under my blue eyes and I'm wearing one of Gabriel's old Nike T-shirts and a pair of his shorts, with a belt tied over the material to keep them up. I'm the definition of skin and bones.

'Is the purpose to call Gabriel or your mother?' St Nick says.

'Gabe,' I say.

St Nick moves over to the oval wooden table, tripping over the cape on the way, and takes a seat next to the broken me. He doesn't have to pull out the chair, it's already out from the table, and broken me doesn't look up from staring at the candle she's about to light.

'I'd read that a spirit could cross realms after hearing my call. I'm plucking up the courage to speak to Gabe,' I say, as I move over to stand behind St Nick.

'Good idea,' he says. 'It's usually painful for spirits to cross back onto Earth. That's why they tend not to do it, unless there's an absolute need to get a message over or they can hitch a ride on a séance,' St Nick says.

'I'd have thought this would have qualified as an absolute need and an easy ride for Gabe. I was falling apart,' I say. I try to push away a niggling thought about Gabriel not loving me; it doesn't move.

'And seeing Gabriel would have made you better?' St Nick asks.

'Seeing him, at that time, would have made me want to be with him even more,' I whisper.

'And Gabriel would have been told that in his lessons. Although, just a few weeks in, the poor boy was probably still adjusting...' St Nick says and then pauses.

'Lessons?' I ask. 'What do you mean?'

'I shouldn't...' He pauses. He sighs. 'We continue to learn wherever we end up,' he says. He looks up at the ceiling. 'Whichever realm your Gabriel's in now, he will have a guardian; someone will be guiding him and helping him adjust.'

'Like in heaven?' I say. There's a sarcastic edge to how I say 'heaven'.

'Like heaven, but different,' he says. I want to ask more, but when I look at him he's looking at broken me while still talking. 'You're a bit rubbish at contacting the dead. You do realise you need a minimum of three people to do a séance?'

'No one wanted to be involved. Everyone I told said I should leave the dead alone,' I say. 'If you look closely...' I point over at the chairs next to where broken me is sitting, opposite St Nick, 'you'll see I've put two of the teddies Gabe gave me on those two chairs.' St Nick stands to lean over the table.

'Clever,' St Nick says, nodding his head as he sits back down. I can't help but smile. 'How are you going to communicate?'

'Spirit rapping,' I say.

'Classic,' St Nick says with a broad smile. 'Old school, but effective,' and then the broken me starts to speak.

'Gabe,' she says. 'I think I've already summoned you, but I don't really know for sure. I'm going to ask you some questions. I mean, I will when I've lit the candle and stuff. If it's not too much trouble, I'd like you to answer by rapping on the table. So, a single rap means yes or if you want to say more, then complex raps can be used to spell out words and complete sentences. Let's say that the number of raps for each letter will match with where it appears in the alphabet. Look, I've written it all down for you.' Broken me points at a piece of paper on the table. It's covered in letters with the corresponding number of raps under each letter.

I smile.

'Wow,' St Nick says. I turn to him and he's smiling. He nods at the paper in the table. 'You're a pro.'

'Shut up,' I say and turn back to broken me.

'I know text speak's not your bag, Gabe,' she says. 'But I'm thinking it might be a little bit quicker and helpful today.' She laughs, it echoes like she's trapped in a tin, and then the sound ends.

'I remember that laugh. It was almost as if I'd felt I'd been talking to him. I'd let my guard down and then was hit by the reality of what was happening,' I say.

'You're only little,' St Nick says.

'I'm not that much older now,' I say.

'Yes, but look how you're changing,' he says. 'Can you see how much stronger you are already?'

I look at broken me and I nod. The word 'defiance' jumps into my head.

'Yes, defiance in the eye of the storm that threatened to engulf you,' St Nick says. 'Already you're through the worst and already you're unaware just how you made it through. You've forgotten how you managed to survive. All that you know for sure is that you're not that little girl anymore.' He points at broken me. 'The storm failed to conquer you, my defiant Theodora Quirke.' He pauses. 'There are times that test our souls.'

I watch as broken me lights the candle she's holding and places it in the centre of the oval circle. Next, she stands and moves over to the light switch, turning off the light and moving back to the table. Just before the table she stops to lift a small jar of flowers that were picked from our former foster mum's garden and a slice of white bread that's waiting to be part of the séance.

'Internet told me bread and soup, but that's all I could find,' I say.

'You really are good at this,' St Nick says. 'You should consider it as a career. A kind of ghostbuster or something.' He chuckles to himself.

'Stop being a nobhead,' I say.

I watch as broken me places her hands on the table.

'This is the part where I needed someone to hold my hand and for a circle to be formed,' I say. 'I felt so alone.'

I move over to the broken me. I crouch down beside the table and place a hand on her hand. St Nick does the same with her other hand and we join ours together.

'Spirits of the past, move among us. Be guided by the light of this world and visit upon us,' broken me says.

We wait. Nothing happens. I look at St Nick and he shrugs his shoulders, making our arms lift. Broken me's arms lift too. She lets out a little squeal.

'She thought that was a sign,' I say. 'I remember feeling excited.'

'Beloved Gabriel, we bring you gifts from life into death. Be guided by the light of this world and visit upon us,' broken me says.

'I'd been told that I had to be patient and wait for the spirit's response,' I say. 'But I wasn't feeling very patient.'

'Gabe, are you there? Rap once for yes,' broken me says. Her voice is agitated and breathy.

'You dare,' St Nick says, glaring at me as I break our circle and make my hand into a fist.

'But she needs hope,' I say.

'No,' St Nick says. His face is serious, the smile is gone.

'Gabe, one rap,' she says. Her voice is louder and higher in pitch. 'Just let me know I meant something to you.' Tears stream down her cheeks. I'm crying too. I'm crying for her, for how very broken and alone she feels.

'She just needs hope,' I whisper, locking my eyes on St Nick's.

'No,' St Nick says. 'She needs to continue on the path she's on. Don't change this moment. This one needs to unravel in exactly the same way.'

'So why bring me here? What's the point of this?' I say, waving my arms out wide with my voice rising to a shout.

'So you can see that,' St Nick says. He points to something behind me.

THEO (THEODORA QUIRKE)

I turn quickly and just in time.

What the actual fuck?

I see Gabriel being restrained by a pretty woman, maybe in her twenties. She must be strong because he's thrashing about under her grip. Her hair's black, flattened on top and then to curls that frame her beautiful face. Her skin's porcelain, her eyes kind, her clothes outdated or possibly retro. She pulls him back by his arms; she must be pulling and pulling, as she's moving backwards slowly and no amount of Gabriel's restraint and trying to get into my foster mum's kitchen is working. It's like she's on a conveyor belt, being pulled back to someplace I don't know, and Gabriel's trying his best not to go with her.

'Let him stay,' I shout, trying to avoid chairs and cuddly toys, and falling over my feet in the process.

One of her feet disappears through the closed, wooden door. Her arse in her retro dress is going next. Her face is still pretty, even though she's straining and pulling. Gabriel's shaking his head and shouting something. He's trying to shake his arms free, but her grip isn't breaking. He's looking at broken me. He can't see this me.

'I can't hear him,' I say. 'Gabe,' I shout. I hurdle those two steps forward to the door. But just as I get there, the woman connects eyes with me. She must have somehow heard my shout and I can't pull my gaze away from her to turn and ask St Nick what the fuck's happening. The woman shakes her head. A warning. Her eyes are like ice; she wants him for herself, she won't let me near him.

She wants me to back off.

The woman pulls Gabriel through the closed, wooden door; he struggles but she wins. I can't stop him leaving.

'No,' I scream. I pull open the door and expect to see Gabriel standing there. He isn't there. Of course he isn't fucking there, but the door opening scares broken me. She screams and runs from the room crying.

'Well, that went *well*,' St Nick says. He reaches for the slice of bread, rolls it into a sausage shape and stuffs it into his mouth.

I look through the open door. I want Gabriel to appear. I want to understand where he's gone. He can't have just disappeared, can he? And who the fuck was she? Has he moved on already? Found someone else to love?

'Is that all I get? Is that my wish to see him again granted?' I ask. 'Because if it is, then you're a shit genie.'

Low murmurs come from the lounge. It's other me. I'm talking to the ceiling in there, apologising to Gabriel for breaking the séance. I'll give myself a hard time over that for the next few days.

'I just wanted to say goodbye,' I say. 'This fucking Christmas magic is useless.'

'It doesn't work like that,' St Nick says.

'He was here though,' I say. 'My séance worked?' I ask and St Nick nods.

'Yes,' St Nick says. 'Bess showed him the way.'

'Bess?' I ask.

But St Nick answers, 'They both braved pain to be here.'

'But why bother? Why come all this way and then not rap?' I ask.

A pause while St Nick appears to scan the room. My best guess is that he's looking for food.

'St Nick?'

'We're back to my initial question, Theodora Quirke,' St Nick says. He spins on the spot again, throwing out the front of his cape like he's being dramatic. 'Would seeing Gabriel have helped you?'

I shake my head. He's so weird. 'Not then, no,' I say and then I whisper, 'but it has now.' I pause. 'Where is he?'

'He's safe,' St Nick says.

'If I die, will we see each other again?' I ask.

'Perhaps, but only if your death is natural,' St Nick says. 'If you take your own life, you'll end up in a different realm.'

'You mean in hell?' I say. A blast of cold runs down my spine as I think about my mum.

'Of course not. There's no such place,' St Nick says. 'Those who take their own lives are cared for and nurtured, before they're "rebooted",' he makes those weird air quotations when he says 'rebooted' and nods to the ceiling, 'and then reborn.' He pauses. 'All you need to know is that to see Gabriel again, you need to end up where he is now. And...'

'And?'

'It's complicated,' St Nick says, as if that's helpful.

'So let's get this straight. Santa Claus is made up, and there's an afterlife of different realms, with none of them being heaven or hell?' I say.

'In simple terms, yes,' St Nick says, seemingly ignoring my sarcasm. I have no idea what's going on, but I've just seen Gabriel. He looked alive. He looked like him. But some other dead woman had her hands all over him.

'Has he found someone else already?' I whisper. I feel sick. 'They looked like they were together. Is that why he didn't communicate with me? Because of her.'

The word jumps in to my head and flashes like it's on a

huge neon sign; jealousy. And I can't help but scrunch up my face at the realisation I've reached a new level of weird. I'm jealous of a dead woman being with my dead boyfriend in a realm full of other dead people. Someone call the police; I'm officially off my head.

I think I hear St Nick mutter, 'For fuck's sake, Theodora Quirke,' as he grabs my hand. 'You're stubborn. Have it your way.'

I don't try to stop him or anything like that. No point; he's fifteen times my size and he's a fucking time traveller.

'Your wish is my command,' St Nick says.

MY STORY – BY DOTTIE SMITH

(Founder of Spitfire Saint Nicholas Umbrella Collective)

I didn't sleep much that night. Jack being angry with me wasn't sitting right. I felt full of grief, like I'd lost someone else I cared 'bout loads. It was like another person from my little family had gone away. That feeling that now that Jack was angry, then everything else in my life was going to go tits up. That made me brim with guilt too. Like it mattered if Jack didn't want to be friends no more. Like that was suddenly the worst thing that could be happening to me. It was like my head was telling me that I was cheating on the memories of Noah, Betty and Neil. I'd not realised how much Jack meant to me until then.

Next day, Mr Belsnickel called the sweetshop, but I couldn't speak as it was during the lunchtime school rush and I was on my own. I ended up having to call him back myself and we were on the phone for ages, to the point where I was serving customers whilst still chatting.

He said that Spitfire wanted the public to know all 'bout Saint Nicholas and all them wonderful things he'd been doing without folk noticing. He said it was time Saint Nicholas was getting some recognition. He said Spitfire were all 'bout helping Saint Nicholas. He said that their involvement would be minimal. He said that we, the group, just needed to keep doing what we was already doing. He said nothing would change for us and that Spitfire's involvement would be in public relations. They were only interested in raising Saint Nicholas' reputation and making sure that knowledge of all the good work he was doing reached the general public. He was nice, was saying all the right things.

At that stage he didn't say nothing 'bout how he'd make that happen. The only thing Spitfire really wanted was to have their name tagged onto our group name. That seemed fair enough to me and I thought it might give us a bit of legitimacy at the same time. He talked 'bout how Spitfire would help raise our profiles too, how all eight of us deserved some fame and attention for our dedication to Saint Nicholas over the years. He talked 'bout making us social media stars and 'bout how we'd end up being verified on Twitter. I didn't even have no Twitter account then and don't get me started on Snapchat.

If I'm being honest, most of what Mr Belsnickel was saying that day made little sense to me, but his enthusiasm was infectious. He made me want something I didn't fully understand. I'd like to say that I wasn't being swayed by a promise of a change in public opinion towards me. I liked the thought of people believing me when I talked 'bout Saint Nicholas and for all them who'd thought me capable of murder being proved wrong.

I think I even liked the thought of being famous for bringing Saint Nicholas to the people. Like I was providing a service and doing the best thing ever for the true meaning of Christmas. I'd had this niggle in my stomach, right next to where my hope lived, for ages. It was this feeling that my future was to be linked to Saint Nicholas and them Christmas miracles.

Then, and this was right out of the blue, Mr Belsnickel said how Spitfire wanted to give all of us a little financial incentive. Five thousand pounds each. Tax free. A gift. He was offering money and I had none.

It was only going to go one way, wasn't it? I said I'd talk to the others.

MY STORY – BY DOTTIE SMITH

(Founder of Spitfire Saint Nicholas Umbrella Collective)

I couldn't think of nothing else all the rest of the day at work. I tried to talk to Jack, but he wasn't having none of it. He heard it was me on the phone and he hung up. That night I sent out an email to everyone. I detailed what I knew, which I figured weren't really that much when I started trying to formulate sentences, and I stressed how five thousand pounds would be a nice treat for us all.

Of course, Jack was the first to reply. He was adamant that he didn't want none of us to be involved with Spitfire. He said how they were an organisation driven by commercialism and how they only wanted to be associating with Saint Nicholas to help launch their sale of toys. He said that we owed Saint Nicholas so much more than selling him out to commercial wankers.

The others soon started with their agreeing with Jack. They said how they felt uncomfortable gaining financially from Saint Nicholas. I tried to argue that Saint Nicholas would want us to be happy and even that people could donate the five thousand to charity, if they wanted.

That's when Jack replied saying how money didn't buy no happiness and that if I'd not yet figured that out, then I wasn't the kind of person he wanted in his life. That was the last time I heard from him.

Christina replied though and she supported me. She said we'd be crazy to be turning down the opportunity of five thousand pounds for doing nothing. The others said they'd think 'bout it.

Mr Belsnickel called my work first thing the next day. I'd only just been getting through the before school rush when the phone rang. I told him that there was some concern from the others and, before I could begin my explaining any of them concerns, he said that Spitfire would up their financial gift to twenty thousand pounds each.

Twenty thousand tax free pounds for doing nothing.

I didn't reply straight away. I was blown away by the amount. Thing is, Mr Belsnickel took that as my hesitating to say no, and so he threw in how they'd also give us online vouchers to buy anything we wanted from their website. He said they could stretch to nineteen thousand pounds of shopping vouchers each. He was talking life-changing money, for all of us. I honestly and truly thought Jack would appreciate what I did next.

Because I said yes. I said it quick before he could be changing his mind. After all, establishing the Facebook group was all my idea, so I felt I had the controlling vote.

You should know that I did it for the others as much as for myself though. None of us were flush. But maybe more than that, maybe I thought I was giving my friends a chance to have a life-changing amount of money without no guilt, as I'd be shouldering all the responsibility for having made the decision. Like I was giving them another one of them Christmas miracles, even though it wasn't December for a few more months. I even considered how we could all have a holiday together and how it could be all luxurious and posh.

Mr Belsnickel was chuffed when I said yes. He said he'd come to the sweetshop the following day, so that I could sign all the paperwork and legal forms.

THEO (THEODORA QUIRKE)

And then I blink again and we're someplace else. Someplace inside and someplace that still isn't Dante House.

I look at St Nick. He's back to wearing that pair of grey trackies but no vest this time. His belly's hanging over the elastic waistband of the trackies and he stinks of sweat. He's still holding an umbrella in one hand, his sausage fingers gripping the handle. I think the handle might be ivory; it looks old and might be worth a bit of money.

'Why no top?' I say, but then I'm distracted as I look around the room we're in. It's familiar in a way that's making my heart beat too fast and my belly flip like I want to throw up on my shoes. I'm standing in a doorway between two rooms, a kitchen in front of me and a hallway behind me. I know where I am.

I step forward into the kitchen, a modern design, bright red tiles and black cupboard doors; there's a huge American-style fridge to my right. The magnets spell out 'GABE + THEO' and there's a photo of Gabriel and me in front of the lovelocks down by Albert Dock. I reach out my hand and my fingers connect with the surface of the photo.

I can feel the surface. This is real. What the fuck is going on? I'm in Gabriel's house. I'm standing in Gabriel's kitchen. I look to the window and it's starting to get light outside. I spin on the spot. I'm looking for clues. I'm desperate to figure out where I am on my timeline. There are no Christmas decorations. When is this?

'This might freak you out a little but...' He pauses. 'But you have to remember that—'

'What the fuck?' I whisper, as I spin on the spot, back around to face into the hallway. My spinning is slow; I'm back wearing my puffer jacket again. It feels too tight. I'm back in my work clothes again. It all feels wrong. I think I might be sweating a new world record.

'That there is a greater purpose. I'm giving you what you wanted,' St Nick whispers, but I'm not responding. I'm standing in a kitchen, not just any kitchen but Gabriel's kitchen. I can see him. He's there. He's standing in the hallway.

He's tall, with a thin face. His cheekbones are sharp; his lips are plump. That brown curly hair, still wet from his shower. His blue eyes are slightly dull. I can tell that something's wrong but I can't move. My entire body is shaking. Every one of my trillion cells are jumping for joy.

'Gabe,' I whisper, tears already streaming down my face.

My beautiful, my caring, my handsome, my dead boyfriend is standing at the bottom of the stairs. He's looking up to the landing, as if waiting for a response.

'Mum,' he says, 'I can't find the headache tablets. I need to get ready, bus'll be here soon.'

'Bus?' I say. 'Is he going—' I stop talking.

He's clearly not seen me. He's clearly not heard St Nick and me. He's clearly not dead. He turns towards us.

'Gabe,' I say.

I want to rush to him, to be scooped into his arms and to feel his lips on mine. I don't understand why I'm not running towards him, I don't understand why he's not looking at me. I don't understand what the fuck's happening, but it all seems to be in fast-forward.

Gabriel walks towards us, but he's looking through me. It's as if I'm not here, it's as if I don't exist, as if *I'm* dead. Three strides later and I'm shuffling backwards into the kitchen, avoiding Gabriel as he starts flinging open cupboard doors. He's flinging things about – Tupperware boxes, an empty Quality Street tin, a cat toy – not caring about the noise. He's desperate.

'What the hell is this?' I ask, turning to face St Nick. Snot's dripping from my nose and I reckon I look like shit, but I can't think about that and I can't stare at St Nick for long. I need to watch Gabriel; all of me wants to soak in every detail. He's here, he's alive; is this an actual Christmas miracle?

Gabriel's walking around the house wearing only shorts. He was always hot, winter, spring, summer, autumn, always turning down the central heating and leaving his mum thinking the system was fucked. She even called a heating engineer out to fix it. The bloke charged the hundred quid call out fee and spoke to her like she was thick. Gabriel got a proper bollocking that night.

His chest muscles are defined from hours at the college's gym; hours we spent there together and I don't understand how he's still like that. How he's still all buff. It's been ten months since we worked out together. No, more than that. St Nick said months had passed. What's going on? I want to touch him. No, I want to loop my fingers with his. I want to hear his voice again. I want to sniff his armpits.

I don't want this moment to end.

'What kind of magic is this?' I ask, my eyes still on Gabriel.

'Theodora Quirke, it's trust,' St Nick says.

'You give people their heart's desire, yes? And what I want most in the world is for Gabe not to be dead,' I say. I gulp in the middle of the sentence, the enormity of this hitting me. I can't help but hope that this is going to be the best moment ever. I can't help but think that St Nick's working his magic. That he's not full of shit. He's bringing back my Gabriel. He's making Gabriel not dead. He's giving Gabriel and me that future I thought was lost. I'm getting my family back. He's giving me hope. This is his plan to save me.

I think I've forgotten to breathe. I'm lightheaded. I feel sick. I feel like I want to jump for joy. Don't crumble. Stay in control. I can't fall apart and miss any of this moment. I can't—

'No, you wanted to see him again,' St Nick says, interrupting my thoughts, but I don't want to listen. 'A chance to say goodbye. That was your heart's—'

'Gabe,' I say.

He doesn't hear me; he doesn't even turn towards the noise. Has he got an ear infection? Maybe his headache's caused some inner ear thing, maybe some problems with his sight too.

But I don't move from the spot.

'Mum,' he whispers. It's as if full volume will hurt too much. I don't know how but I can feel what he's feeling. Not the pain, but the fear. Like everything's tumbling in on him and he can't find a way out.

'The pain in my ears,' he says.

I still don't move.

He's bent to his knees now. Clutching both ears. His eyes roll backwards and forwards. He vomits over his chest; he retches bile again and again.

'What the fuck? Do something,' I scream, punching St Nick on the arm.

'Theodora Quirke, you know the rules. I can't—'

'Mum,' Gabriel whispers towards the floor as he curls and shudders with pain.

'Francesca,' I scream.

I run to the bottom of the stairs, screaming for Gabriel's mum. I scream out her name again and again. I try the pockets of my puffer coat but of course my phone's not there. I try to find their house phone; I'm spinning again and struggling to focus.

'Theodora,' St Nick says, 'come, be near Gabriel.' His voice contains a warning that stops me mid-spin, a tinge of something that makes me turn and shuffle back into the kitchen.

'Francesca,' I scream again as I walk. She doesn't reply. A wave of helplessness makes me clammy. I reach the kitchen and that's when Gabriel sneezes and that's when I realise what I'm seeing.

'Take me back to Dante House. Right now,' I yell at St Nick, but he doesn't respond to me. He's sitting on the floor next to Gabriel.

'It's going to be okay, son,' he whispers.

I look down at St Nick, cross-legged in grey trackies, stroking Gabriel's hair, his umbrella on the floor beside them both. Gabriel's in shit loads of pain and I can't bear it. He sneezes again. St Nick moves my boyfriend onto his side; Gabriel's eyes roll again.

'Do something,' I yell at St Nick.

Gabriel sneezes a third time, then a fourth, then a fifth. Each sneeze makes him floppier; each sneeze makes his body shudder.

'I can't change this,' St Nick says, 'but *you* can help him. He's scared, Theodora. He needs to know that you'll be okay without him.'

I rush to the floor, my fingers on Gabriel's curls; they're soft and wet, no product has been applied yet. He sneezes, his eyes still rolling, wee seeping into his shorts, vomit and bile covering his torso and around him.

'I'm here,' I say. 'Don't leave me,' I say. Tears and snot drip from me. I'm out of control, I don't want this to be happening again.

'Pure of heart,' St Nick whispers.

'I can't lie,' I whisper, 'I'll never be okay without him. Not really.'

'Theodora, I promise you—'

Two more sneezes and Gabriel begins fitting. I can't stop him and St Nick's not helping. I call out, shout to Francesca, but she can't hear me. I move Gabriel back onto his side, attempt a recovery position, but I've no idea what I'm doing.

'It's okay,' I say. I bend close to his ear, kissing the lobe. My snot and tears drip over his sore ear. 'I'll be okay, I promise,' I say. 'You can let go,' I say. 'You're right Gabriel, you were always right. What we have is better than all that bullshit love out there. What we have is raw and real and so fucking ace.'

'Good girl,' St Nick whispers.

'I wish we'd overused I love you, I wish I'd said it a million more times until you groaned and told me to stop,' I whisper. 'You loved me at my darkest.'

'He turned on your light,' St Nick whispers.

My tears fall into Gabriel's hair, his body shudders and I try to grip him and pull him closer, to pull him back. I don't want to lose him. Not again.

'People lie, Gabriel, actions don't,' I whisper. 'Your actions were the best.'

'Through death, we discover life,' St Nick whispers.

'Goodbye,' I whisper. 'I love you.'

Gabriel's body stops convulsing, and then the atmosphere feels lighter. Bubbles pop in the air; for a few moments they're the only sound.

I look to St Nick. Tears are streaming down his cheeks.

'You could have saved him,' I whisper.

'It wasn't my choice, Theodora,' he says. 'I follow orders.'

'Fuck your orders and fuck you,' I say.

I clutch Gabriel's body and pull him up onto me. He's lighter. My gorgeous, my caring, my dead boyfriend has gone again. This body isn't him, this isn't Gabriel.

I've no fucking idea what's going on.

THEO (THEODORA QUIRKE)

We sit on the kitchen floor in silence.

'What the fuck just happened?' I whisper. I don't even know if I want an explanation.

'You were there when he needed you most,' St Nick says.

'But what about me?' I say, but hearing the words makes me want to punch myself in the face. I'm being a selfish twat. This was never about me.

'What'll I do without him?' I ask. I sob, my entire body vibrating.

St Nick hums *Rudolph the Red Nosed Reindeer*. What the fuck? I keep pulling Gabriel's empty body into me and rocking to the melody. I've no concept of passage of time. We're frozen in this spot.

'People expected me to get over him quickly,' I say. 'Some were trying to be kind. Said things like, "Plenty more lads out there", or, "You're still young, you've got your whole life ahead of you". It seemed that him *just* being a boyfriend meant I wasn't entitled to grieve for long.'

'How long were you allowed?' he asked.

'I was back in college a week after he died. Those in charge of me thought it best I worked through my grief, that I got back to normal as soon as possible.' I pause. 'Is this my normal now? This me having no idea what the fuck's going on or what day it even is.'

'February 5th,' St Nick says.

I move my hand back to Gabriel, stroking his hair again, begging his remaining warmth to seep into my fingers.

'When people hear about someone dying, when it's someone else's partner or child, there's a moment when they pull their loved ones in that little bit closer. There's a fragment of time when they cherish life and all that they have. They value love. Yet that passes. It seems to me that it takes death for that fleeting realisation that life's worth living.

'But when it's your own partner or child who dies, well that's different. Life ceases to contain its worth and it stops having the same purpose. When someone you truly love dies, everything changes. I spent days, weeks, months, longing for a rewind. I wanted my life to go back, for the chaos to be removed. I fantasised about how much I'd appreciate every single moment, how I'd never whinge again, if I could just go back.' A pause. I wipe my snot onto the sleeve of my puffer jacket. 'My life is now split into three: before Gabe, Gabe and after Gabe. Having Gabe in my life was the best time. I can't imagine ever feeling that level of joy again.' I look down at Gabriel. His body is a shell. His heart's already gone. 'But I'm okay. I'm doing okay. I find tiny bits of joy nowadays…'

'We hide death,' St Nick says.

'I was called into the college office,' I say. 'I knew something bad had happened when he'd not sent a text to let me know why he wasn't in college. I'd tried calling him—'

A tear falls onto Gabriel; I look down. I'm covered in Gabe's vomit and pee.

'Within a few hours there'd been an outpouring of grief on his Facebook wall. People who hardly knew him, people who'd given us both shit for years were suddenly posting bollocks like "gone too soon but forever in our hearts" and talking about how their hearts were breaking. *Their* hearts.'

I'm shouting, my breath is ragged. It's like I'm back there again. Living that time again. I want to pick up Gabriel and run away with him. I want us to turn back time. Even just to before meeting St Nick. I was sorted. I was moving forward. But now I'm screwed again. Now, I want to steal Gabriel's dead body. Now I want anything but my life. I want anything but this pain. I don't know if I'm strong enough to survive losing Gabriel all over again. I want to not be me anymore.

'What have you done?' I say. 'I was doing so well and now this...' I nod at my dead boyfriend. What the fuck is this life?

'Keep going,' St Nick says. 'Tell me more.'

'I can't,' I say but St Nick nods at me, his head moving vigorously; he wants me to keep talking.

'People claimed him, but he was mine, I was his,' I say. 'I started commenting under their Facebook wall posts, telling them to stop spouting bollocks, telling them to fuck off. I wrote paragraphs pointing out times when the person had been a dick to me and to Gabe. I started telling people how they had no right to grieve... I was a nobhead. Wasn't my proudest time.'

'Grief is pure, Theodora, don't worry about that. We all behave poorly at some point or other. It's when you're a constant *nobhead* that you need be concerned,' he says.

I can't help but giggle, even though I'm a mess of snot and tears. The word 'nobhead' sounds wrong when he says it.

'I think Gabriel would have liked you,' I say, looking up at St Nick. He's looking inside the fridge, but then he closes the door and turns to me. Two slices of ham in one hand and a strawberry yoghurt in the other.

'Spoons?' he says. I point to a drawer behind us, shaking my head but still smiling a weak rainbow of a smile.

'He drank Dr Pepper. He didn't use product in his hair on a Sunday. His favourite piece of clothing was a T-shirt from last summer's Parklife Festival; we both had them, we matched. On special occasions, he smelled of One Million, a gift from his mum the Christmas before he died. He never refilled the kettle after using it; that annoyed both me and Francesca. He had a season ticket for Tranmere Rovers and went to every match with his mum. His mum was from the Wirral you see, no dad on the scene. Kids at school used to take the piss.' I pause. 'Gabe took me once, then afterwards said it was the only place in the world he preferred to be without me. His phone number ended in sixty-nine.' I laugh. 'He passed his driving test first time. He drove his mum's blue Ford Fiesta. He was an Aries. He died on Feb 5th... he died today.'

'He supported Tranmere Rovers?' St Nick says. He laughs between mouthfuls of yoghurt. Some of it spills onto his beard and he leaves it there. It drips down the hair like pink snot. He's given up on the spoon and uses the ham to shovel the yoghurt into his mouth. My stomach turns. I look back at Gabriel.

'I can't bear the thought of forgetting him,' I say.

'But remembering hurts too much,' he says and I shrug my shoulders.

'I can think about him now, you know, back in December. But I've not turned my old mobile on since a week after he died,' I say. 'Bought myself a cheap Pay as You Go, one without the internet. Stopped me popping off on Facebook and I couldn't be arsed with all the texts and people wanting to know more about it. I mean, who'd believe that a healthy eighteen-year-old would die from sneezing? People were more interested in the details than trying to understand how I was feeling.'

'A brain haemorrhage, which was triggered by the fit,' he says. 'They will find there's a genetic cause.' He pauses. 'Do you not know this?' he asks and I shake my head.

'After the funeral, I couldn't face his mum again. We haven't spoken since and—'

'You overheard her,' he says and I nod. I look towards the doorway, half-expecting her to be listening.

'Francesca's best friend was comforting her. They'd hired a hall, caterers had supplied the food, so many people had wanted to say goodbye to Gabe. I'd been looking for his mum, to tell her that I loved her and that I wanted to always be part of her life.' I pause. 'I'd been a fool back then, thinking that I was important to her, thinking that I was part of their family. But they were the only family I'd ever known. Her and Gabe made me feel like a belonged somewhere. First time in my life and—'

I can't continue. I can't allow myself to think about losing Francesca. I used to laugh and call her Mum. I thought she'd felt the same way about me. She even said I was the daughter she'd always wanted. Liar.

'But you know Francesca didn't speak the words,' he says. I shake my head.

'Francesca was saying how guilty she was feeling for not being able to comfort me and that's when I heard her friend's reply. They were standing outside the hall; Francesca was having a ciggie, even though she hadn't smoked since she was a student. Anyway, her friend said that I was "just Gabriel's girlfriend" and she spoke other words too, about how Gabe would have had loads of different girlfriends at university, what with him being so handsome.'

Tears stream down my face again. I'm hit with a double punch of loss and loneliness that I've spent the last ten months trying to push away.

'Just a girlfriend,' St Nick repeats. I pull Gabriel into me again, the lightness of his being feels wrong but still I'm grabbing this time with him. I can't let go.

'My sob was loud, I guess. They both turned and looked at me. I ripped my name necklace off and threw it at them. I ran off, left the wake. I never contacted her again. Refused to see her. Two different foster homes since but then they gave up on trying to place me and got me a room in supported accommodation at Dante House,' I say.

'That feeling that his mother had put up with you?' he says and I nod.

'That she'd not meant any of those wonderful things she'd said to me. That she'd been so terrified that she'd lose Gabe, that she'd used me to keep him close to her,' I say. 'And being *just* a girlfriend was the worst thing anyone could have said. He was my everything... He still is.'

I look at his empty shell, once so noisy and bold. I smile, a weak smile. I put my hand in my puffer jacket's pocket. They're still there. I take the lovelock and key out and place it on the floor next to Gabriel.

'What is it with adults?' I say.

'You're asking the wrong person,' he says. 'In all my lifetimes, I've never quite mastered being one.' He laughs.

'Why do they criticise what they don't understand? We'd talked about marriage, but we weren't in any hurry, we had forever.'

'Francesca was grieving,' he says. 'You didn't give her time to speak.'

'It seems to me that blood relationships are everything, but my blood relationships are all screwed and broken and dead.' I pause. I think about my mum. 'That's what I thought back then. And Gabe and Francesca were all I had. Being *just* a girlfriend seemed to mean that I wasn't *entitled* to feel the overwhelming, all-consuming grief that was smothering me. But that not being entitled didn't mean that I could "snap out" of it or think about all the other boyfriends who were waiting for me in a fabulous future. A fabulous future without Gabe.'

'Grief is complicated,' he says.

'Adults spout bollocks,' I say. 'And they fear children who know that they spout bollocks.'

I hear him laugh. 'I think you might be right, Theodora Quirke.'

'I miss him so much,' I say. 'I miss him every single day. That the world continues to spin amazes me sometimes. As do people. But I soon got tired of being angry with strangers. I spent a month or so swearing at people with kids, at people holding hands, at people in love, at people wasting love. Some of those days I hated him so much. But then I realised that that wasn't the kind of person I wanted to be,' I say.

'You've a pure heart, Theodora Quirke,' he says. I nod, tears and snot dripping beyond my control.

'I still hate him, just a little bit, for leaving me.' I hold up my thumb and forefinger, showing a tiny gap between them. 'He taught me so much,' I say, wiping even more snot and tears on the jacket's sleeve. 'But he failed to teach me how to live without him.'

'Did you find them, love?' It's Francesca. She's coming down the stairs.

'No, quick,' I say, moving Gabriel's head to the tiled floor.

'Please,' I beg, standing up. St Nick looks at me as he lifts his umbrella. 'Please don't let me see her finding—'

'Touch it,' he says and I do.

MY STORY – BY DOTTIE SMITH

(Founder of Spitfire Saint Nicholas Umbrella Collective)

I felt sick when I pressed the send button on the email to the others. I waited until everything had been signed and sealed and there wasn't no going back. I even changed the name of my Facebook group and added Spitfire to the start of it.

Josette Borg replied first. She talked 'bout how the money would allow them to have much needed financial security. Laurence Rosseau and Sofia Beckerman couldn't quite believe that they each got the money. That was double the shopping vouchers too. They thanked me for taking the decision out of their hands. Lucas Edwards said he'd use the money to help others having to travel abroad for operations and Birgitte Jesson talked 'bout the charity she'd set up to help underprivileged children. She was going to spend her online vouchers on Christmas presents for them all. Christina Milano said she'd been praying for a miracle, as her finances were dire and how she'd use the money to have more 'work done' on her face. She wanted to look her best for all the media attention that was to be coming our way.

No matter how many times I emailed him, Jack didn't reply. Everyone else supplied their bank details for Spitfire, but not Jack. He spoke to Laurence though and asked him to tell me that I wasn't to contact him again. I sobbed down the phone when Laurence called to tell me. I was inconsolable. Laurence had to pass the phone to Sofia but it didn't make no difference. I wanted Jack.

Things changed quickly after that. Money was in each of our accounts within a week. Not Jack's account though. He refused to have anything to do with Spitfire. He even removed himself as admin from my Facebook group. We were seven members now, but I refused to acknowledge that. For me, there were always eight of us.

Then everything was upped a notch and everything changed again. I guess though that was good, as I didn't have no time for dwelling on Jack.

The first change that Spitfire made was to want to increase our membership numbers. That seemed fair enough. If we wanted to raise Saint Nicholas' profile, then we were needing more people to be liking our Facebook page. Thing is, Spitfire wasn't happy with just a few likes. They wanted loads of them. They talked 'bout trending and going viral and a whole load of other terms that weren't even in my vocabulary. They talked 'bout entitlement and how they didn't want just anyone thinking they could be rewarded.

That's when Mr Belsnickel from Spitfire said we should charge a membership fee.

The theory was that anyone could be liking our pages and getting access to basic information, but that real and true fans should be identified. He talked 'bout legitimacy and how people would take us and Saint Nicholas more seriously if they were paying for the privilege. He said something 'bout charging a nominal amount being a proven marketing tool and how if people paid, they was more likely to respect the group.

It was 'bout inclusion, you see, 'bout making people feel like they belonged. He talked 'bout how we would all have to commit to building our brand and how that could be a full-time job. He talked quickly, he was confident and convincing. He was one of them blokes who folk swore could sell ice to them Eskimos.

So I agreed to what he said. We started accepting paying members, and that brought with it adverts in the tabloids and articles being written 'bout us.

It weren't long, I'm talking two days, before he advised me (and I agreed) to give up my job in the sweetshop. Spitfire were offering to pay me a wage that was almost ten times the hourly amount I was getting for working in the sweetshop.

Although there was a team at Spitfire who were happy to sort out the emails into those that required a response, there'd been a surge in people wanting to join our group. They needed me to put my name to all online communication.

And so I was given training on how to answer emails, update various social media sites and keep everyone up to date with the developments in our search for Saint Nicholas. Everything I put online had to be checked first by Spitfire, and they changed almost everything I wrote. I hardly recognised myself online; they made me jolly, clever and proper confident.

THEO (THEODORA QUIRKE)

'Why would you do that?' I whisper.

We stand on a flat roof; it's a perfect square, no outdoor furniture, no chimney, nothing. I spin and see that an ocean or sea surrounds us; we're on a single building on a small island. It's not warm, it's not cold, there isn't any snow. I'm not even going to ask why we're on a roof or which roof it might be. He's St Nick. He's got magic powers. I can't even begin to consider all of the other possibilities and reasons we might be so far from Dante House.

'Your heart's desire. You said you wanted to see him again,' he says. 'One last time.'

'Not that... I didn't want to see *that*,' I shout. 'Why the fuck would you think I'd want to see *that*?'

I walk to the edge of the flat roof. I think about jumping, wondering if I'd hit rocks or sea. I turn to St Nick and I glare at him.

'I am not going to let you jump,' he says. His voice is flat; matter-of-fact flat, matter-of-I'm-in-control arsey. I could hate St Nick, I want to hate St Nick, yet I don't.

'*Let me*? Who the fuck do you think you are?'

I don't know why I'm angry. I wouldn't actually jump. Even in my darkest moments, I've not considered suicide. Not really. I mean I've thought that it would all be easier if I died, but that tiny niggle of hope still flickered. It's more that I hate his tone. That he's telling me off. That he thinks he's the boss of me. No one's the boss of me. I mean, apart from Stacey. But, thanks to St Nick, I think I'm now unemployed, probably homeless and maybe off my head.

And then I'm shaking; tears are streaming down my face and my breathing's caught inside me. But it's not anger, not really. It's all emotion. It's the depth of what I've just seen, it's swimming around inside my head.

Gabriel's dead.

I feel raw. I am explosive. Yet, if I'm being honest, I want to say thank you and tell St Nick how grateful I am. Knowing that Gabriel wasn't alone when he died means everything.

Mine was the last voice he heard. We managed a tiny rewrite of Gabriel's history into an end that I can try to live with. Into an end I can't ever explain to another living soul without them locking me up in an asylum. But, fuck that, this rewrite's mine forever.

Still, there's this other part of me that wants to curl into a ball and never stop crying. I've lost him. I've lost Gabriel all over again and right now that's making me want to punch the man who I know was trying to help me, in his own entirely screwed up way.

'*You* asked me to grant *your* wish.'

'What kind of a man are you?' I ask. 'Are you the devil in a fluffy red coat?'

He shakes his head and points at his naked belly. He's smiling and I don't know if he's deliberately messing with my head or if he's the kindest man I've ever met. He's the unlikeliest of people to be so very full of magic.

'Are you trying to make me kill myself?' I say. 'Is that what you did to my mum?' The words have no conviction. They're unnecessarily cruel. I'm being a bitch.

St Nick shakes his head again. I've made him sad. I look down at my clothes, Gabriel's vomit and pee no longer cover the front of them. Nothing is as it was, nothing is as it seems. I've no idea what day it is or what year we're in. There's magic everywhere.

'I know what you're doing,' I say. 'With all this Charles Dickens bollocks.'

'Charles Dickens *bollocks*? Theodora Quirke, my dear, you are going to have to be a little more specific,' he says.

'This shit *Christmas Carol* remake,' I say. 'We did it for GCSE English Lit and I've read its *York Notes*. The snow, you being a twatting ghost and it being Christmas Eve. Showing me my past, making me the *embodiment of winter*. You're wanting me to *transform*, to be *renewed* and to *become spring*. And you're a shit Charles Dickens,' I say. Silence. St Nick rubs his belly and he smiles.

'Let's not talk about Charles. After everything I showed him and him not giving me the slightest nod of credit for the creative seed. Bastard.' He winks. He still has yoghurt in his beard. 'I simply help people who are searching for answers.'

'You don't half spout—' I start to say but then I stop. I pause, then, 'And I want my lock back.'

'Sorry, no can do. It's back with Gabriel,' he says.

I think my head might pop with questions, thoughts and grief. So much fucking grief. I put my hands into the pockets of my puffer jacket and look out to an unknown sea. Deep breaths in, long exhales out. The sea grounds me, it brings me back to my purpose, back to that desire I've had since that first time travel back to toddler Theodora; to be the best version of me. Yet now I've no idea what evening it is or how everything that's happening tonight is going to alter me.

'How many times have you been in love?' I ask St Nick.

'Once,' he says.

I watch as he walks and stands near the edge of the flat roof, looking out over the unknown sea but in a different direction to me. He's got one finger up his nose, twirling around and searching, and the other hand's still clutching that weird looking umbrella. Without his costume he doesn't look like Santa Claus at all. Now he looks like that fat bloke who runs a comic book store in *The Simpsons*, but with grey hair and the scraggiest, dirtiest beard I've ever seen.

'What happened?' I ask.

I see something glitter around his neck. It wasn't there before. A necklace. A thin gold chain with a delicate oval shaped locket dangling onto his hairy chest. It looks out of place and I don't think it belongs to him. St Nick takes the finger from his nose and touches the oval.

'What's that?' I ask. The necklace disappears. I blink.

'She died a long time ago,' he says and I nod. 'Falling in love in your teens is the best kind of love. It's free, it doesn't have to consider the practicalities of mortgages, of house prices, of retirement funds, of that desperate need to conceive a child.' He pauses. I watch him, but he's not looking at me. He's sending his words out across the water. He's sending his words out to her.

I hope she's listening. I already know that St Nick is lonely. His longing is familiar. I don't think he's got any family left either and that makes him the same as me.

'If I'm being honest, Theodora Quirke, I've failed to live without her,' he says and then he turns to look at me. 'But my situation is different and complicated. I am Nikolaos of Myra. I cannot die. I am entirely immortal. I have lived many lives, yet I have lived none since her death.'

'I don't understand what that all means,' I say, because I honestly don't have a fucking clue what's happening. But I want to. That's the only thing I know for sure.

'You'll understand eventually. But for now my task appears to be to save you. Even though, as you can see from this current body, my current life, still without her I should note, appears to have taken a twist in a negative direction and I think my communication with the higher powers…' He pauses and looks up to the starless sky. 'I think it might be buggered. That note I got was super confused. Took me hours to try and sort out the letters. Anagrams are not my favourite things to do. I'm more a Sudoku kind of guy. But you don't see me trying to take my own life, do you? No, you do not.' He pauses again, his eyes now locked on my face as if scolding me for something I've not done.

'But you're immortal. You can't die,' I say and then I smile.

'That's not the point,' he says, shaking his head. 'Even if I could die, I wouldn't want to kill myself.' He stops talking.

'You never loved again?' I ask and St Nick shakes his head. I think I've either pissed him off or made him sad.

'So that message you got to save me,' I say. I'm keen to try and bring St Nick back into focus. I mean he's got to have a plan. He must know why I'm on this flat roof in the middle of, literally, nowhere. 'You've done that now?'

'Maybe the thought of loving someone again and them dying is what stops me. Or, maybe it's because I could never love another as much as I loved her.' A pause. I don't know what to do or say. I mean what's the appropriate response in this situation?

'Some days I believe that my happiness died with my love,' St Nick says. 'So now I exist, or possibly I endure.'

There's a clap of thunder. Loud, actually like a thwack sound. I think it might be directly over St Nick's head. What the fuck? What if he gets struck by lightning? What if he dies? I'd be stuck on this roof. No food, no water, no–

'Bloody control freaks,' St Nick says. He shakes a fist at the sky. 'Apparently this isn't about me and I really am supposed to be putting a positive spin on living. How am I doing?'

CAROLINE SMAILES

I take a good look at his eyes. They're tiny pools of blue lost in a hairy moon face. He's staring at me, waiting for me to reply.

'I've no one living who cares about me,' I say and he shrugs. 'How insane is that?'

'We never had children,' he says. 'Left no one behind who would care.'

'And now you help kids all over the world?' I ask.

'Not quite, Theodora Quirke,' he says. 'You've been watching too many films about *him*. Mainly, these days, I help adults.' He laughs and snorts. His sounds are becoming comforting.

'They make your face kind in the films and, usually, you keep your clothes on,' I say.

I can't help but look at his belly again. There are streaks of brown on it. I hope that it's mud but I've got a horrible feeling it might actually be shit. My face scrunches.

'If only real life were like the movies, young Theodora,' he says.

I exhale. The sound is heavy and full of loss. I can't remember the last time I sighed. The sound shocks me; it forces a giggle to escape. I don't want to laugh, not now, not after losing Gabriel all over again. What kind of girlfriend would that make me? I'd be like they said, I'd be 'just a girlfriend'.

'I know, Theodora. I really do know how you feel,' he says and that's when I realise that he's being truthful. He understands.

'No one at college had gone through anything similar, so they didn't know what to say and how could they possibly begin to understand? Older people talked about how only a widower, after thirty years of marriage, was entitled to feel such intensity of grief. That sense of entitlement made me want to tell the world to fuck off,' I say and St Nick nods. 'Young people aren't allowed to know love. Only old people, who've spent years together and probably sent dick pics to strangers on the internet. They're the only ones who know what love is.'

'I don't think all old people have sent—'

'Well, bollocks to them all. My love for Gabe was pure and beautiful. My love for him didn't have a chance to turn jaded and sour,' I say.

'Not everyone feels that way,' he says. 'About young love. She was a teen when I met her.'

I wait to see if he'll say more but he doesn't.

'I'd known Gabriel for seven years when he died, we'd been best friends for seven years, we'd admitted we were in love three years ago. He's the only person I've ever kissed on the lips, the only man to see me without any clothes on.'

'But you were *just* a girlfriend,' he says. I nod. 'Have you ever felt that you were enough?'

I shake my head. 'Not since Gabe's funeral,' I say. I pause, and then I add, 'I knew Gabriel better, differently, absolutely. And she had no fucking right to devalue all that we had. She made it seem like a pointless relationship, like I'd wasted all those years—'

'You didn't waste those years, Theodora,' he says.

The rain pounds down at that moment. Large drops bouncing off my head, large drops dancing along the flat roof. I smile. I lift my arms into the air and I twirl a clumsy twirl.

I keep spinning and twirling and then I'm shrieking and I'm laughing. I don't care if I'm near to the edge; I know St Nick won't let me fall. In that moment, I'm entirely free. The raindrops offer rhythm and I spin.

'Fucking adults,' I say. 'Fuck them all.'

SPITFIRE SAINT NICHOLAS UMBRELLA COLLECTIVE ☑

COMMUNITY

Hello friends! DOTTIE SMITH, founder of the SpitfireSNUC, here again. Since my last post about one of the miracles that Saint Nicholas performed, there have been numerous new questions and much scepticism. I've had to block some people, because of their rude and unnecessary comments, so do be aware that all haters will be blocked. If you've nothing nice to say, then you've joined the wrong Facebook group.

Again, I hope my answers to your questions make sense, but if they don't leave a comment below and I'll get to it as soon as I can. Thanks for all your support, especially those of you who jumped to my defence in the comments of my last post! Really appreciated the love. Consider yourselves on my good list.

WHY IS SAINT NICHOLAS LINKED TO SANTA CLAUS?

It is alleged that some felt a conflict between the belief that Saint Nicholas visited all children to leave gifts and his standing as a saint. It is said that a representation of Jesus was created to replace the notion of Saint Nicholas being a gift giver.

A child known as Christkind/Christkindl was created and said to visit children and leave gifts. The date of the celebration was moved from the eve of December 6th to the eve of December 25th, to honour Christ's birth. Eventually, some say that this occurred during the nineteenth century, the figures of Saint Nicholas and Christkind and Father Christmas blended (incorrectly) into the formation of one being – Santa Claus.

Some believe Santa Claus gained his red clothing due to Coca-Cola's use of him in their advertisements, but others say this is not the case and that his 'red' clothing existed before the first advertisement was released.

Whatever the truth behind the origin of Santa Claus's clothing, I believe it to be almost irrelevant. The fact is that the public move to gift giving on Christmas Eve served as a distraction and merely created opportunity for the actual, immortal, Saint Nicholas to carry out his own work, undetected.

Originally, I created The Saint Nicholas Umbrella Collective because Saint Nicholas changed my life. He saved my life, and the lives of the other original seven group members. **We, the eight of us, have first-hand evidence that he exists.** I want to acknowledge and honour him, and thanks to Spitfire I am now reaching a wider audience.

DO YOU BELIEVE SAINT NICHOLAS IS STILL ALIVE? HOW IS THAT POSSIBLE?

I believe that Saint Nicholas is immortal. I believe that he continues to gift miracles and selfless acts to a chosen few, during the eve and early hours of his feast day every year.

DO YOU HAVE EVIDENCE TO SUPPORT THIS CLAIM?

Yes, I do. Each of the original members of our small group have received a Christmas miracle from Saint Nicholas, in his many guises, on the eve of December 6th or during the day on December 6th. This has united us, but has also led to further investigation. There are many reported miracles, acts of kindness and sightings plotted throughout history and for as long as records have existed on or around December 6th. I believe that they are all linked to Saint Nicholas. Is this the best-kept secret? I believe it was, but now I feel that it is time to share Saint Nicholas with all of you.

THEO (THEODORA QUIRKE)

I don't know how long I spin with the rain, but my throat's aching from all of my shrieking while rotating.

'You did good tonight,' he shouts over my shrieking.

'When?' I say. I stop mid-whirl. My head flutters with the dizzy throb and I turn to face him. The rain continues to lash down. Life continues; it does that, the bastard, yet I've no idea if I'm currently in my past, present or future. The rain bounces off us both. It continues to leap and hop as we stand still.

'He wasn't alone,' he says and I shrug my shoulders before my breath jumps; a sharp intake and then it hides in my throat.

The grief hits me; it's fresh, all-consuming, smothering my voice. The sound that escapes me is animalistic. A cry of loss, of anger, a cry for all that I'll never have. Gabriel was the one person in this world who kicked my arse and forced me to have purpose. He was the person who gave me hope and guidance. He'd found me when I'd been at my lowest; he was the best friend. My only true friend. There have been others who've tried to be my friend since, but trusting people kinda seemed to be beyond me. Sally, my neighbour, she was trying to be my friend. Leaving cookies and not giving up on me; that was her way of showing me. Unconditional too, because I've given her nothing in return.

But in the last ten months I've learned to live without him. I've not buckled under grief. I've been my own person, not Gabriel's girlfriend or another statistic in the care system. I've found my own purpose, a different direction, I've not relied on anyone but myself. And, if I'm being entirely honest, I'm quite proud of that. The odds, the stats, other people's expectations too, they were against me – I mean they've been against me since the day I was born – but I kept going. I survived without becoming a bitter and twisted mess of a person. We've all met that kind of person who carries a hatred for the world on their back – hunched over, smelly, shrinking with the seasons.

I'm just not sure I can do that whole survival thing all over again.

I mean the thought of having to go back to February 5th and reliving those early days and that pain again, well that makes me want to vomit on my work pants.

'It doesn't make you weak that you're not strong enough for twice,' St Nick says.

I turn to him. He clutches his still-closed umbrella in one hand. With the other he pulls together his wet beard and squeezes a stream of rain from it. I watch as he bends forward and shakes his head from side-to-side, whipping the water in my direction like a wet dog.

'Whoa,' I say, holding out my palms, as if that'll protect me from a St Nick shower.

He ignores me until he's finished shaking, then he stands up straight and looks out to sea. All the time he clutches that closed fucking umbrella. It makes no sense.

'Why don't you use your umbrella?' I ask. 'You do know it'd stop you from getting wet?'

'It's a parasol,' he says. He holds it in front of him, as if he's inspecting it or perhaps he's checking to make sure it's the correct one. 'Why does everyone think it's an umbrella?' he asks. I shrug my shoulders. I feel I should know the difference between a parasol and an umbrella, but I've not got the foggiest.

'I never asked for anything for Christmas,' I say. 'That way it was easier when Santa Claus forgot to visit.'

'I always visited,' he says. 'On the eve of St Nicholas Day. I left candy in your shoe.'

I shake my head. He never did.

'I did. I pride myself on never having missed a child. It'll be the legacy of my reign.'

'Your what?' I ask. I'm no longer howling, the anger's been replaced with silent tears streaming out in a steady flow.

'My reign of the Christmas World. Don't they teach you anything at school?' St Nick shrugs his shoulders. 'Are you ready to travel?' he says, before I've time to ask if he's actually a king. I've no idea how long we've been on the roof. Maybe minutes have passed, maybe months. I've no concept of time anymore.

'Am I going to be visited by a new ghost now?' I say, looking around the flat roof and up to the starless sky. 'I've had four scenes from the past, so is it the present next?'

'Haven't we been through this? That's an entirely flawed concept,' he says. 'Why would I show you your present? You're self-aware, you're living it, Theodora. The past though – that has moulded you and knowing more about it will have a direct influence on your present and future,' St Nick says. He moves to sit on the edge of the flat roof, with his legs dangling over the side. He pats the space next to him and I move to be nearer.

'I'm glad I got to see my mum,' I say. I swing my legs out over the drop.

It's time to admit that I like being with St Nick. He's refreshing, although I accept that's perhaps a word people use to describe something they can't quite put into a nice neat category. Time travel's much better than wiping old people's arses.

'A couple of weeks after Gabe's funeral, Sarah from CAMHS had been looking through my file again. She'd been reassessing because I was deteriorating. I wasn't being happy quickly enough for her. She was looking for triggers and reasons and I was refusing to talk about Francesca and the funeral.' I pause but St Nick doesn't say anything. Instead, he nods his encouragement, he wants me to continue.

'In my file… well there were details about my mum. I knew she'd died. I just didn't realise that she'd killed herself.'

'You didn't know she had taken her own life?' St Nick says.

'No, not until nine months ago. I'd known she died but I'd never asked how or why. What kind of a person does that make me?'

'A survivor,' he says but I shake my head.

'I've spent nine months thinking I must have been a really shit child for her to want to kill herself and leave me with no one,' I say.

St Nick shakes his head. His eyes look sad. Not a patronising kind of sad though, and that makes me want to tell him stuff. I think I can trust him.

'You know different now though?' St Nick says and I nod.

'Apparently there was an academic report saying that how a parent dies strongly influences their child's risk. My Young Person's Adviser had noted something like "losing a parent to suicide at an early age can be a catalyst for suicide and psychiatric disorders". Sarah read that out to me three times and she said something about losing a parent increasing a child's risk of committing a violent crime. She said I needed to take medication straight away.' I pause. 'I guess they wanted to control the beast within me. She'd already made an appointment for me at the personality disorder clinic. I tuned out from her around about then. I swear she was ticking boxes on a spreadsheet while talking.

'Then she said she'd be in touch with more details and to see if the medication was working. She gave me a number to ring, if I was feeling suicidal. But the number could only be rung weekdays during 11 a.m. and 1 p.m. Then she dismissed me,' I say.

We're both silent for a few moments. Raindrops bounce off the flat roof; the sound's calming.

'Silly woman,' St Nick says, breaking our stillness. 'There are many others involved in CAMHS who are exquisite—'

'Have you ever felt like you're a bomb and someone's just switched you on?' I interrupt to ask, but St Nick doesn't answer. 'So basically, I was told there was no hope for me. I walked out of the meeting and decided to prove everyone wrong.'

'Did the medication work?' St Nick says, but then speaks again. 'Not that you were forgetting Gabriel, more that the chaos in your head was shifting, just a fraction in a positive direction?'

'Never took it,' I say.

'Any person, even someone who hadn't just been through trauma, would be freaked into hysteria by her statistics and prophecy. She should have known better than to add to your already fragile mind,' he says and I nod.

'I think it actually helped. I've been a statistic all my life and it gave me a focus. I didn't want her to be right. I didn't want all kids with parents who'd committed suicide to be brushed aside and dismissed. Two days later I picked up a book and managed to read four pages,' I say. 'That was the start of my battle with my head.'

'Suicide's not genetic,' St Nick says. 'It's not an irredeemable mental condition. It can be prevented. That's what I was told and my sources are vast, international and varied.' He pauses. 'Perhaps that's why I was sent – to save you from suicide.'

'I wasn't suicidal though.'

'Perhaps I was sent to help break your silence and to listen to your pain.'

'But then what?' I ask.

'I think I've figured it out,' St Nick says and then he laughs. 'The lines have been rather muffled.' He lifts his eyes up to the heavens.

'Oh Christ. You're a religious nut. Before you start trying to convert me—' I say.

'There's no God, well not in the way—' St Nick says.

'There's no God, there's no heaven or hell, but Father Christmas exists?' I ask.

'No, Father Christmas is made up, but St Nicholas exists,' he says, his voice full of impatience.

I can't help but laugh. He's too easy to wind up. I swing my legs backwards and forwards. There's no breeze, there's no warmth, but there are loads of raindrops that aren't making me shiver or feel at all cold. They offer the beats and rhythm.

'Do you realise how screwed up this situation actually is? I think it might have been easier if you were a serial killer,' I say.

'Things are not always as they first appear, Theodora. Wait until you see my profile picture on Twitter. It looks nothing like me, yet I have many admirers and on several occasions have been referred to as "a bae".' He pauses. 'Now, is there anything you would like right now?' he asks.

'I'd like a cigarette and a bottle of vodka,' I say, sounding like an A-class brat. He coughs and I look at him. A lit cigarette's balancing on his lip, whilst he's still gripping the handle of his umbrella, and he's got an open bottle of vodka in the other hand.

I can't help but smile. His magic is still unexpected. 'I've never smoked before,' I say. 'And vodka makes me vomit. I had a bad experience on the beach in New Brighton. Vodka, sunshine, empty stomach…'

'Youngsters today,' he says, pulling a drag before spitting the cigarette over the edge. He takes a swig from the vodka bottle, shaking his head to help the liquid sink down his throat. 'Don't know why I bother. Not like I can get drunk. To be honest, that's about the only thing I have in common with Jesus. Our nights out together in Larry's Bar are the talk of Valletta.'

I look at him. 'What the fuck are you talking about now?'

'Nothing, forget it,' he says, jiggling the vodka bottle in the air.

'Anyway,' I say. 'Are there other *stops*?' I ask and he shakes his head. 'So my time's up? I go back to my old life?'

Why does that thought scare me? How the fuck do I go back and pretend none of this ever happened?

'Your travelling is up,' he says. He throws the bottle of vodka over the edge of the roof. I wait to hear the splash as it makes contact with the water. There's no sound. 'I felt it important that you have a firm sense of who you are. But now we head back to Liverpool. Time to act. I've ignored Spitfire for too long. They're about to cause us far too much trouble.'

'Spitfire?' I ask.

'Did I say Spitfire? Shit. No. I didn't say Spitfire.' He's doing that weird hand waving dance again, trying to erase the word.

'On that note, when we first met. It definitely said Spitfire—'

'I said shit and fire. But, yes, back to Liverpool we go. It's time for me to tell you all about my proposition,' he says, touching my arm, and with that the rooftop spins away.

PART TWO

MY STORY – BY DOTTIE SMITH

(Founder of Spitfire Saint Nicholas Umbrella Collective)

Within a week Josette Borg, Laurence Rosseau, Sofia Beckerman, Lucas Edwards and Birgitte Jesson had all changed their lives too. We were all now employed by Spitfire. We were on a high hourly wage with a bonus for every new member. The media wanted to know all of us. Christina Milano was off having 'work done'. She'd wanted to look her best for all the media attention, but hadn't figured the speed with which that would be happening.

There was Instagram, Tumblr, Snapchat, Podcasts, a YouTube channel with daily vlogs. Spitfire expected us to perform. We all had to run individual social media outlets, all of us under the strict guidance of our individual Spitfire social media experts, as well as having to contribute to the main group channels. Building the 'online brand' bollocks was now a full-time job for each of us and that wasn't what our little group had expected, or wanted.

Of course their Christmas advert was the first one to be released. A tearjerker that went viral; a Leonard Cohen track, a Santa Claus in a Spitfire-branded sleigh, an orphanage full of crying babies, a dying grandma reaching out for the ghost of her already dead husband, a three-legged dog, a homeless pregnant woman and a focus on how gifts bought from Spitfire made even the direst situation entirely better. The public lapped it up.

People from all over the world were clamouring to sign up for membership of Spitfire Saint Nicholas Umbrella Collective. They weren't doing it to celebrate Saint Nicholas. They were doing it because they wanted something for nothing. They were being promised stuff. They were being told that being a member meant they had a legitimate claim on a Christmas miracle.

Viral, trending, hashtags; people were talking 'bout us founding members and our private business. Details of the deaths of those I loved were being printed left right and centre. Folk were posting photos of hands praying and inspirational quotes alongside a hashtag #ripSmithfamily. Photos of Neil, Noah and Betty were being posted online.

Every single thing that was happening was beyond my control and I hated every single part of it.

Spitfire had decided that early membership should cost thirty pounds. For that people would receive a membership badge (SpitfireSNUC on it, alongside a traditional illustration of Santa Claus), a weekly e-newsletter and access to a private members only website and forum. They made it sound like there was loads of secret stuff on the forum and website, but there wasn't really. It was all just a rehashing of the limited stuff we knew 'bout Saint Nicholas. But the actual selling point was probably the members-only Spitfire Saint Nicholas tracking app.

Lucas was assigned to be the face of that one. Someone at Spitfire updated it hourly with sightings from the public. Lucas focused all his daily vlogs on tracking news. Of course, they were all uploaded a day late, so that information was out of date to the average person. Those who had the app, as in the actual members, got the info hourly via SMS, as well as an email with location links. The fact that many of them locations had a shop or restaurant that paid Spitfire for advertising seemed to be missed by the public.

The final selling point to get people to sign up, was the claim that only members of the Spitfire Saint Nicholas Umbrella Collective would be eligible for a Christmas miracle. That point didn't sit too comfy with me. Both Laurence Rosseau and Birgitte Jesson were on the phone straight after that went live, but there was nothing I could do. I didn't have no control over nothing by that point.

Membership was easy. The form was online, as was how payment was taken. We had five thousand, three hundred and seven paid members in the first three weeks. That was almost one hundred and sixty thousand pounds. And as each one of them membership fees equalled a bonus in our wages, our wages that first month were insane.

THEO (THEODORA QUIRKE)

'Where the fuck are we this time?' I ask.

I look around. It's a modern place, open plan and spacious. A blank canvas. There are loads of large objects around the room, all wrapped in Christmas paper, and with the biggest red bows that I've ever seen tied around them.

'So, is *this* your grotto?' I ask.

I mean there's no crap Christmas music playing and there's a distinct lack of elves. Also, it's not like I'm suggesting I'm in the North Pole or anything like that; it's got more of a 'presents in a sterile place' feel. Possibly in a psychiatric ward in the future, or an outer space waiting room, or a meditation area in heaven.

'For crying out loud,' St Nick whispers, and then, 'so this is how it's going to be, is it?' He shakes his fist up at the ceiling. He's back in his Santa pants and black boots, but doesn't have a top on. 'Give me a hand, Theodora Quirke,' he says. He points at the wrapped goods.

He starts ripping off the wrapping paper, throwing it into the air behind him. I stand watching. An unwrapping frenzy. He's how I'd imagine a small child to be on Christmas morning. An unhappy, ungrateful, possibly spoilt child. He grunts with each rip. The wrapping paper, that's covered in cartoon santas, floats up into the air, twirls and dances, but then as it hits the carpet it disappears.

'What the actual fuck?' I say, pointing to where the wrap should be. St Nick doesn't say anything. He's too busy grunting away to himself.

A few minutes later, with me standing all open mouthed and in awe of the wrapping paper magic and St Nick rushing around the room in an unwrapping whirl, he's bent over huffing and puffing and I'm taking in my new surroundings. Squishy white sofas, a large TV, a wooden dining table with four chairs, all overlooked by a small kitchen. It's all whites and chromes and there's a desperate need for a splash of colour. St Nick's umbrella now sits in a weird pot, that looks like a tree trunk, next to one of the two sofas; there's a white glow around the pot. I can't help but think that it might be recharging. A Christmas tree sprouts up from the corner. It's actually growing out of the carpet. Sparkling with lights, it's magical. Glittery silver baubles, huge snowflakes that'll never melt, silvery tinsel and an abundance of hanging silver ornaments; mainly santas and polar bears. It's very matchy and not at all how I'd expect St Nick to decorate a tree.

'Is this heaven?' I ask, immediately aware that I sound like a nobhead. He's already told me there's no heaven.

'No, Theodora Quirke, it's Liverpool. This is our new home,' St Nick says.

'This is where you live?' I say. 'In Liverpool?'

'It's where I live *now*. I can only live in cities where I'm the Patron Saint and, clearly,' he shakes a fist at the ceiling and jumps on the spot a few times, 'with you needing to be saved, I've been relocated *here* for the time being.'

'Fuck off, Liverpool's the best city in the world. You should—'

'I was living just outside Verona,' he says and I shrug my shoulders. I like living in Liverpool.

'In a one-off lakefront liberty style villa located on the sunny shores of Lake Garda. Lush Mediterranean gardens, featuring a tower, extensive terraces with panoramic views, outdoor heated pool, sauna and spa area,' St Nick says. 'Until I answered the message to save you. Before that I was in Siġġiewi. Before that in Manhattan.' He lets out a huge sigh. 'Now I've been relocated here and given a new face and *this* body.' He grabs his naked belly and jiggles it. 'The higher powers organised all of this.'

'Higher powers?' I ask.

'My bosses,' St Nick says. He spreads out his arms and raises his eyes to the ceiling. He tuts, clearly not impressed with the new location or the interior design or his new look, but I think it's wonderful.

'Three bedrooms, one is your room and it has an ensuite. One is mine and the other room is already full of Spitfire—'

'You keep mentioning Spitfire. What is it?'

'Shit. No, no, no. You are mistaken. I've never mentioned them—'

'You keep doing that too. Denying you've said Spitfire—'

'No, no, no. Shit and fire.'

'It was on that note you showed—'

'Always shit and fire. The room is full of shit and fire. I say it all the time. I think you'll be very comfortable here,' St Nick says. He shakes his head in an exaggerated manner.

'We're going to live together?'

'Only while you're training—'

'Like for a marathon?' I ask.

St Nick shakes his head. 'Do I look like a marathon kind of guy?' he asks, pointing to his overhanging belly. I shrug. 'All will be revealed.'

A pause. I'm hoping he's not about to whip out his dick.

'It's for something else and only when I'm absolutely convinced that you're ready,' he says, then he winks.

Please don't let this be about his dick.

'Ready for what?' I ask. 'I'm not a danger to myself or anything like that. I mean I don't really understand how but I reckon I've changed dramatically since we met a couple of... months ago?' It's a question. 'You should be available on the NHS. Imagine all those minds you'd be able to make better. I should ring Sarah at CAMHS and tell her to do one.' I laugh.

'A couple of months?' Nick says. 'Oh.'

'Oh?' I repeat.

'Theodora Quirke, you know how I said time travel alters your timeline.' He pauses, I nod, and then looks at his watch. 'You've been missing for almost...' Another pause. He uses his fingers to count. He stops on his seventh finger. 'Seven months. It's the twentieth of July.'

'I've practically missed all of being nineteen. I'm nearly twenty. But, how—'

'You're missing, presumed dead. A neighbour alerted the authorities after cookies outside of your flat weren't collected.'

Oh God, Sally. I hope she didn't think I was rejecting her and her cookies. We might have actually been friends. One day.

'Your boss... what's her name?'

'Stacey,' I whisper. Bet she had to work the Christmas Eve shift. Bet she's still slagging me off about that.

'Vile woman. Never considered you missing, just sent you a stream of vulgar texts with reasons why you'd never amount to anything,' St Nick says.

'Nice.'

'Oh, and she fired you by text,' St Nick says and I nod. Sounds about right. Doubt she'll give me a reference then.

'No body has been found. Obviously. But there was a small service.'

'I don't imagine anyone attended,' I say and St Nick doesn't respond.

My stomach turns. It's a cooking pot stirring up a giant bowl of loss and anxiety. I feel it bubbling in my belly and a wave rushes up – leaving blotches on my chest and all up my neck – reaching my face. There's no one left to care if I live or die. I'll be forgotten already.

'But there's a Christmas tree up,' I say. I point at the tree. 'That means it can't be July.'

'Oh Theodora Quirke, if only life were that straightforward,' he says.

'How can you look so weird, yet have such a kind and wonderful heart?' I say and St Nick laughs.

'Isn't that how your society works? You dismiss and judge on appearance alone? How many wonderful souls are left silent because society deems them unfit for public consumption? I didn't choose to look like this,' St Nick says. He rubs his hands over his naked belly. 'I'm given a face and body to reflect the society I live in. I don't mean just Liverpool, I mean the UK as a whole. This is what they,' he looks to the ceiling, 'think is the best disguise for here. In Verona I was thinner, and I had two married lovers, but that's a different story.'

'I've no fucking idea what's going on, St Nick,' I say and he nods.

'All will be clear soon,' he says.

I doubt it ever will be, but I nod anyway.

THEO (THEODORA QUIRKE)

I'm checking out my new bedroom – a wicker hanging chair in front of the window, a wall mounted fish tank with several Nemos swimming about, a chalkboard wall with the words 'WELCOME THEO' in lime green chalk. A faux fur rug, a round bed, fancy plush bedding and a million pillows in various colours and textures – when St Nick shouts that he wants to talk to me.

'Best not to have a shower for the next half hour or so,' he says as I walk into the living room. I don't ask why, I have an ensuite anyway, but I nod instead. I'm still lost for words. How do I now have a bedroom as amazing as that?

'Because there's a five-foot snowman in there. Said he'd go when he's finished though,' he says. I still don't ask.

'Anyway, about that job proposition,' he says. 'Perhaps you should sit down.' He pats next to him on the squishy sofa and I move to it. I perch on the edge, excited to hear whatever St Nick's got in mind. It's got to be better than wiping old person arse.

'Have you heard of Gustave Doré?' St Nick says and I shake my head. 'It doesn't matter. He was quite a character, a French artist and I think you would have rather liked him.'

I smile at that.

'He was a lovely chap; I met him once, accidentally of course. He happened upon one of my angels and I had to step in and diffuse the situation.' St Nick pauses.

He shuffles a little closer to me, the sofa's cushions bouncing with his weight. I wait for him to speak but instead he rubs his belly again, as if there's either a tune playing in his head or he's making a wish.

'One of your angels?' I mean, I had to ask. Surely it's okay to ask when what he's saying is off its head.

Angels, St Nick, Christmas miracles – it's basically the plot of a Hallmark movie on Christmas 24. Just need to add someone who is grieving and has lost their way and then—

'*La Nuit de Noel*, it's a painting. It shows the figure of an angel sitting atop a snowy chimney pot. Have you seen it?' I shake my head. I've no idea what he's talking about. 'One second.'

He bends forward, his hand scrambling about on the floor. A few seconds later and he's sitting back on the sofa with an Etch A Sketch on his knee. What the fuck? Where did that come from?

A number of twists of the white knobs, forwards and backwards, and he passes me his creation. 'See. The angel is clutching a bundle of toys with one arm, whilst dropping a toy down the chimney with the other hand. You must have seen it?'

Again, I shake my head. What he's drawn is possibly a shit SpongeBob SquarePants in the middle of a wonky square next to a rectangle. I guess that's supposed to be a roof and a chimney. He tuts. He's not used to dealing with someone as unsophisticated as me.

'Anyway,' he throws the Etch A Sketch into the air and it disappears before hitting the coffee table, 'Gustave Doré created the original, using watercolour and gouache over pencil lines. After my discussion with him, of course. He even helped out with the Christmas miracles in 1873.'

'Christmas miracles in 1873. How's that even possible?'

St Nick's hand shoots out again, his finger pushing on my

lips. It smells of fish. I wriggle my head away. When did he last wash his hands?

'In the end Gustave Doré decided to support our movement.'

'Your movement?' I say.

This time he smiles, nodding his head vigorously.

'Yes, Theodora. I'd like you to support us too by becoming one of my Christmas angels,' St Nick says.

My mouth actually drops open, and apart from shouting, 'Shut the fuck up,' there's nothing else I can possibly say.

'Since that message I received, and seeing as you're not suicidal or even in need of actual saving, it's the only remaining conclusion to be reached,' he says, then he pauses before adding, 'I think.'

'A Christmas angel,' I say. An echo. What the actual fuck is this life?

'You'd be joining the Christmas World, here on Earth,' he says.

'Christmas World,' I repeat. Because repeating words is all I seem to be capable of doing. Then, 'In the North Pole?' I ask and St Nick lets out a grunty groan.

'No. In Li-ver-pool,' he says. He says 'Liverpool' proper slowly, like I'm a bit stupid.

'You'd be joining a team and it's an honourable profession. You'd be self-employed, so responsible for your own tax return, with five projects per annum to manage. There's an annual meeting where all the Christmas angels get together, usually in the first week of the new year, although that's open for negotiation. If I'm being honest, it's a bit of a jolly, although for an unknown reason next year's meeting appears to be in Milton Keynes. You'll have to watch out for Alfr—'

This time it's my turn to pop a couple of fingers on his lips.

'You're going to have to slow down a little, St Nick,' I say and St Nick licks my fingers. I pull them away. He's such a weirdo. 'I've no idea what you're talking about, mate.'

'It's simple really,' St Nick says and I nod for him to continue. 'The whole concept of Santa Claus living in the North Pole and visiting children all around the world on Christmas Eve is, what you call, *bollocks*.'

I hear jingle bells. I search the room; it's fairly possible that I'm even looking for a reindeer. I glance up and that's when it starts to snow. From the ceiling. Not fake snow. It's actually snowing *inside* the flat. Large flakes are falling from the ceiling. Landing on my legs and melting. I bend my head back and watch them flutter down; a snowflake lands in my eye.

'What the—'

'Behave,' St Nick shouts. At first I think he's shouting at me, but then the snow stops. The flakes disappear instantly. I look at my legs and it's like there was never any snow. What the—

'As I was saying, the entire concept of Santa Claus is ridiculous. I'm definitely not him because *he* doesn't exist.'

'I figured that out a long time ago, St Nick. Can't say my pre-Gabe Christmas mornings were anything other than disappointing.'

'Yes, but what you failed to figure out is that Christmas miracles occur on, or during, the eve of December 6th each year. On my feast day. I feel that I'm repeating myself.'

I shrug my shoulders; yes he's repeating himself, but it still doesn't mean that any of this really makes sense. I mean, he's asking a lot of me, isn't he? I've only just accepted he's magic and now he's talking about me being a Christmas angel.

'Did you really never find a small toy or a coin or even

a sweet in one of your shoes on the morning of December 6th?' he asks and I shrug my shoulders. He's already asked, I've already said no.

'I put one there, every year,' he says. 'Never missed a child.'

'And I failed to notice?'

'Alas most do these days,' he says and all I can do is nod. 'Most dismiss the gift as an inconvenience, as if it's been dropped in there by mistake, but not all. Each year, and this is aside from my traditional small gift giving in shoes to every single child in the world, you'll find five people to go on my "good list". We're expanding... or maybe I'm just creating a new position for you. Either way, you'll monitor their progress all year and come the eve or day of December 6th, they'll receive gifts or miracles; selfless acts of kindness. It's all about bringing back the true meaning of gift giving at Christmas, and rarely simply about money.'

'Five people, every year?' It's mainly a question for me. It's me repeating words until I get my head around what he's saying. 'But how will I find my five?' I ask.

'By using social media, local newspapers, internet searches and personal knowledge, my Christmas angels scour each country for those with pure hearts. You'll be responsible for Great Britain. That's what I mean by your five projects.'

He pauses, perhaps waiting for me to speak. This is somehow too much information and not enough. But, mainly, I'm hit by the fact that both me and Mum were someone's one in five. I'd always considered myself the unluckiest person in the world, but the fact that I'd received one of St Nick's Christmas miracles is mind-blowing. I was chosen for something that was *actually* miraculous.

'You've already said how meeting Gabriel was my Christmas miracle,' I say and St Nick nods. 'And Mum was set to get one…' I stop. That memory's still raw. I think about how many people must give up on life just before a miracle's about to occur. Just before their life's set to change direction again.

'Our gifts bring joy and those chosen to be Christmas angels must have a purity of spirit.' He pauses. 'That's why I was called to help you. Or at least I think that's why I was called to help you. That's still not been made clear and I'm not entirely convinced I decoded the message correctly, but—'

'So by being one of your Christmas angels I'd have paid work and I'd be bringing joy. I'd actually have a purpose?' I say. My heart's thumping though.

'Yes, but it comes with a price and there will be sacrifices that you'll have to make, so it's not an easy decision,' St Nick says.

'It all sounds amazing, where do I sign—' I say.

'Slow down. You need to understand that the job's not what it used to be. We're fighting a losing battle within this society. Consumerism is rampant, the UK's political system is entirely corrupt and, as a result, it's becoming increasingly difficult for us to do our jobs. That's why I'm not entirely convinced that I've reached the correct conclusion. An unorthodox appointment, when your society is entirely broken, doesn't quite ring true,' St Nick says.

'Unorthodox?' I ask.

'Yes, my Theodora Quirke, for you would be the first ever female Christmas angel. That's why I was initially apprehensive and asked you whether you were transitioning. Primarily, all that I had to go on was, "*Save Theo – Spitfire and oral*",' St Nick says.

'And here was me thinking you simply preferred little boys,' I say. 'There's still no way I'm giving you oral, by the way.'

He shakes his hands out in front of him as if to rub out the words I've said. He shakes his head too. 'No, no, no. Nothing like that. Tradition dictates that Christmas angels must be boys,' St Nick says.

'Why?' I ask and St Nick shrugs. 'You're not going to try and convince me that men are better than women.'

'I wouldn't dream of offering such an argument,' St Nick says. 'An angel, or angelos in Greek, is a male being, and so male angels have always been sought. Yet on becoming a Christmas angel the angel is almost androgynous.'

'Almost androgynous,' I say. I'm repeating words again. 'Does that mean I'd still have tits?' I say and I watch as St Nick looks at my chest. 'For fuck's sake,' I say.

St Nick rushes his palms up to his face, hitting himself in the eyes and holding them there as if he's playing peekaboo. 'No, no, no,' he says.

'It's okay, St Nick,' I say and he slowly lowers his hands. His eyes search my face. I reckon he's checking to see if I'm pissed off. I shake my head and smile.

'This really isn't a feminist issue,' St Nick says. 'Mainly we're concerned that society has stopped giving and instead society's focused on taking. Christmas is suddenly all about what a person owns and how many presents they receive. It breaks my heart that the gift of joy is dismissed in favour of gifts that promote ownership and financial worth.'

'What's the gift of joy?'

'The gifts that *bring* joy,' he says. He sounds perplexed.

'Like Gabriel becoming my friend,' I say and he nods.

'On a larger scale, yes, the experience is unique to those who receive it. There was a time when finding a small gift in your shoe unleashed a sense of magic,' St Nick says.

So I'm in a flat in Liverpool, unsure how I got here, with no concept of time, listening to an almost naked, hairy man who might be a political radical, serial killer, anti-feminist, Santa Claus. I should be running to the River Mersey and jumping in. Yet instead, I'm nodding and thinking that he's the wisest and kindest man I've ever met.

'After seeing the purity of your heart and hearing how lacking focus and direction you've become, I can *only* conclude that my saving you is so that you can become a Christmas angel,' he says. 'And so your training will begin.' He flings his arms out wide in a dramatic gesture and whacks me in the tit. 'No, no, no,' he says. 'I wasn't trying to touch your... your...'

'My tit,' I say. 'It's fine, St Nick.' I shake my head mainly because this entire situation is ridiculous. St Nick's cheeks are beetroot and I think he's sweating under all that facial hair.

'Just over four months until the big day, so you'll be shadowing choices already made this year. Of course, there's a strict job specification and you're not quite ticking all the boxes yet, so I've been told to stress that a job will not be guaranteed after training,' St Nick says.

'Told?' I ask.

'It's a tough job,' Nick says.

'I'll do anything,' I say.

'There's also the fact that you'll need to be immortal and the consequences of that decision, but let's not think too much about that for now. Let's have a cup of tea and I do believe there's a triple layer chocolate fudge cake in that tin on top of the microwave,' St Nick says, as he points into the kitchen. 'Unless *they've* turned it into mince pies. Again.'

'They?' I ask, but St Nick is pushing himself up from the sofa and waddling towards the tin.

SPITFIRE SAINT NICHOLAS UMBRELLA COLLECTIVE ☑

COMMUNITY

Hello friends! DOTTIE SMITH, founder of the SpitfireSNUC, here again. Since so many of you are asking about the membership fee, I thought I'd respond and explain why we charge members to join our group. Hope this helps you to understand and encourages you to sign up, but if there's anything that's still not clear, leave a comment below. Thanks for being interested in joining SpitfireSNUC!

WHY ARE YOU NOW CHARGING A MEMBERSHIP FEE?

Thanks to Spitfire we have seen a recent surge in interest in Saint Nicholas. Due to this increased attention, our original members have had to give up their paid employment and their free time to answer emails, update various social media sites and keep everyone informed with the developments in our search for Saint Nicholas.

As many of you are set to receive financial reward when we eventually make contact with Saint Nicholas, and under the guidance of Spitfire, we feel that a yearly membership of thirty pounds is a fair amount. For that money, you will receive a membership badge, a weekly e-newsletter, access to a private members only website and forum, as well as the Spitfire Saint Nicholas tracking app that is updated hourly. We can also guarantee that only those who are members of the Spitfire Saint Nicholas Umbrella Collective will be eligible for a Christmas miracle.

We have decided to cap membership numbers shortly. Remember that only members of this group will be entitled to a life-changing Christmas miracle, so be sure to join TODAY.

DOES CHARGING A MEMBERSHIP FEE AND NOT ALLOWING ANYONE TO JOIN CONTRADICT YOUR FORMER AIMS FOR THE GROUP?

No! We feel that we are providing a community service that meets the demands of our public. We have adjusted our group aims accordingly.

WHAT IS YOUR NEW AIM FOR THE GROUP?

We aim to connect those entitled, and only those who are genuinely interested, with Saint Nicholas. He will listen to their claims and reward them accordingly.

THEO (THEODORA QUIRKE)

We're sitting at a small wooden table in the small kitchen. St Nick's on his third bowl of Coco Pops but I've only nibbled the corner of a piece of jam on toast. I'm assuming he's got trackies on, but his hairy top half's naked.

'So you'll live forever?' I say.

I've lived here ten days now. I'm told it's the last day of July, but that still makes no sense to me. How is it nearly August? I'm adapting to the ways of the Christmas World but I don't think I'm adapting fast enough. St Nick's not said as much, but sometimes the way he tuts makes me feel rubbish. Sometimes I don't see him for hours. I've no idea where he goes. I'm trying my hardest, but I ask him to repeat things too often. Because, despite everything I've seen, I can't seem to get my head around the fact that he's immortal. I can't seem to shift past that.

I've even wondered what'd happen if I chemical poisoned him *Heathers* style, or shot him in the head *Pulp Fiction* style, or electrified him in the bath like a film that does that. Not to hurt him. I just want to know what'll happen next. If it'll be like on those machines in the arcade, where there's a funny sound and then the game restarts a few steps back from where the life ended. And, also, I want to know if his number of lives is never-ending, or if he's only immortal for say seven deaths. Too many questions really, all about the same aspect, and possibly not enough of me focusing on that job offer to be a Christmas angel.

'Kinda the definition of immortal, Theodora Quirke,' St Nick replies.

He lifts the bowl to his lips and sucks up the chocolate flavoured milk. Most of it drips into his beard. The bowl's white with 'I believe in Santa Claus' written around it in a festive candy cane font. Four days ago all of our original white bowls were replaced with this set. I don't know who did it or why. St Nick was furious about it. He threatened to put them in the bin if the originals weren't returned. That still hasn't happened but no bowls have been binned. Clearly St Nick's desire to eat Coco Pops outweighs his hatred of all things Santa.

'Like a Greek god?' I ask and St Nick nods. 'So you can travel anywhere you want in the world.' I pause. 'Like, you can travel to heaven for the day and—'

'There's *still* no heaven,' he says. His voice is abrupt. 'And immortality in the Christmas World is earthbound. I live forever, but can only travel along an earthbound timeline. I cannot venture to another realm.'

'So when people die, there's an afterlife? But you get to live forever on Earth, so you never get to go there…' I pause; St Nick doesn't respond. But I've got to keep asking, as I've been thinking a lot and I've so many unanswered questions. 'Does that mean you have to keep seeing people you love die? And that you'll never see them again?'

'This isn't what you really want to talk about,' St Nick says. He puts his empty bowl back on the table.

I stare at my toast to avoid eye contact with him. It's on a plastic plate that's decorated with Santa Claus on a sleigh. There are additional festive items appearing daily, much to St Nick's annoyance. 'Higher power humour' was the only explanation I got. Whenever he talks about the higher powers he looks to the ceiling. I think they might live upstairs. Still I don't understand how they're getting in this flat without me noticing. Must be

144

when I sleep, but the thought of strangers clattering around in our cupboards, without either of us waking up, is terrifying. St Nick laughed when I told him that I was scared of that. He laughed and laughed until I thought he was going to throw up. I've still got no idea what was funny.

'If you decide to become a Christmas angel, you'll never die. Instead, you'll stay living solely on Earth until this world ends,' St Nick says.

'And that means that I'll never see Gabe again?' I ask. I look up and search St Nick's face for clues about what I should say or do. Coco Pops dangle, like mini brown baubles, from his scraggy beard.

'Not necessarily,' St Nick says. 'If Gabriel chooses to be reborn onto Earth again, then there's a chance, albeit a slim one, that your paths will cross. Do you understand what I am saying?'

I nod. 'But—'

'A small and improbable chance of you meeting with him, but it's not unknown. True love is a powerful beast. However, there's no guarantee that Gabriel will be born a man again, or that you'll recognise him in his new form... And on top of that, the chances of you actually being in the same place at the same time—'

'But if I die, I could see him again?'

'That's not quite as straightforward either. If you die by natural causes, then yes, there's a chance you could see him again. Your essence would have to find itself in the same realm and, in theory, there's a one in six chance of that happening.' He pauses and I nod for him to continue. 'However, it's highly likely that your essence is similar to Gabriel's so the same realm would be matched. Another complication comes from the need for Gabriel to still be in that realm when you arrive.

There's the possibility that he chooses to be reborn,' St Nick says.

'So even if I don't become immortal, it's still not guaranteed I'll see Gabriel again? But if I decide to become an earthbound immortal…' *Santa Baby* starts playing into the flat. It's loud. I have to raise my voice to be heard. 'He'll remain in a different realm, until he chooses to be reborn, and then I'll only see him if a million things fall into place for us,' I say.

'And that's why becoming a Christmas angel has to be your decision. You're giving up a lot, or very little. I guess it depends on whether or not you feel the odds will be in your favour,' St Nick shouts. 'Anyway, apparently it's work time now.'

He points at the ceiling and shakes his head. It's a new thing the higher powers are trying out. Christmas songs are played to mark when they feel we should be working. That sense of being watched constantly freaks me out.

'Do you think there's a chance that Gabriel won't wait for me?' I ask.

'I can't answer that,' St Nick says.

'That girl he was with at the séance, will she—' I start to say.

'Perhaps you need to consider that there's a chance you could meet someone else.'

I shake my head vigorously but St Nick continues. 'You're young, you could turn down my job offer and fall in love with someone you meet in another job. There could still be a happily ever after on Earth for you.'

If looks could kill, this immortal, definitely not Santa Claus, would be dead right now.

'It happens,' St Nick says, holding up his palms to fight off my killer glare.

'Stop spouting bollocks like an adult. You know how I feel.'

'I do, but even I have had other dalliances,' St Nick says.

'And how many times have you loved like you did with—'

'I have one true love,' he says. We connect eyes and I see that he understands.

'What do you think I should do? Do you think he'll be waiting for me?' I say.

'It's not in my job description to influence. Rather I'm merely inclined to present you with my experience and your options. But remember we're in training at the moment, so live in this present. The final decision will be made in four months and I'm still not entirely convinced you're the right person...' St Nick stops talking as he pours Coco Pops into his bowl for the fourth time. The music plays a little louder but St Nick shakes his head.

'I can't be expected to work on an empty stomach,' he shouts at the ceiling.

I reckon the ceiling's really thin and there are loads of elves upstairs, with tin cans to the floor, listening in on what we're saying.

'I'm this close,' St Nick clasps his palms together, like he's praying, 'to contacting my union rep.'

MY STORY – BY DOTTIE SMITH

(Founder of Spitfire Saint Nicholas Umbrella Collective)

There was no resting on the success of the ridiculous numbers of paid members. Mr Belsnickel from Spitfire said they had more plans. They wanted thousands more members and they were talking 'bout a Spitfire Saint Nicholas Umbrella Collective clothing range.

I was spending my days posting tweets 'bout Christmas miracles that Spitfire had written, getting my Facebook posts approved and altered by Spitfire before I was allowed to post anything, and updating my Instagram with my private photos that were in that box Saint Nicholas had delivered. I was sharing my memories and my secrets with strangers, but also I was letting the world know 'bout Noah, Betty and Neil. I was conflicted.

It wasn't long before I was invited on *This Morning* and *Loose Women*. I even had a literary agent asking if I'd considered writing a book 'bout my experiences. He suggested *How Santa Claus Saved My Life* as a crap title. He was saying he could get me a seven-figure advance, record amounts for a non-celebrity memoir, and that he already had someone to help with the writing too.

My life had changed. I was getting attention and folk were listening. I had everything I thought I wanted, yet somehow I had nothing.

I was living on adrenalin. There were phone calls and exciting news occurring daily. I was being invited to swanky film premiers and I was being asked if I wanted to try makeup, shoes, a handbag, drinks brands, you name it. There were even folk offering to pay me to tweet out 'bout their products. My endorsement meant

148

guaranteed sales, apparently. I was aspirational for the common person, apparently.

It wasn't just me that was experiencing this either. It was all seven of us and somehow, in amongst it all, we stopped talking to each other. I'd look at them online from time-to-time, but sometimes I'd feel myself getting angry if Christina looked to be getting more attention, had a designer shoe brand chasing her or when, for a few hours, she had more followers than me. I think they must have felt the same. I started resenting their lack of gratitude and I started hating the popularity contest that was occurring.

Saint Nicholas had stopped being our focus and I'd not even realised.

From the outside it looked like I had everything. I did, in terms of attention and financial shit. I wasn't happy at all though. I was the loneliest I'd been for years. Since I'd lost my family. I was missing Jack.

I was also hating that he'd been right.

THEO (THEODORA QUIRKE)

We sit not talking, *Frosty the Snowman* blaring out. Me not eating my toast and St Nick slurping away at his fifth bowl of Coco Pops. I can't bring myself to watch him eat. When the glugging stops, I look over at him. He's staring at me.

'Ella Fitzgerald,' he says.

'Was that who you loved?' I say.

'No, it's her. The one singing. How don't you know Ella?' he says. He points to the ceiling and sings along with the female voice. I shrug my shoulders. There's lots I don't know – how to sew on a button, how to bake a cake, what it feels like to receive a birthday card with 'daughter' on the front, who the fuck Ella Fitswhatever might be.

'I've lived for thousands of years,' St Nick says. He's still talking loud to be heard over the music. 'I loved once. We married and she was my everything. But then I failed to age and she did. I watched her growing older and becoming weaker.' A pause. I nod for him to continue. 'She knew who I was and what I was, we held no secrets, yet my not aging broke her very being. That is the reality of being an immortal.' He pauses again. I wait. 'She thought her wrinkles were foul. She lived waiting for me to leave her for someone younger,' St Nick says.

'But you wouldn't?' I ask.

'She was the most beautiful woman to have lived,' St Nick says. 'To truly love is to see what is within and to embrace the changes that occur with life's seasons.'

He pauses and the music changes to *2000 Miles*. Francesca

loved The Pretenders. I wonder how many nudges, how things each day, bring Francesca and Gabriel into my thoughts. I'm always going to miss them. I know that already.

'Her beauty matured with each crease that appeared on her striking surface, her sadness accompanied each drop of grey that replaced her roots. Her mind didn't age. Yet she walked through seasons and I behind, constantly hoping to catch her again. But...'

'But?' I say. An echo. A bump.

'She pushed me away.'

His empty bowl is on the table. One of his podgy fingers strokes its rim, and even though he's talking to me, his eyes are looking at the ceiling.

'Do you have a photo of her?' I ask.

'No.' His response is abrupt. I wait for him to continue. 'Personal mementos are forbidden within the Christmas World,' he says.

I want to ask about that gold, oval locket that I'm sure I saw him wearing. I don't though.

'She died three days before her fifty-eighth birthday and it was around that time that people started to ask questions. We had tended to move around and, as Alice grew older, she would tell strangers that I was her son.'

'Alice,' I repeat. It feels like saying her name breathes into her memory. I reckon that if we talk about dead people, they continue to exist.

'That way, we would avoid questions about how I remained looking in my twenties. But she was ill for a few years before she finally passed and so we'd settled in a village. That was where the rumours started.

'People suggested witchcraft. And so, shortly after Alice's death, I had to move away from our home. I lived without shelter for a number of years, always relying on the kindness of others. Years later I woke to learn that my face had changed and I could no longer speak Greek.'

'You're Greek?' I ask.

'Remember I was Bishop of Myra, around the fourth century? My powers were slightly altered then. I was able to bring four butchered children back to life.'

'I thought you couldn't bring back the dead—' I start to ask.

'That was then,' he says. His voice is firm. 'Now I don't have such skills.' He pauses. He wants me to understand that he won't be bringing Gabriel back from the dead. I nod. I'd figured that little gem out already.

'The Christmas miracles are my only constant. Infinite lives mean that I often forget everyday moments. There have been too many, but not the miracles. Each miracle matters,' St Nick says. 'It's beyond my control that my face changes and that I acquire a new mother tongue when it's time for me to move on. When we met I had been speaking Italian for years and I've already explained that I certainly didn't look like this.' He looks down at his naked belly and I'm sure I see a frown spreading across his hairy face.

'What this means, Theodora, is that each time my face changes and each time I acquire a new mother tongue, I'm seen as an intruder and forced to move on. How can I possibly form new friendships and relationships when my having to leave or them dying is inevitable? What's the point in loving when there's a limit to it?'

'But isn't that true of everyone?'

'Yes, people tend to deny that their only certainty is their death,' St Nick says. 'People seem to have missed that life is chaos. That life and all that they believe to be true will change in an instant.'

'Fear came into my life the day that Gabe died. It took my hope away too. Until I met you,' I say. I smile, but St Nick isn't looking at me. I think that my questions have made him sad. 'Perhaps it's best that people don't consider the chaos and cruelty in the world.'

'Perhaps,' he says. He's still running his finger around the rim of his cereal bowl. 'Can you hear a turkey?'

'A what?' I ask.

'A turkey. An actual, live, turkey. Listen.' I can't hear anything over the sound of the Christmas songs blaring into the flat. 'They make a range of sounds. This one's yelping a series of notes in a sequence. He's telling me that he's here.'

I can't hear anything but Chrissie Hynde. St Nick stands, kicking the wooden chair backwards until it hits one of the kitchen cupboards. Then he starts walking in a weird way, with his head bobbing back and forth. He clucks with each head bob.

'What are you doing?' I ask. Has he actually lost the plot? Was it only a matter of time before he cracked and I figured out I was actually being drugged by a serial killer?

'Talking to the turkey,' he says.

As if that makes any sense at all.

MY STORY – BY DOTTIE SMITH

(Founder of Spitfire Saint Nicholas Umbrella Collective)

And thousands more members is what they got.

Within three months there were over forty thousand paid members. That meant that the income from membership alone was over a million pounds. Merchandise – T-shirts, caps, beanies, hoodies, flags, pin badges, backpacks, umbrellas – was selling out within hours of being restocked and emails were getting to the stage of being unmanageable. Fake and replica merchandise was being sold on eBay and Wish, and being shipped over from China, and Spitfire seemed to think this was because of us all hinting online at the possibility of capping membership numbers.

Spitfire Saint Nicholas Umbrella Collective featured in a tabloid newspaper at least once a day and #SpitfireSNUC trended daily. The fact that Saint Nicholas was getting his name known should have been celebrated by us seven original members, but it wasn't long before it was clear that folk who were becoming members weren't interested in the origins of Saint Nicholas' story. They weren't interested in the little edible gifts that were left in a shoe or how Saint Nicholas had once stopped a desolate father from forcing his daughters into prostitution. None of that interested the paying members.

Instead, their emails and letters were 'bout how they were looking forward to Santa Claus arriving on a sleigh. Their emails and letters were all 'bout outlining what they wanted Saint Nicholas to give them. Their emails and letters were Christmas lists and explanations of why they deserved every single item. They were never a request for one small thing. They were always 'bout getting as much as they possibly could.

The thing is, I couldn't blame none of them. Spitfire had told them they were *eligible* and that had somehow translated into them being entitled and 'you will probably get anything you ask for'. Greed's a terrible thing. There was nothing pleasant or festive 'bout my inbox. Mainly though, the number of people calling Saint Nicholas 'Santa Claus' was making me realise that what we'd set out to achieve had not only failed, but had also failed on the biggest level possible.

Of course, me being me, you know with my desire to be liked and maybe my need to feel important, I felt I must reply to each and every email. Mr Belsnickel told me there was neither need nor was it advisable, but still. I started with simple replies like 'Your requests have been logged and will be passed on to Saint Nicholas' but that would start a dialogue. They'd then reply wanting to know when the goods would be delivered. They'd want a reference number, a delivery time, a Royal Mail tracking number and sometimes they'd even reply with more things they wanted adding to their 'order'.

THEO (THEODORA QUIRKE)

He talks to the turkey for a good twenty minutes, before I leave the kitchen and he follows me into the living room. He picks up his laptop from the coffee table. He opens it up. Something on the screen catches his eye. He flops back into the squishy sofa and balances the laptop on one hand, near to his eyes, while scrolling with the other hand. He leans in closer, then even closer, to the words.

I want to ask if the turkey told him to look online, but I don't. Instead I watch St Nick typing, sighing, shaking his head, staring at his screen, typing some more, huffing, then puffing.

There's a large decal of Rudolf on his laptop's lid. I hadn't noticed it before.

'That sticker's not very you,' I say.

St Nick shrugs. 'Buggers upstairs,' he says. He points one finger to the ceiling but doesn't take his eyes off the screen.

I wait for him to continue the conversation, but something's distracted him. His typing's frantic. He's sighing and grumbling and snorting more than usual. His eyes flick across his laptop screen at super speed. Like he's on drugs, or he's been fast-forwarded, but different. He scrolls and reads and clicks and types. Something's disturbing him. The lights from the Christmas tree twinkle in time with St Nick's typing; the effect's hypnotic. I wonder how much time is passing. I feel myself drifting—

'I'm far from perfect, Theodora Quirke, but I can forgive myself. I've lived many lives. I've manipulated and I've lied,'

St Nick says and then he pauses. He looks up at me, over his laptop.

Is he waiting for me to add to the discussion? Is he wanting me to confess to something awful I've done? Has he read something about me online?

'I've accomplished things that I'm not proud of, but I've learned from my actions. And that's why I can forgive myself and move forward,' he says. 'Because people make mistakes. People screw up and that's what makes them human beings and not robots. Embrace it and own your shit.'

'Okay,' I say – extending both the 'o' and the 'k' because I've no idea what he wants me to say or what's prompted his outburst. This man smells of sweat and he eats food he finds in his beard, yet here he is offering life advice in its purest form. I'm hit with a wave of thoughts; I'll lose him one day too. That fear catches in my throat.

'Will you leave me?' I ask. St Nick nods, his eyes back locked on his screen. 'Bastard,' I say. I laugh. 'Can't you lie and say you won't?'

'You're too fearful of the future,' he says and this time I nod. I am, but I reckon that's pretty understandable. I've nothing stable in my life. I've no roots, nothing firm under my feet. 'You need to learn to live in moments and not in the fear of those moments no longer existing, Theodora Quirke,' St Nick says.

I take a moment to try and unravel what he's saying. Easy words for someone with job security and immortality. I've basically got no idea where I'll be tomorrow, in an hour, in ten minutes even. *I Saw Mommy Kissing Santa Claus* plays into the flat.

'I hate this song,' St Nick says, possibly to himself. I've no idea who controls the soundtrack. The higher powers have a playful side. I like them, even if the concept of them existing's a bit terrifying.

'Wait a minute,' I say. St Nick's views on love and loving, on things ending replay in my head. 'You don't live in this now.'

'Like I said, I'm far from perfect,' St Nick says. He types a beat to his words. 'Things become a lot easier when you no longer expect victory.'

'Did you just read that on the internet?' I ask and St Nick nods.

'You're a survivor, defiant Theodora. We both are,' St Nick says. His eyes flick up from his screen to meet with mine. 'So let's get on with surviving.'

'And part of that is admitting that my mum killed herself. I need to embrace that she didn't die a natural death. I think I always knew that. I think I always knew when that lie was being told to me. I could sense it in the air around the speaker and see it in the way that eye contact was avoided,' I say. 'Does that mean that I'll never see my mother again?'

'She's been rebooted and the darkness was removed. She was last reborn in Bari, Italy. I was glad about that. Their week long Festa di San Nicola is a firm favourite of mine,' St Nick says. His voice is matter of fact, yet what he's telling me is entirely overwhelming.

'Is she happy?' I ask. I'm trying not to cry.

'Entirely,' St Nick says. 'I visit her once a year, in May.'

'That sounds wonderful,' I say.

Really wonderful, but fuck – now I miss my mum too. I miss all that we never experienced together. I miss having a chance to know her.

'I worried that if I'd been a better daughter then she'd have had more to live for. But you've shown me—'

'That there's no need for perfection,' St Nick says.

'Just because a parent takes their own life, it doesn't mean the child must follow suit,' I recite. With each time they're spoken aloud, the words are bedding into the universe that little bit more. Fuck statistics. And fuck the people who think telling a young adult about them is helpful.

'You were never on that path, Theodora Quirke,' St Nick says. 'But, believe me, now we have very real and very current concerns to deal with.' He turns his laptop around and points at the screen. 'I think those bastards at Spitfire are close to figuring out my true identity.'

'Shit and fire?' I say.

St Nick juggles his laptop on his belly, as he stands and walks over to me. I look at where he's pointing on his laptop's screen.

'Spitfire Saint Nicholas Umbrella Collective? Like on that note you got: *"Save Theo – Spitfire and Oral."* Is this a problem?' I ask.

'Possibly,' he says.

'Still not giving anyone oral,' I say.

'Thank the lords,' St Nick says.

'What can I do?'

'Nothing. The hunters are almost here,' St Nick says.

'What?'

'They're coming to get me,' he says.

'What the actual fuck?' I ask. I'm on my feet. I look towards the front door. Expecting a shit load of men in combat gear to batter the door down in the next minute. 'Are they going to kill you?'

'Worse than that,' he says.

Worse than killing him? Torture. Rape. Skinning him alive.

'We need to call the police—' I say. I need to protect St Nick. I can't let anyone hurt him.

MY STORY – BY DOTTIE SMITH

(Founder of Spitfire Saint Nicholas Umbrella Collective)

It was around that time, when membership was out of control, the comments being left on my Facebook group were hideous and us founding members were no longer speaking to each other, that I happened to see a tabloid's headline. 'I AM ST NICK'S LOVE CHILD' it said and there was a photo of a middle-aged woman wearing a too tight and very tiny Mrs Claus costume. That was when I decided I'd had enough and that I'd not let no more members join my group that year.

And that was when the accusations really started.

Folk didn't like hearing that they weren't allowed to join. I was called every name under the sun. My email address and phone number were given out online. You can imagine the text messages I started receiving. My actual address soon found its way there too and I had to be moved to a hotel. People were saying I'd murdered my kids; others were saying how I was the worst mother ever because I'd been out drinking that night they died. Everyone had an opinion on me and my business. I was being blamed for membership closing. I was being branded a 'Christmas hater'; I was somehow now the face of Spitfire.

Mr Belsnickel loved it all. For him, no publicity was bad publicity. Spitfire were getting more press than money could buy. The fact that my life and my reputation was being ripped apart meant nothing to them.

Then things took a step that even I wasn't expecting. There were newspaper articles, tweets and blog posts all linking Saint

Nicholas to child abuse and rape. It, and by it I mean *The Sun,* was even saying that Saint Nicholas had captured a vulnerable teen and was holding her against her will. They were calling her his suicidal sex slave.

It was around that time that Josette Borg, Laurence Rosseau, Sofia Beckerman and Lucas Edwards resigned. They were worried 'bout their reputations and they wanted nothing else to do with Saint Nicholas. They all made a big deal 'bout leaving. Stories were sold and they all earned their final piece of fame. By that point we'd all made small fortunes. There was no need to be making more money from renouncing the man who'd saved us all.

I didn't do none of that.

I didn't believe a word that was printed. Saint Nicholas had saved my life and I would be forever grateful to him. Thing was, I was to blame for the change in public opinion. I mean, not from the members of Spitfire Saint Nicholas Umbrella Collective, not yet.

I only got two emails saying they didn't want to be part of no Christmas miracles from a paedophile and asking for a refund, but the rest of the group members were reserving judgement. They were waiting for their big pay-out before deciding which side to be on.

Greed does that, don't it? It puts morals and ethics on hold until a time that best suits.

THEO (THEODORA QUIRKE)

I'm still in bed, but I'm sure I hear St Nick outside my bedroom door. 'St Nick,' I shout. He's been avoiding me. No more though. I need answers about the hunters and Spitfire. 'It must be...' I look at a chalkboard wall with the word 'OCTOBER' in hot pink. There's a smiley face next to it. Seems the higher powers send an elf or something into my room each month to write on my wall. I'm trying to see it as them helping me keep track of time. That way I won't get freaked out about a stranger being in here while I sleep.

'Must be mid-October by now, so I think it's time to put up more Christmas decorations. Maybe even some pumpkin ornaments on the Christmas tree. The higher powers will love that.'

No response. I wriggle out of bed, hopping across the fake fur rug. I hate how the fake fur tickles my feet. I'm stepping out of my room and stretching, when I look over at the third bedroom.

I never go in St Nick's bedroom and he never enters mine. It's not about being *allowed*, it's more that we've fallen into a nice little routine and boundaries sorted themselves out without us making a fuss. Also, why the fuck would I ever want to go in St Nick's bedroom? There's a third bedroom though. That door's always been locked and St Nick refers to it as the 'storage room'. There's so much paperwork involved with being in the Christmas World and I always imagined that room to be chock full of newspapers and letters. I mean, St Nick's been doing this for a long time and all the paperwork must go someplace. And sometimes, when I can't find St Nick, I've listened at the door and heard him mumbling in there.

It's never really interested me more than that though, if I'm honest. But today it looks different and I need answers.

'Hello?' I say.

The doorway to the third bedroom's covered in wrapping paper. Huge cartoon santas and smiling snowmen decorate the space. I walk over and touch the paper. It's flimsy; probably one of the cheap rolls from Home Bargains. There's a light on in the storage room so I can see that the door's open behind the wrap. I can make out shapes and I can even hear St Nick talking on the other side. He doesn't sound happy; is he talking to himself or has he got someone in there with him?

'What the fuck?' I say.

I cough, pretending to clear my throat, mainly so that he knows to put on his boxers.

'Come in,' he says. 'Bloody higher powers.'

'How?' I ask.

'Have you never broken through a wrapping paper door, Theodora Quirke?' he asks. I shake my head. He doesn't respond, probably because he can't see my head shaking.

I press a finger on the paper. Nothing happens. 'Punch it,' he says, and so I do. I punch and I kick and the paper rips. I tear and I pull and I laugh. It doesn't take long before there's enough space for me to walk into the room.

I take a step in and then I look around.

'What the—'

It isn't at all what I expected. A box-shaped room with no window. Next to one of the four walls, there's a desk, with a computer on it and a chair tucked under it. St Nick's in the centre of the room. He's spinning slowly on the spot and talking to himself. He's in a pair of red briefs that are possibly a size too small and they nip into the skin under his belly.

I hear the words, 'Saint Nicholas Umbrella Collective,' and, 'fuck,' a few times. I'm about to speak, mainly to remind St Nick that I'm there, when I glance over at the other three walls of the room. They're covered in paper: articles, printouts from the internet, grey pictures, some colour photos too. There are pieces of red string joining images, Post-it Notes in multiple colours and barely an inch of wall space left.

I walk further into the room. I know St Nick's seen me, as he's stopped talking, but I'm not quite ready to speak yet. I walk around the room, taking in the display. At first I think it might be to do with all of the people chosen for this year's Christmas miracles, but it seems to mainly focus on the same eight people. Someone called 'Dottie Smith' features the most. But then I see words like 'umbrella' and I see printouts with the subject line 'FINDING SAINT NICHOLAS' and 'ST NICK SPOTTED IN LIVERPOOL'.

Fuck.

This isn't about the Christmas angels' chosen people. This is something entirely different.

I turn to St Nick.

'I think we've got a problem,' St Nick says.

'You *reckon*?' I say. My eyes still flick around. 'So that mention of being hunted and all those slips about Spitfire that you dismissed—'

'Spitfire are *possibly* a *little* problem,' St Nick says. I think he's trying to be funny.

'Well I'm glad the room's not full of shit and fire,' I say and offer a crap smile. St Nick frowns. 'And obviously this has been an issue for a few weeks?' I say.

'Their interest in me has been going on for a number of years,' St Nick says, 'but the higher powers never considered it a concern.'

'And now?' I say. I point at a printout of a Facebook group

called 'Spitfire Saint Nicholas Umbrella Collective'.

'It started years ago. One person became a little obsessed with the idea that Nikolaos of Myra was real. That's not a new thing, many adults have reason to believe in me. I'm rather a big deal in Europe, you know.'

I nod. He's mentioned it a few times.

'But then through online bits and bobs, that one person found other like-minded people and they formed a group. That person, Dottie Smith,' he points at an article about her, 'recalled having seen St Nicholas outside her bedsit,' St Nick says.

'And did she?' I ask.

'Yes. I had a different face then. It was back when I was living briefly in Quebec, but she was one of the Christmas angels' choices. She'd had a horrific time, lost all her family in a house fire. Beautiful children; a boy and a girl, both under five, and her husband was an absolute gent.'

'I like that you remember,' I say.

'Always will,' he says. 'I'd left a box of precious memories outside her bedsit. Photos mainly, that she'd thought destroyed in the fire. Hadn't expected her to be more interested in the deliveryman than the contents of the box.'

'You do good work,' I say and St Nick nods. This is the St Nick I met outside Dante House; a focused man with the purest of hearts.

'The thing is, when the Christmas miracles are performed, I always have my parasol with me. It's tradition and the higher powers—' He pauses and looks up to the ceiling. 'They've got my having to carry it into my job description. It's magic, of course. That was why the group was originally called "The Saint Nicholas Umbrella Collective" and that's how these people found each other. Not that they even know the difference between a parasol and an umbrella. Imbeciles,' St Nick says.

'People?' I say.

'There were eight of them and they're from all over the world.' He points at printouts of eight faces. 'They had all connected online and were never of concern to me. They had their little online group and met once a year, on St Nicholas Day, to celebrate all things me. I liked to watch them meeting up. The eight of them had all had difficult pasts and, increasingly, you know I've been watching them for a few years now, they've formed bonds. They were a tiny family all connected through having been chosen to have a Christmas miracle by one of our Christmas angels,' St Nick says. 'I like to keep an eye on my own.' He winks at me and I smile.

'That sounds like a good thing,' I say. 'So why all of this?' I point at the displays on the walls.

'It was a good thing. There was a sense of gratitude and their search to find me was to thank me, not to expose the truth. I've been leaving gifts in shoes for hundreds of years, and the number of actual Christmas miracles have increased over the years with the size of my team,' St Nick says. 'But then this company heard about the Facebook group. Spitfire.'

'You never explained who they were,' I say.

'They're an up-and-coming internet-based retailer. Like Amazon, but smaller. Recently they branched out into selling toys.'

'And with Christmas fast approaching…' I say, nodding. I can guess where this is going.

'Yes, *someone* in their marketing department decided that it would be a good idea to jump on-board "The Saint Nicholas Umbrella Collective" and their "Search for St Nicholas" nice and early. They believed that by helping the organisation and exposing the Christmas miracles, they would gain much press and be seen as being full of community spirit, and not the money grabbing evil that they truly are.' He pauses. 'A Mr Belsnickel contacted Dottie Smith. He's the brains behind the company. Let's just say that his motivation isn't straightforward, but there's much press interest. He claimed to be against commercialism, yet his company sells products online at discount prices and are promising new members exclusive access to me,' St Nick says. He pauses.

'So The Saint Nicholas Umbrella Collective had a database of evidence? Is that what this is?' I say, pointing at one of the walls. There's a printout of the original list. The years of each December 6th miracle fills one column and then there are the names of the recipient and the details of their miracles in different columns. 'So Monika Czacki received a visit from a sister she had thought dead in 1965?'

'Yes, but Mark Franklyn didn't receive a mermaid girlfriend in 1986. I've no idea who he is and what happened in his bedroom, but it definitely wasn't from me,' St Nick says. 'Mermaids are just not my style. Anyway, they get way too grumpy if out of the sea for longer than a few minutes. Trust me, a grumpy mermaid is zero fun. And look at this one.' He points at a newspaper article with the title 'I AM ST NICK'S LOVE CHILD' and the photo is of a blonde with huge tits popping from a very tiny Mrs Claus costume.

I can't help but laugh and St Nick scowls at me.

'And you know the worst thing?' St Nick says and I shake my head, because I don't. I'd not even try to guess what the fuck it could be.

'I've just found out who this Mr Belsnickel really is,' St Nick says. 'And this situation,' he waves at the walls, 'just got one hundred times worse. The reindeer shit's just hit the fan.'

MY STORY – BY DOTTIE SMITH

(Founder of Spitfire Saint Nicholas Umbrella Collective)

It was around 'bout that time, that Spitfire decided to switch their focus and up their search to find Saint Nicholas. There was proof that Saint Nicholas was hanging out with a girl, Theodora Quirke, who was supposed to be dead. That's how the rumour 'bout her being kept as a sex slave was started. Spitfire had hunted out CCTV footage from outside where the girl was living. Her name was trending constantly. It was either #saveTheodoraQuirke or #ripTheodoraQuirke. Folk couldn't make their minds up.

It never occurred to them that Saint Nicholas might have been helping the girl or maybe even saving her life. Instead, damage limitation I guess, but the hunt to find Saint Nicholas and to save Theodora Quirke shifted up a gear.

I looked at the images of Theodora Quirke. She was a petite blonde with the brightest blue eyes, that spoke of pain beyond her years. Tiny features, porcelain skin, she was a doll of a girl. I spent a few days googling her and I found her boyfriend's mum's blog. I read every word 'bout Theodora's past, 'bout how Francesca had been piecing together Theodora's last few days. Francesca's anger at finding out what that lady from CAMHS had told Theodora, her own despair at not being able to reach out to Theodora, what was overheard at Gabriel's funeral, what was left unspoken. I read 'bout Francesca's despair and loss. She'd lost a son and a daughter too. I recognised her pain.

There was nothing I could do to stop everything from unravelling for Saint Nicholas.

The thing is though, even in and amongst all of that shit – I mean I'd lost everyone I cared 'bout, I had no friends, I'd managed to screw up the reputation of Saint Nicholas and perhaps destroyed any possibility of Christmas miracles occurring again — somehow I still had hope.

Me and hope, eh? It's like we're practically the same thing. It seems like when I'm faced with choice, I always pick that path named hope.

THEO (THEODORA QUIRKE)

I've spent the last twenty minutes walking around the room, reading the articles stuck to the wall and trying to figure out what the actual fuck is going on.

'You're really crap at not being seen,' I say and St Nick shrugs his shoulders.

'Only eight confirmed sightings. Seems that the Christmas magic doesn't always work when I'm delivering the Christmas miracles. A bit of a glitch in the system. Stopping time is a complicated thing.'

'What?' I ask.

'Nothing, nothing, really... nothing. Most is speculation though and a lot of it is so far off the mark,' St Nick says. He points at some of the highlighted details on the list. There's a lot more than eight on that list.

'Since Spitfire got involved, all these people are coming forward saying that I've done a vast variety of horrific things,' St Nick says. Again, he points at copies of newspaper articles stuck to the wall. My eyes scan over one of them with the headline 'PEDO RING INSIDE ST NICK'S WORKSHOP'.

For fuck's sake. All those people who'll have read that headline and believed every single lie in the article. All those people out there who'll be talking shit about St Nick.

'In the first three weeks, the reported sightings of me went from eight from around December 6th, because I'm careful and rarely make mistakes, to thirty-seven thousand and seventeen sightings all year round.'

'And it's still rising?' I say.

'The higher powers are estimating they'll reach over one hundred thousand sightings and new stories within the next week,' St Nick says. 'And you know what the killer is in all of this?' St Nick asks and I shake my head. 'The miracles received were selfless acts. No calling card was left, no clue or hint that the Christmas miracles were anything other than that – miracles. Everything that was given was to make a difference and to steer people onto the right track. We try to save lives. Don't get me wrong, it doesn't always work out as we plan…' He pauses. I think about my mum. 'But we've got an impressive success rate.'

'Is that a membership form to join SpitfireSNUC?' I ask. I point at a printout. 'And the fee to join is thirty pounds a year?'

St Nick sighs and nods his head. 'They had over five thousand paid, new members in the first three weeks. That's a lot less than how many have "liked" the free Facebook group, but paying is said to get members many "additional extras". You do the sums – over five thousand at thirty pounds each in just three weeks. Dottie Smith gave up her job and the others weren't far behind them. Now, they've thousands more paid members, merchandise and are "extending their reach".'

'But how did Spitfire get the original members to agree to all of this?'

'Money. Is it not always about money?' St Nick says. 'One day Mr *Belsnickel*…' His face twists in disgust when he says the name. 'That's not even his real name. I mean if people took a minute to google his name—'

'What did he do?' I ask. I need St Nick to stay focused.

'He posted on their Facebook wall for someone to contact him. Dottie Smith took the lead and messaged him, before discussing it with the others. That was a shame, as although she has the purest of hearts, she remains the weakest of the eight.'

'In what way?' I ask.

'Mr *Belsnickel*,' another twisting of his face, 'pressed all of her buttons. He told Dottie Smith the group had lost their focus. Then he offered them each a financial incentive, as a goodwill gesture, to allow Spitfire to take control of their group. All but two of the eight, Dottie and Christina, were initially reluctant, but Dottie got Mr *Belsnickel*,' another twisting of his face, 'to up their incentive and she agreed on behalf of the others. Seven of the eight got twenty thousand pounds, and online shopping vouchers of almost the same amount. Not Jack though. Nice lad.'

'How do you know all of this?' I ask.

'I've been monitoring them,' he says. As if that's enough of an explanation. I look around the room again. This is so much more than casual stalking.

'And the initial eight are all people you helped,' I say. 'I mean, you gave them miracles that changed their lives and they handed over all their research to Spitfire?'

St Nick nods. 'But not Jack.'

'Well that's still fucked up,' I say.

'Mr *Belsnickel*,' another twisting of his face, 'has jumped on it all. Let's face it, it's excellent PR in the months leading up to Christmas Day. Suddenly there's a Twitter account for SpitfireSNUC and each of the original members have thousands of fans and their own Twitter accounts too. The online world makes the borders of sea and continents disappear. There's Instagram, Tumblr, Snapchat, Podcasts, a YouTube channel with daily vlogs and people from all over the world are jumping to sign up for membership, in the hope that they'll get something life changing. Viral, trending, hashtags, you name it. It's spiralling and spreading, and the information they hold is all leading towards me,' St Nick says. 'They're posting and reposting details daily, sometimes hourly, of Christmas miracles that have been occurring on December 6th around the world and for hundreds of years. They even have people out hunting for me.'

'Do they know about your new face?'

'They have footage of us talking outside Dante House,' St Nick says. 'And two days ago they figured out that we were back in Liverpool.'

'So we move,' I say.

'The higher powers are refusing to let us move until your training's complete,' St Nick says. 'But, and Theodora Quirke, this is something you really need to think about, people have identified you. They know you're not dead and there's a Facebook page all about you… as well as a police hunt to find you.'

'Shit,' I say. He points to a printed out headline that claims '(UN)SAINTLY NICK AND HIS SUICIDAL SEX SLAVE'.

'Fuck,' I say, as I scan the article. 'And you didn't think I needed to know about all of this?'

'I was trying to protect you,' he says. 'I mean, we can sort all of this.' He waves at the walls. 'I didn't realise who Mr *Belsnickel*,' another twisting of his face, 'was at first. That's been the hardest part of the investigation. I haven't seen him for a number of years and he's got a new face too. But now my need to keep you from Mr *Belsnickel*…' another twisting of his face, 'that's my biggest challenge.'

SPITFIRE SAINT NICHOLAS UMBRELLA COLLECTIVE ☑

COMMUNITY

Hello friends! Mr Belsnickel, executive director of Spitfire, here for you today. Dottie Smith would like to thank you for the outpouring of kindness after her last post. We love how many of you support Dottie's belief that if you've got nothing nice to say, then you've joined the wrong Facebook group. You, dear friends, are the best!

Those who want to be negative about the membership fee really are failing to embrace the spirit of this group. It does seem though, from the hundreds of comments left, that you love reading about the work Saint Nicholas has been doing and we, as a group, are devoted to bringing you details of all the wonderful acts on and around December 6th. These gifts were often to seemingly normal, insignificant people, which begs the question – **do you want more money than you could ever dream of having?**

On December 6th, 2014, a lottery ticket was stuck to the door of Emma Murray's bedsit. That evening Emma's ticket was a winner! Thirty-five million pounds later, and Emma's life changed forever. I cannot find an update on what Emma did with the money, but her belief (at that time) was that whoever left the ticket was an angel. Obviously, we now have evidence that suggests that the anonymous patron was indeed St Nicholas.

For details on how to join SpitfireSNUC to be eligible for a Saint Nicholas Christmas miracle, go to www. SpitfireSNUC.com/becomeamember

THEO (THEODORA QUIRKE)

We're back on the squishy leather sofas. I couldn't concentrate with all that information plastered to the walls in the so-called 'storage room'. Too much to look at. St Nick's got his laptop open and he's trying to remember a password to some site or other.

Think he's tried three variations of 'Santa Claus is a...' so far. None of them were 'twat'. He told me to wait while he logged in but I need answers. I'm done with waiting until everything's all fucked up and broken before anyone tells me what's actually going on.

'I think it's time you told me everything you know,' I say. I'm trying to sound assertive and in control. 'Who is Mr *Belsnickel*?'

A sigh. I think he's typed in the wrong password again.

'St Nick,' I say.

'He's Krampus,' St Nick says.

'Fuck off,' I say. I'm staring at him but his eyes are fixed on his screen. 'There's no such thing as Krampus.'

He points at himself. 'You said that about me,' St Nick says. Like that's proof that I'm not actually losing the plot. 'Do you even know who Krampus is?'

I shake my head. I've heard his name. I'm sure he's like a made up bogey man. I think there was a horror film about him but I never watched it. Think he might be terrifying.

'Here, read this.' He passes me his laptop. The WikiPage for Krampus is already open.

It takes me a few minutes to scroll through it all.

176

'So you expect me to believe that there's a horned half-goat, half-demon out there, who's somehow set up an online company, selling toys at bargain prices? I mean, that's quite a shift from hunting naughty children and eating them.' I laugh, because what I've said is ridiculous but what St Nick's suggesting is even sillier. St Nick doesn't laugh though.

'Where do you get this information?' St Nick says. I point at the WikiPage he's just handed me but he shakes his head. It's like he thinks I've made this stuff up about Krampus and not that all I've actually done is read what *he* told me to read.

'This is the problem, really,' he says. His tone, his folded arms across his chest, his full on bitch face – he's pissed. 'This is why Krampus is the way he is. So many lies about him. If his identity was established he'd—'

'There was a film about him though,' I say.

I think he might mutter, 'Imbecile.'

'But—'

'Sharp claws. Echoing cloven hooves and rattling iron chains. Forked tongue, half-goat. Said to kidnap children. This is what your society does,' St Nick says. 'It whips people up into a frenzy of hatred against the innocent. *You* made him the way he is.'

'I've done nothing,' I say. I sound like a sulky kid.

I mean, when he says 'you', I'm not stupid, I know he doesn't actually mean *me*. I just want him to stop blaming me for other people being shit. That said, I've no idea what St Nick's talking about or what the fuck's happening, in terms of Spitfire and those folk who should have been worshipping at St Nick's feet, not selling him out to the highest bidder. I mean, how does a half-goat even fit into all of this?

'Look,' St Nick says. He takes his laptop back, taps a few keys, sighs too many times, and then he turns the laptop around so I can see it. He points at the screen. He's pulled up what looks like an old Myspace account. He's pointing at a photograph.

'You were on Myspace?' I say, but he doesn't answer. Instead he prods a finger at the screen again. 'Okay, okay,' I say, bending in closer to the laptop.

A black and white photo, a little blurry, possibly scanned in and then uploaded. There are two men. Dressed the same; two old fashioned suits all buttoned up and making them look stiff and formal. They both hold top hats, neither are smiling. Might be brothers, they might be lovers, I've no idea how old photographs work. One's darker, the other's fairer. One has a goatee and sideburns, the other's clean shaven. They're possibly in their fifties but sometimes people in the olden days looked proper old even when they were still young.

'Should I know who they are?' I ask, nodding at the photo.

'That's me,' St Nick says, pointing at the man who doesn't have a goatee. 'And that's my brother.'

'You have a brother?' I say. 'So we're not the same. I thought you had no one, like me.' Again, I sound like a sulky kid.

Why didn't he tell me? How does that even work? St Nick's immortal. Has lived many lives. Yet somehow he's got a brother who's also survived? Does that mean his brother's immortal too?

'A twin,' St Nick says

But—'

'His name's Krampus. We've not seen each other for over one hundred years.'

'What the fuck?' I say.

'Looks like he's going by the name of Mr *Belsnickel* these days,' St Nick says, his eyes still on his laptop's screen. 'Pretentious *nobhead*.'

SPITFIRE SAINT NICHOLAS UMBRELLA COLLECTIVE ☑

COMMUNITY

Hello friends! Mr Belsnickel, executive director of Spitfire, here. I'm still standing in for Dottie Smith and it's a short post today. This post is also a reminder that one of the reasons why Dottie founded the group was so that we could bring you details of all the wonderful acts, miracles and donations that Saint Nicholas has given the general public, all over the world, on and around December 6th. These gifts were often lifesaving, which begs the question – **wouldn't you want Saint Nicholas to save your life (lives) too?**

On December 5th, 1660, a ship sank in the straights off Dover. It was noted that the only survivor was a Hugh Williams. Then on December 5th, 1767, another ship sank in those same waters. It was recorded that 127 people lost their lives, and, again, the only survivor was a Hugh Williams.

For details on how to join SpitfireSNUC to be eligible for a Saint Nicholas Christmas miracle, go to www. SpitfireSNUC.com/becomeamember

THEO (THEODORA QUIRKE)

Mainly I'm still staring at St Nick's laptop. This makes no sense. How is St Nick related to a half-goat, half-man? I look at St Nick's feet. Hairy toes but no cloven hooves. I look at his nails; bitten down. Does he have a forked tongue?

'It might help if you understand the Christmas World a little more,' St Nick says.

'You think?' I don't mean to be quite so sarcastic, but I'm pissed off. Wouldn't it have been useful to have known all of this shit from the beginning? I mean I don't know where or when he could have slotted in about him being the twin of a goat man, but still.

'So I'm Principal of the Christmas World. I reign—'

'Like a king.'

He holds up his palm. I think that's because he doesn't want me to interrupt. 'Yes and no,' he says and I nod.

'And the higher powers?'

He points up to the ceiling. 'Invisible cameras. They oversee all of the realms. Six realms in the afterlife, four earthbound realms, three otherworld realms.'

I honestly thought they lived upstairs and that the floors and walls were super thin. That they have cameras everywhere makes a lot more sense.

'So they're the boss of you. Like high tech Greek gods?'

St Nick tuts. I don't think he likes the idea of anyone being his boss.

'That's perhaps the closest comparison. We're simplifying, but the *condition* of my reign and of people celebrating The

Feast of Saint Nicholas on December 6th, is that I deliver a gift to every child. If I fail to deliver to even one child…'

A pause. Is he being dramatic? Am I supposed to ask? I reckon at least a minute passes, so that's probably a day in the real world of me waiting for him to finish his sentence.

'What? What happens?' I ask, nudging him to continue.

'Then I'm deemed as having failed in my role and I lose my reign,' he says. 'On December 7th, someone else takes over.'

'Harsh,' I say, and St Nick laughs.

'It would pass to the next in line for the reign. That person would step forward, their feast day would be given significance and mine would fade away.'

'And that's not good?' I say, because I don't see how a bit of variety's a bad thing. St Nick's been doing this gig since the fourth century. I mean maybe, and clearly I'm not saying this out loud, but maybe it's time he let someone else have a turn.

'It is… the next in line's my brother,' he says. 'Krampus would reign over the Christmas World.'

Shit just got complicated.

'How would that work?' I ask.

'The Christmas World would shift its focus to Krampus and his needs. The Christmas angels would work for Krampus and Krampus Night would be the pinnacle of the year's activities.'

'And that really would be a bad thing?' I ask, catching up with what St Nick's actually been saying.

'My brother kidnaps naughty children and keeps them in his underground lair for a year…'

What the actual fuck?

SPITFIRE SAINT NICHOLAS UMBRELLA COLLECTIVE ☑

COMMUNITY

Hello friends! Mr Belsnickel, executive director of Spitfire, here. Yes, I'm still standing in for Dottie Smith. I have heard, from a reliable source, that she is spending some of her vast fortune and enjoying a road trip around the USA. We, of course, send her our love.

Unexpectedly, most of you seemed to love that last post about Hugh's double survival. Thanks for all the links to further research you've been doing and we love that so many of you now reply to the naysayers for us. You are the best! Some of you have been asking for details of the miracles that Saint Nicholas has performed to other original group members, so I thought I'd write about another one today.

As you know, Dottie was devoted to bringing you details of all the wonderful acts, miracles and donations that Saint Nicholas has given the general public, all over the world, on and around December 6th. These gifts were often to seemingly normal, insignificant people, and always life changing, which begs the question **– would you like to find true love?**

This is a story Dottie told me when I first met her. On December 6th, Sofia Beckerman and Laurence Rosseau both received an email at 13:22 hours. The sender claimed to be Saint Nicholas, the email address supporting the assertion, and the contents of the email were entirely to introduce the strangers to each other. This then led to an exchange of emails from the singletons and, after many months of daily interaction, the travelling from France to the US for an initial meeting. They are now married with a second child's arrival imminent, and cite Saint Nicholas as being the reason they found the true love that had previously escaped them.

Sophia and Laurence are two of the original eight members of the Spitfire Saint Nicholas Umbrella Collective.

For details on how to join SpitfireSNUC to be eligible for a Saint Nicholas Christmas miracle, go to www. SpitfireSNUC.com/becomeamember

THEO (THEODORA QUIRKE)

Apparently, I've not been outside of the bubble of this flat for three weeks now. It only feels like days. I'm finally accepting the time passing differently – guess it makes every minute matter that little bit more.

The shop downstairs seems to change its purpose every couple of weeks and St Nick's said that the higher powers like to spice things up and keep the tenants altering to avoid our detection. We currently live above a fish and chip shop. Thankfully we have a roof terrace, so we can get some crisp early November air, but even that's been a little risky in the last week.

Because it seems that Mr Belsnickel – well, Krampus has now got the local newspaper onside and the editor in chief seems to have a bee in his bonnet about finding St Nick. He's put a positive spin on it all, of course, about how it'll put Liverpool on the world map. Clearly he's spouting adult bollocks, as Liverpool gave the world Steven Gerrard, Sporty Spice and The Beatles. Liverpool's well and truly already on the map. The newspaper's offering cash too, although St Nick seems to suspect that the cash is coming from Krampus, but the people of Liverpool are joining forces and everyone's wanting to be the hero of the hour. Basically St Nick is more or less the devil and Krampus is doing everything in his power to make sure as many people as possible know about it. Everyone in the city thinks I'm St Nick's sex slave and they're all after saving me. We love a good rescue story in this city.

'Can I publish a statement, telling everyone to fuck off?' I ask St Nick, but he shakes his head.

St Nick's said that it's too dangerous for me to go into town. He's reasoned that we're more likely to be spotted together and that he can't guarantee the magic will always work. I don't know if his umbrella, or whatever other magic he seems to use, works all the time, but over the last three weeks he's hardly been going out and instead he's been focusing on the Christmas miracles more. A month left. As he keeps saying, that's what we're here to do.

So we're working hard on my training. I've got eight on the list now, only three reserves left. We're monitoring them all daily. Two people fucked up pretty quickly thanks to their social media addictions. One for joining Tinder and sending dick pics to two women (even though he was supposedly happily married), the other for his cruel (anonymous) trolling of a YouTuber on a weird site called Chitter Chatter.

Still got my favourite on my list though. She's called Elsie and she's from Preston. She's a dinner lady during the morning and then she spends every afternoon cooking. Every single day she cooks more than her and her husband need, so that she can deliver hot food to the homeless in her town. No one knows what she does; she never seeks thanks or praise. I'm hoping she can hold it together but I can see the trouble she's in. The debt's rising each month and she's already at the stage where she's hiding unopened letters from the bank in a drawer in her kitchen. She spends too much on food, even though she shops around for the cheapest prices. And now it looks like her husband's about to lose his job. His hours have been reduced and they've missed two mortgage payments even before his income's taken away. He's not told her yet. I'm scared for when he does.

What if it all gets too much for her? What if she gives up before the Christmas miracle happens?

I've got to search into any social media accounts she might use. Please don't let me find anything. I start my search on her name.

'Fancy being the first ever female Christmas angel,' St Nick says.

I look over at St Nick. He's lying like a beached whale, in a too-tight sliver thong, on the squishy sofa. I'm glad he's lying on his back. Not convinced I want to see his arse and a silver slither of material sinking down his crack. I'd thought he was asleep. I'm not sure if he's talking to himself or to me. He's told me daily about how he's a little confused by this new direction.

'They really are spicing up the Christmas World,' he says. He doesn't open his eyes. This is the most he's spoken to me in days.

'Are you worried about your job security?' I ask.

I scroll through Facebook profiles. This is the first time I've been allowed internet access without St Nick peering over my shoulder. St Nick laughs. It's more sarcastic than jolly.

'Have you never been female?' I ask, and St Nick laughs again.

'Why's the concept of a female St Nick so hilarious?' I ask. I'm not sure if I'm trying to wind him up or if I'm actually interested.

'You're entirely missing the essence of my being,' he says. His voice is full of arse and that makes me want to annoy him even more.

'First, there'll be a Christmas angel, then there'll be a cluster of females running the Christmas World,' I say. He tuts. 'One day you'll be born with porn star tits and an enhanced vagina.' St Nick doesn't respond. I look up from the laptop screen and see that he's giving me the finger. Eyes still closed though. I try not to smile.

'I've not had a period since I met you,' I say. St Nick doesn't respond. 'That's a Christmas miracle in itself,' I say. St Nick doesn't respond.

'Just for future record,' I say, holding up one finger. 'Number one is periods.' I hold up two fingers. 'Number two is porn star tits.' I hold up three fingers. 'Number three is your brother.' I hold up four fingers. 'And number four is Spitfire.' I pause and this time St Nick shrugs his shoulders. He's refusing to look at me.

'They're the four topics that can't be discussed. Yes?' St Nick doesn't respond, but I'm sure I hear someone giggling. I think it might have come from the ceiling. I look up and smile at the higher powers, and then I focus back on my scrolling through profiles.

'The UK's one of the easier countries to research,' St Nick says. 'Everyone here feels the need to put all of their business on the internet.' He pauses. I look over at him, waiting for a little more. 'I learned last week that people put filters on photographs of food. Filters on *food*!' His voice is dramatic. I wait for him to settle. I watch him move his body around, sucking sounds escaping as he unsticks his sweaty flesh from the sofa. Reminder to self: rub a Dettol wipe over the leather later.

With St Nick's laptop I've got access to all social media. So even though a person's account could be private or locked or under a ridiculous pseudonym, I'm told their true identity and get to have a look at all of it. That includes private messages and anything that's been deleted. The other week St Nick showed me some examples of what I could discover. It's amazing how someone can appear to tick all of the criteria, then I get to read their private messages on Twitter, often with a stranger, and I'm shocked (and sometimes a little bit queasy). I can also access internet histories, deleted text messages and St Nick has a programme on his laptop that lets me see the person, at any time of the day and regardless of what they're doing. I swear, it offers a whole new twist on 'he watches while you're sleeping'.

Privacy doesn't seem to matter in the world of Christmas miracles, but that's only because finding the right five is vital. This first year is pretty straightforward though, because St Nick had already selected the five (and five reserves) and the other Christmas angels have been running checks. I'm simply monitoring them, to see if I can spot something that would disqualify them, so I guess it's a test or an in-job interview of sorts. At the same time, I've been told to keep an eye out for next year's five.

I look over at St Nick; I think he's sleeping. I delete Elsie's name and type *'Sophie Vallance'* into a Facebook search. She used to inbox Gabriel all the time. Her surname's quite unusual, so my search only pops up five profiles. I recognise her picture and click on it. She was one of the first to say how Gabriel's death had broken her heart. I scroll down her Facebook wall. It's all photos of her with duck lips and excellent brows. I've scrolled back a few months and there's not been one post about Gabriel. He clearly wasn't that important to her.

I stop scrolling when I see a photo of me. It's possibly the least flattering photo I've ever seen. I'm in my school uniform, in the crowded school canteen, with half a sandwich stuffed in my mouth. The image is a bit blurry, as they've obviously zoomed in on me. Above the photo it says *'MISSING?'*

'For fuck's sake,' I say. 'Is that the best photo they could find?'

'What?' St Nick says and I jump.

'Nothing,' I say.

A pause as I wait to see what he'll do next. St Nick doesn't open his eyes, so I keep reading. The comments start with mainly '*lol, have shared xxx*' and then there's a few people saying how I took Gabriel's death '*badly*'. I give the screen the finger, then keep scrolling. The last few comments are about my probably killing myself. The final one is from Sophie, saying how she always thought I was '*a bit odd*' and if I didn't want to be a sex slave, then I'd '*have probably escaped by now*'. Two hundred and nine likes on that one comment.

'Bitch,' I shout. 'Just wait until I bump into you in town—'

'What're you doing?' St Nick asks. I look up and he's glaring at me. Caught in the act. I push the laptop closed.

'Nothing,' I lie.

'Gabriel's mum's profile photo is a picture of the three of you,' St Nick says.

'I don't want to know,' I say. I shake my head vigorously. I don't want to think about Francesca.

'It's of you, Gabriel and Francesca,' St Nick says. 'All of you in matching festive jumpers. It—'

'I don't want to know,' I repeat, this time with me glaring at him.

No good could come from me looking at Francesca's profile. It's time to leave her in the past. Any contact from me would remind her of losing her son and the last thing I want to do is cause her more grief and pain. I miss Gabriel every single day and I can imagine what she's going through too. I miss her though. I miss how easily she could embarrass Gabriel. I miss her hot chocolate with marshmallows and cream. I miss being part of her family.

For fuck's sake. I wipe away a tear.

'You okay, Theodora Quirke?' St Nick asks and I nod.

St Nick believes that the quicker I get my training out the way, the quicker we'll be relocated, but I want to know what Spitfire being involved will mean to the Christmas miracle team. *Wonderful Christmastime* sings through the flat.

'Krampus won't give up now. Too much public interest and that brother of mine's all about attention,' St Nick says. He's reading my thoughts again. 'The higher powers are talking about the need for our absolute isolation.'

'Maybe the North Pole—' I start to say, but then catch St Nick's glare and stop talking.

He rolls back and forth, getting momentum to sit up. The leather squeaks and suckers and strains with each limb shifting.

He's up. He paces around the living room. His silver thong, which is somehow managing to be both inappropriate and perfectly apt, shimmers when the light catches it. I really don't want to be this fascinated with St Nick's crotch area.

'Have you any idea what kind of temperatures we'd be dealing with, living there?' St Nick says. 'This body,' he jazz hands a shimmy over his fat belly, 'does not like clothes.'

'But Rudolf and the reindeers—' I say. St Nick's stare is entirely poisonous. 'No reindeers?' I ask and St Nick shakes his head. Apparently this isn't the time for humour.

In the past three weeks, Spitfire have been a constant in the headlines of every major and local newspaper. They've been the talk of radio shows and the topic of meetings in schools. Apparently, they've shown the biggest rapid growth in an online start-up business, since online businesses began. They had a double page spread in *The Sun* last weekend, announcing that Santa Claus did not deliver presents on Christmas Eve and detailed why and how. They said that Saint Nick had killed him. As if I needed another reason to hate *The Sun*.

Decades of secret keeping by adults and the devilish organisations combine, secretly controlled by Krampus, to decide that it'll be a surefire way to force St Nick out of hiding.

Of course, that never happened and so St Nick has been branded a villain and people are hunting him down to bring Christmas justice to the masses. Krampus has singlehandedly destroyed Christmas magic for millions of kids, yet the media's declaring St Nick to be to blame. It's such a fucking mess.

'I hate being trapped in here,' I say. 'It's driving me insane.'

'That there's the definition of irony,' St Nick says, as he keeps pacing. 'All that matters is that the chosen few receive their Christmas miracles,' St Nick repeats. 'You let me worry about the children. You concentrate on your checks.'

It's his daily mantra, but each day he's becoming less convincing. His shoulders are slumped that little bit more, his skin tinged that little bit greyer, his belly that little bit saggier and his voice lacking any oomph. Society's eating away at him. Krampus is currently edging ahead. My only solution is to work as hard as I can, to complete my training and transform into a Christmas angel. We're in a race against Krampus though; I'm not sure of the rules and what'll happen if we don't win. The higher powers have attempted some more festive tricks, a giant Christmas pudding, an entirely annoying kindness elf called Simon, eight milking maids (and their cows) dancing around the flat, but St Nick didn't even react. That he didn't shake his fist and shout, 'Fuck off,' at the ceiling is too unlike him.

I spend my days worrying about St Nick, missing Gabriel, resisting stalking Francesca's social media and hoping that the chosen five are deserving. If I get this wrong, if I miss something—

'You can sell your story to the press,' St Nick says. 'Tell them all about what a beast of a man I am.'

'I'd never do that,' I say. I glare at St Nick but he refuses my eye contact. His pacing is manic. He's scaring me a little.

'People do strange things when money's involved,' he says.

SPITFIRE SAINT NICHOLAS UMBRELLA COLLECTIVE ☑

COMMUNITY

Hello friends! Mr Belsnickel, executive director of Spitfire, here. I'm still standing in for Dottie Smith. In response to your questions, no, I don't know when Dottie will be back from her super-expensive holiday, and no, of course she isn't seriously ill. I wouldn't lie to you. She is simply taking a well-deserved break and spending some of the vast amounts of money you lot have helped her earn.

As you know, one of the reasons I founded SpitfireSNUC was so that I could bring you details of all the wonderful acts, miracles and donations that Saint Nicholas has given the general public, all over the world, on and around December 6th. These gifts were often to seemingly normal, insignificant people, which begs the question – **how high would you like to aim? Would becoming President of the USA be on your wish list?**

On December 5th, 1792, George Washington was re-elected in the US. Do you really think that him running unopposed was a mere happening without external interference? There was never a question that George would be re-elected, thanks to behind the scenes actions of Saint Nicholas.

For details on how to join SpitfireSNUC to be eligible for a Saint Nicholas Christmas miracle, go to www. SpitfireSNUC.com/becomeamember

THEO (THEODORA QUIRKE)

Another week passes, St Nick's on the front of a tabloid every day.

'SANTA CLAUS GROOMED ME ON FACEBOOK.'

'SHOCKING MOMENT: ST NICK SHAVED MY PUBIC HAIR OFF.'

'EXCLUSIVE: MY NIGHT WITH THE BIG GUY.'

'ST NICK: THE ILLEGAL IMMIGRANT WHO DODGES PAYING TAX AND KILLS KITTENS.'

'CHRISTMAS EVE: HE'LL RAPE YOU WHILE YOU'RE SLEEPING.'

I'd been reading them out to St Nick, but with each headline and each claim being made, it's like his very being is getting chipped away. Like he's actually breaking in front of me and I'm scared – not of what he might do to me, but because I can't stop his spiral.

Krampus is on a roll and, as a result, St Nick's the shadow of that man I met nearly eleven months ago outside Dante House. All traces of his humour and sass have gone. Conversation between us is strained and I'm trying to ignore the niggle that it's somehow all my fault. He's broken, he feels worthless and, if I'm entirely honest, I think he's not even sure who he really is anymore.

All the claims about him being an abuser, a bully, a serial killer, an estranged lover, a kitten killer and even a taxidermist, well at one point even St Nick declared that he was confused as to which of the stories were real. He can't quite understand why people would want their moment of fame at his expense. I tried to explain *Big Brother*, *The Jeremy Kyle Show* and *Love*

Island to him. Telling him how the public used the internet to pile on people for fun. I tried to explain how the people stopped being humans and became property the minute they stepped into the public eye. How most of the public didn't even realise that their taking the piss was actually bullying. Seems to me that my society's idea of entertainment is poking people until they fall apart. But no matter how many examples I offered, St Nick couldn't grasp what I was saying. It made no sense to that kind man.

Finally, this morning, and with St Nick stinking because he's not washed for the last week (or moved off one of our squishy, now almost-grey, sofas), I lost it with him. I mean my training has stopped, no festive music plays in the flat and he blanks any request I have for guidance. I'm stumbling through my Christmas miracle checks. I'm set to fail at this rate and I need his spiralling to stop. Even the flat's Christmas tree looks weary and less twinkly.

In the end, I waited until St Nick went off for a shit and left his laptop unattended. That's when I found a group chat that he'd set up with the Christmas angels. There were only usernames, with @angelAngle123 the most active, so their actual identities were still protected. I had no choice. I hoped they wouldn't mind. Desperate times, and all that.

I sent a message, explaining about St Nick's '*deterioration*' and about the shitty headlines and articles that were being printed. I explained how I was '*lost*', '*pissed off*' and how my '*training had stopped*'.

One of the angels, @angelQuick, responded instantly with an email address for the head of their trade union, someone called John Smith. I then had to email John Smith, all of this from St Nick's laptop and during his ten minute morning shit slot, asking him to step in.

To my relief, he replied within one minute. He said he'd spoken to the higher powers and they'd found a solution to my St Nick problem. The instructions were very specific: '*both of you must go to Bold Street Coffee immediately*'.

Now, forty minutes later, we're out and about. St Nick pissed with me because I made him wear clothes.

Of course I felt the need to confess what I'd done, and, of course, St Nick isn't happy.

'You're an imbecile,' is the only thing he says as we walk up Bold Street.

I'm ignoring him. Shop workers are putting up Christmas decorations in their windows. The second week in November and the city's festive preparations are in full force. I love it. All the smiling Santas, oversized candy canes and excessive amounts of fairy lights. I read in the local newspaper that the main Christmas trees are already up in town. Huge baubles and twinkling lights that'll brave the winter weather. Despite St Nick and despite the concerns about Spitfire, I can't help but feel flickers of excitement about the festive season. If I can just get my five candidates right, I'll have achieved something this year.

'Only imbeciles jump from one commercial scam to another,' St Nick grumbles, but I still hear him. I don't respond.

I push open the door to the coffee shop and *Here Comes Santa Claus* blasts out. I can't help but smile and wonder if the higher powers are in charge of the music here too. I pull off my bobble hat and scarf, shoving them in my pocket and scan the shop for the higher powers, press, police or all of them.

'Why are we even here?' St Nick says. 'I've got a million things I need to be doing, and being in public isn't one of them.' I let him shuffle into the warmth first.

'I'll buy you a hot chocolate,' I say.

'Double chocolate, hot chocolate with extra marshmallows,' he says.

We stand at the back of the queue, him with his umbrella being all huffy and puffy, in the coffee shop.

'Music's too loud,' St Nick says. 'Might go and switch it off myself, the—'

He stops talking. I don't turn to look at him. I'm not pandering to him. I'm looking at the cutesy display of wooden hearts, cinnamon sticks, dried oranges and fairy lights. They feel authentic and true to St Nick's origins. Francesca would love them. I turn to point them out to St Nick, as he speaks.

'It's you,' St Nick says. 'I have died every day.' It's a whisper, but I hear it.

THEO (THEODORA QUIRKE)

I had thought that he'd used his magic on us and we weren't being seen, but the couple of people in front of us turn. They heard his whisper too.

'You've what?' I say. I turn to look at St Nick, but he's not looking at me and he's certainly not talking to me and soon he's not even standing next me. He's jumped the queue and now he's standing staring at the barista.

'Nick,' I say. I try not to shout. I've dropped the 'St' bit like that's enough to disguise who he is.

Everyone's already looking at us and I know that it's only a matter of time before people connect the dots. I mean the whole of Liverpool's been buzzing about hunting down St Nick for weeks. But St Nick doesn't care. His interest is on the barista.

She's about my age, tall, skinny, two lip piercings, a half-sleeve tattoo on her right arm. She's wearing a red jumper with two sequined Christmas puddings on her tits. I swear her hair swishes; it's brown and blue and intimidating in its shininess. She's the type who could be popular. I imagine people are either intimidated by her or want to look like her. I want to look like her – she's fuck off hot.

None of the customers are moaning directly at St Nick. I mean they're tutting and glaring, but St Nick's a big bloke. He's round and saggy. I actually imagine most people think he's homeless and are too scared to speak to him in case he whips out a copy of *The Big Issue* and guilts them into buying it. St Nick's oblivious though. All fear of us being caught and Christmas miracles not happening seems to have gone out of the coffee shop's door. St Nick's eyes are fixed on the girl behind the counter.

'Sorry?' she says.

She turns away from the customer she was about to serve and looks at St Nick instead. She's poised, a pen in one hand and a pad of white sticky notes in the other. She nods at her hands; she's ready to take his order. I move next to St Nick, mouthing 'sorry' as each person in line gives me evils. I see a couple of them grabbing for their phones and I wonder if St Nick has already been identified. Shit. Maybe they're texting a journalist or tweeting direct to the local newspaper. I'm on high alert, this all feels odd. *Fairytale of New York*'s now booming out from the speakers, but no one's singing along.

'Do you want something?' she asks.

'I want—' St Nick says.

'To drink,' I interrupt. 'Nick, what's wrong?'

He won't look at me and instead he's still staring at the poor barista. She's smiling, but I'm not convinced it's a real smile. Time is ticking; the reporters will be approaching. I think St Nick's finally cracked and I don't know what to do.

'A tall latte, please,' he says. 'Skinny.'

My breath comes rushing out from me in a noisy sigh, and the person behind me tuts.

Turning to look at them, I say, 'Shut it.'

'What name?' the barista asks.

Her brown eyes twinkle under the ceiling lights. She's beautiful and I can see why St Nick's going all gooey over her, but he needs to get a fucking grip. I swear it's only a matter of time before someone calls the police and reports him for being a weirdo. So that's journalists and police on their way; we just need Krampus and we'll have a full house. I don't want to start imagining tomorrow's headlines.

The pauses between each of St Nick's answers are that little bit too long; sweat's dripping from St Nick's forehead and down onto his bulbous nose. She's still poised, she's scribbled onto her white sticky note and now she wants to write his name onto the disposable festive cup. She has a tattoo of an anchor along the middle finger of her right hand.

'Hurry up, mate,' someone from the queue says. I turn to see who but they all refuse to meet my eyes.

I turn back to St Nick and see that he's still staring at her. Their eyes are connected; he's searching for something. I don't know what the fuck it could be.

Does he know her? Is she on the naughty list? I don't think it's that.

I look from him, to her, to him. I think about the Chuckle Brothers and feel a little bit sweaty. As far as I can see, there isn't a flicker of recognition and she doesn't know him, but I think he recognises her.

'Nicholas,' he says.

'Thank Christ for that,' I whisper and someone in the queue giggles.

'Nick,' he says. He smiles, a true smile, all crooked, yellow teeth and gums.

She doesn't speak. Instead, I watch her spelling 'NIC' onto the red takeaway cup in black ink.

'Taking out?' she asks.

'No.' It's practically a shout.

'Oh, I…' She looks at the festive paper cup. She'd assumed, perhaps, that he's a homeless man and in need of that festive paper cup for his begging on Bold Street.

'Have we met before?' he asks her.

She looks at him. Her eyes flicker over his features. A greying scraggy beard in need of a strimmer. There's possibly

Coco Pops from yesterday's breakfast stuck to some of the whiskers. I know that he doesn't shampoo it, because I've already had that discussion with him. His eyes are a perfect blue, blue like a lagoon, all bright and full of twinkles, but they're small and lost in his fat moon face, hidden under the bushiest eyebrows I've ever seen. Maybe he was good looking when he was younger, or rather it's more that he says he was good looking in a former life. But right now with his yellowing teeth and his bright red nose, it's like I'm in a scouse remake of *Beauty and the Beast* and there's not a hope in hell that this beauty's going to be falling for St Nick.

But right now he's watching her eyes and I'm watching his eyes. There's a yearning; it isn't creepy sexual. I recognise that look. He's willing her to give him the answer he needs. And that's when I realise that he's willing the smallest recognition.

'Don't think so,' she says. She flicks her eyes away from his. 'It's my first shift.' She passes the paper cup to the other barista. She's clearly already forgotten that he doesn't want a takeout. 'Tall latte for Nic,' she says, turning to smile at him before switching her attention to the next customer.

I place some coins on the counter. She picks up the coins, staring at St Nick as she does. There is a flicker. I see it happen, but St Nick's already lost within himself.

'You do feel familiar though. I just can't...' Her sentence trails as she turns towards the customer after me, but St Nick's face is a picture. A perfect picture of joy, longing and matted facial hair.

I'm about to moan about not having placed an order, when I take a look at the next customer; she's ready to scratch my eyes out. St Nick shuffles a couple of steps, waiting in line for his latte but not once taking his eyes from her.

'A latte?' I ask. 'What happened to the double chocolate,

hot chocolate with extra marshmallows? You could have added almond syrup and extra chocolate whipped cream.'

He ignores me. And at that moment I realise. I know what I've just witnessed. A rush of cold flushes through me. I don't care if all the journalists, all the police and all the Spitfire employees in the UK rush through the door. I feel sick in my stomach. I'm full of nerves and full of envy, but mainly I can't help but think about Gabriel.

I understand. The higher powers sent us here, today, for a specific reason.

'Is she?' I ask and he nods. There are tears in his eyes, there are tears rolling out from my eyes.

'I had to be brave, defiant Theodora. Did I play it cool? I think I did. I was calm, wasn't I? I wasn't weird.' He doesn't take his eyes off her. He speaks in a whisper, he speaks quickly through his crooked smile, but I'm standing close to him and I understand.

The questions aren't questions, but I nod anyway.

'For the first time in oh so many years, I feel alive,' he whispers and then he smiles. 'What's your name?' he shouts.

The man in front of him and the angry lady behind, they both turn to look at him. Clearly they're wondering if the hairy old man's talking to them. They don't answer. I reckon that's because they can see that St Nick's tiny blue eyes are fixed on the girl behind the counter.

She turns to look at him. At first, I'm not sure if she'll respond, but maybe she recognises what I see too. There's something about St Nick. Something that has nothing to do with his dodgy appearance. Something that makes you want to be kind.

'Alice,' she says. 'First day, I don't have a name badge yet.' She points to the sequinned Christmas pudding tit and we all follow her finger. It's where her name badge would be. She giggles and it's possibly what a unicorn's voice would sound like.

'Hope to see you again, Nic,' she says and I smile.

'I knew I'd find you,' St Nick whispers. The person in front of him takes several steps away, possibly considering running away without their drink.

'We need to get out of here now,' I whisper, but St Nick doesn't move. I take his drink from the counter and pull at his sleeve. 'They know we're here,' I say and at that moment St Nick switches his attention to me.

I know that's when we become invisible to others; I feel the atmosphere change. I feel the fear in the others, as they search for explanation as to where we might have gone.

But not Alice. Alice still sees us. Alice smiles.

SPITFIRE SAINT NICHOLAS UMBRELLA COLLECTIVE ☑

COMMUNITY

Hello friends! Mr Belsnickel, executive director of Spitfire, here. No further updates on Dottie Smith. I think she might be off enjoying spending all her money a little too much and has forgotten all about us!

This post is different to our usual spreading of the joy, opportunities and the good work that Saint Nicholas brings. Instead, today I'm posting about a missing girl. Her name's Theodora Quirke and she's been getting a lot of press recently. Her name and Saint Nicholas' have been linked and we've all been worried about her.

However, and exclusive to SpitfireSNUC, within the last hour, Theodora was spotted in Bold Street Coffee (Bold Street, Liverpool, UK) with our very own Saint Nicholas. Photos are below. Look at them closely so you'll recognise Saint Nicholas and Theodora.

I cannot speculate or report on the nature of their relationship, but – if you're reading this, and we hope to God you are – we're on our way Theodora!

As you know, one of the reasons I founded SpitfireSNUC was so that I could bring you details of all the wonderful acts, miracles and donations that Saint Nicholas has given the general public, all over the world, on and around December 6th. That remains my aim, at this moment in time. I also have a backup plan if the rumours about and allegations against Saint Nicholas are eventually proven.

For details on how to Be More Krampus, go to www. SpitfireSNUC.com/bemoreKrampus

THEO (THEODORA QUIRKE)

A week since St Nick was reunited with Alice and he's spent most of it in his bedroom, refusing to talk to me about her. I banged and banged on his locked bedroom door, but he wouldn't answer. I hadn't expected his reaction to be quite so extreme. I doubt it was what the higher powers had in mind when they came up with the idea of a reunion. It's already the third week in November, December 6th is fast approaching and time's, quite literally, ticking away from me. I even emailed John Smith, but he didn't reply.

But just now, St Nick's walked into the open-plan living room; it's the first time we've been in the same place since the coffee shop. *It's a Wonderful Life* is on the TV, mainly because I couldn't be bothered turning it off and also because our TV only shows Christmas movies. Higher power humour, apparently. St Nick used to find them ironic, now I find them all really sad. Maybe if someone made a film about St Nick, then the world would be grateful for everything he's done. And maybe if people learned how to be grateful, then the world would be happier. Less greedy. Less entitled. Less fucked up.

St Nick lies down on his sofa, I'm sitting up on mine. He's wearing his Santa Claus costume; the same one he wore the night we met outside Dante House. I can only assume he's being ironic. The Christmas tree has been pushed over and its roots are on show on the carpet. I think he did that while I slept. The tinsel has been ripped to shreds and most of the baubles have been smashed.

St Nick stares at me, but somehow doesn't seem to see me.

I don't know how to make this better. He throws something up into the air and it floats down before landing on the coffee table. I lean forward. I've seen it before. A thin gold chain with a delicate oval locket. The locket is open; inside there are two pencil portraits. A man, a woman, sketched and coloured. I know without asking that they are St Nick and Alice.

'I thought personal mementos were forbidden within the Christmas World,' I say.

'Fuck off,' he says.

'St Nick,' I say. I think he's been around me too long. The higher powers are going to blame me for his swearing. 'You said that it would be enough just to see her,' I say. I'm trying to show him that he's being unreasonable.

'Well, clearly, I was spouting adult bollocks,' St Nick says.

'You said I had to learn to live in moments and not in the fear of those moments no longer existing,' I say.

'More bollocks,' St Nick says.

St Nick's not touched any of the food I've made and left outside of his locked bedroom door. I've not checked on the potential Christmas miracle candidates since we found Alice. I'm told it's been a week but it feels like less. Everything is fucked up and full of sadness. I hate this. I hate that this kind man is so very broken.

'I have died every day,' he says.

'I understand,' I say, because I do. I'd be a hypocrite to lecture anyone on the need to *let go* of dead people.

'The intensity of grief passes, mortals even learn to embrace it. Grief is the price for love and so many are prepared to pay any price, if it means they get to experience true love,' St Nick says. 'But then it creeps up on them. Its intensity unexpected...'

'Grief?' I ask.

'Of course I'm talking about grief,' he says. 'Then there's

that day when they decide that they need to live. They talk of honouring the dead by living. Even you've thought it, even I've said it to you,' St Nick says. He doesn't smile. His heartbreak is fresh. 'When faced with trauma or loss, there's a moment when people realise how precious and how very fragile life is. They'll realise that their time is fleeting, they'll become acutely aware of their own mortality—'

'I won't. I'm training to be a Christmas angel,' I say. 'I'll never feel that—'

'Fuck you,' he says. The viciousness shocks me. He means it. 'You've no idea what it's really like to be me,' he says. He pokes his finger in my direction. 'My only hope was that I would meet with her again one day. I've lived with that hope since she died. I was prepared to give myself to her again, to love her, to allow that inevitable pain, but now…'

'But what?' I ask. 'You can see her every day.'

I've already considered, and suggested through his locked bedroom door, that he could use his magic to see her every day, undetected from the hunters, until my training's complete.

'It's not enough. It fails to quench this thing that's raw within me.' St Nick punches his chest. He punches himself again and again. The punches echo. They catch St Nick's breath. 'It's one hundred times worse now.'

'I don't understand,' I say. I stand up. Move to him. Small steps. I want to grab his wrists and to stop him from hurting himself, but I don't. I can't. I don't know how he'll react. I don't know this version of St Nick. 'You said it would be enough just to—'

'Those fuckers hate me,' he says. He shakes his fist at the invisible cameras in the ceiling.

'Perhaps they were trying to help,' I say. I'm shuffling back to my sofa. I genuinely think they were though. I refuse to think of them as cruel.

'There's something within me, it's red and raw when I picture it. It's exposed and it has been there since Alice died. Over the years, I've tried to ignore it; I've focused on helping people whilst all the time feeling its pulse. I've devoted my life to helping others.' St Nick pauses, but he doesn't look at me. 'I'm Nikolaos of Myra; I've a duty, a role, a fucking purpose for my existence. I bring joy, I ease pain, I help. But what about my needs?'

'I don't—' I try to talk.

'You can't possibly begin to understand. I endure whatever face and body they pick for me.' He glares at the flat's ceiling. 'I'm lonely. I never complain—'

'Well, lately—'

'Fuck you, Theodora Quirke. Fuck you all,' he says. Then he pauses but I dare not speak. 'Your society's sense of entitlement kills all possibility of a joyful human existence. LOOK at me. I'm the embodiment of your society.'

I look; somehow fatter, even though he's been refusing food. Scraggy and matted beard. Stinks of pee and sweat. Puffy and bloodshot eyes. Swollen nose that's red and bumpy. I don't speak. What does he want me to say? I can't take that fuck off massive weight of responsibility for all that's wrong within *my* society. I've spent all the months since Gabriel died clinging to positivity and finding reasons to live. I'd almost learned to value the gift of life, but now St Nick's contradicting my daily mantras.

'When I saw Alice, there was a moment when that rawness went. I felt it heal. There was a moment of absolute bliss when she looked at me, when she recognised something, but then...'

'But now you can get to know her, and perhaps she'll grow to...'

I stop speaking. I'm being ridiculous. There's no way that

Alice is going to fall in love with St Nick. There's not a fairy tale in the world that could make this one turn out happily ever after. And although I know I shouldn't be making this about me, and although I really don't want to, I can't help but think about Gabriel and the future I'm about to commit to living.

When I become a Christmas angel, what if I become like St Nick? What if I spend the rest of my life earthbound, clinging to the hope that Gabriel will find me again? That constant living in a future where everything will be better; that failure to grab all that is now. Never loving, always waiting; a life committed to the happiness of others. A life not lived.

'Look at me, Theodora Quirke,' St Nick shouts. His raised voice scares me. I sink back into the sofa. 'Why have I found her when I look like *this*? Why have they punished me?' He punches his costumed belly, over and over again.

I have to stop this. He's hurting himself. I jump off my sofa and to him. I grab his wrists, trying to stop him from hurting himself. He's strong, but he folds.

'I quit,' St Nick says.

'You what?'

'I'm not doing this anymore. I'm resigning,' he says.

'Can you even do that?' I ask.

'I won't deliver the gifts and miracles, I'll have failed in my role and the Christmas World will appoint someone else on December 7th. Krampus wins. Krampus can be the new Principal of the Christmas World. Long live the new fucking king.'

His sobs shake his entire being. Clarence is talking about his angel wings on TV; I'm entirely alone again.

THEO (THEODORA QUIRKE)

I let him cry. I sit on his sofa and eventually he lies with his head on my lap. I stroke his hairy face, picking out little bits of food and flicking them onto the carpet. We don't talk; the film plays and I almost hope St Nick's listening to George Bailey's voice.

'She judged me. Fat. Old. Hairy. Dirty. I've no choice regarding the look that's assigned.' A pause. I wiggle and crumble a dry Coco Pop that's lodged in his beard. 'In the very first moments she passed her judgment and dismissed me. Why did she fail to realise that I have died every day without her? This rejection…' He pauses again. 'This pain that I'm feeling in here.' He points to his head. 'It's worse than when I first lost her. Because what are the chances of my ever finding her again? This is it, Theodora Quirke. This is my one and only fucking chance.'

A thought – 'How many times have you been to see her?' I ask.

'I've been in twice a day, for a prolonged amount of time, for the last week. Mainly trying to catch her on shift. She's been working all the hours she can to earn more money—'

'You talk to her?' I interrupt. I don't want to sound as shaken as I do. Clearly I've fucked up again. How did I not notice that he wasn't in his bedroom?

I can't help but worry that he's been seen or followed home. I've not been out, but I've been monitoring the online world and there's definitely been a renewed buzz in Liverpool to find us. We were spotted in the coffee shop. Images were uploaded. Krampus, obviously. Rumour is that I'm being tortured; Stockholm syndrome has been mentioned too. The hunt has increased. They could have captured St Nick and I'd not have known. I'd have just thought he was hiding away in his bedroom.

'I've spent lifetimes avoiding new sorrow and hiding from new happiness. My focus has been my saintly role, my direction governed by a hope that one day I'd be rewarded. Can you see that I endured life?' he says.

'But—' I start.

'No,' he shouts. He jumps up, away from my lap, and towers over me. 'My heart trusted.' He's thumping his chest with a fist. 'They have broken me. Now what?'

'Now you try and—'

'Her surname's Fletcher, she likes Christmas movies and she's in an "open relationship" with someone called Tommy Clarke,' St Nick says. He's stopped hitting himself.

'You've stalked her Facebook,' I say. It's a whisper really. I feel the same as I did when I used to play Kerplunk. Sweaty palms and hoping I'm not about to cause a gush of shit.

'Tumblr, Snapchat, Twitter, Instagram,' St Nick says.

'Someone really needs to talk to her about not sharing her life online,' I say, mainly to myself.

'I see everything, Theodora Quirke,' St Nick says. He sighs. He sits back down next to me. 'Usually it's helpful.'

'Can you not be grateful to catch the glimpses of her life?' I ask.

I'm being a nobhead. I know the answer. I know how I'd feel if I'd searched lifetimes for Gabriel and then not being able to be near him when our paths finally crossed. I swear, even if I was immortal, that'd kill me. I think it might be killing St Nick too.

'I've been searching for a ghost,' St Nick says. 'I thought that when I found her we'd be transported back...'

'But now you can't move forward?' I say and St Nick nods. 'So what you're saying is that I need to let go of my past, because it'll never be my present?'

'Shut the fuck up. This isn't about you, Theodora Quirke,' St Nick says. 'This is all *your* fault.'

'Wait, what?'

'Your society is a self-centred pile of shit,' St Nick says.

He twists away from me into an awkward position, his back to me and his arse pushing me off the sofa. I've fucked up. Again. I'm a selfish cow. Our conversation is over. I stand and start to walk out of the room.

'She's the same but different,' St Nick says. 'Her beauty burns me.'

'St Nick—'

'I wasn't joking about resigning,' he shouts. 'Krampus can have his reign. Time for all the little spoilt, entitled brats and parents to get their comeuppance. They think I'm evil? Well, they've not met my brother. Turn that fucking film off.'

SPITFIRE SAINT NICHOLAS UMBRELLA COLLECTIVE ☑

COMMUNITY

Hello friends! Mr Belsnickel, executive director of Spitfire, here. Dottie Smith has clearly forgotten all about us. She's taken her money and run for the hills, but I'm more than happy to take over any reign.

Thanks for all of your photos and possible sightings of Saint Nicholas and Theodora. My team are looking into every single one of them. All three thousand and seventeen. That's because here at Spitfire, we respect and care about our loyal supporters.

Some of you commented on how much you were enjoying finding out more about Krampus. It's hard to believe that knowledge of his many Christmas miracles haven't reached more people. I especially liked the comments left about how he was an underrepresented and under supported festive figure in the Christmas World. You are the best!

If you'd like to find out more about details of the Christmas miracles that Krampus has performed, go to www.SpitfireSNUC.com/bemoreKrampus

THEO (THEODORA QUIRKE)

I'm sitting on the sofas, watching *The Holiday* on TV when there's a knock at the door. St Nick rushes into the living room. He's wearing a green hospital gown. The back ties are gaping open and showing his arse. I've not seen him for days – it doesn't feel like days, but I'm told it's days from the daily newspaper delivery. He sits down next to me, grabs the TV remote to pause the film and places his closed umbrella across both of our laps.

'What the—' I start to say.

The front door creaks open, then it bangs against the wall in the hall. I look at St Nick and he holds a finger to his lips. I know not to speak. I mouth, *what?* but St Nick growls.

'Here I am, *Santa Claus*,' the man says from the hallway.

'Imbecile,' St Nick whispers.

'Come out, come out. I have cookies and milk.' His voice sounds like a crap Barry White impression. All slow-mo sounds, like every word's being dragged out; I think Francesca would describe it as charming. 'Your brother's here to play with you,' he says.

'What the—' I say, as Krampus rushes into the front room.

'Theodora Quirke?' he shouts. His eyes search the room. At one point he looks in our direction, yet somehow he doesn't see us. The umbrella, obviously. 'I heard you. Bang once, if you're here.'

You dare, St Nick mouths, glaring at me.

I think I hold my breath. I think I want to laugh. This should be a tense moment, but instead it feels ludicrous. I'm wearing a candy cane onesie and reindeer shaped slippers, I appear to be invisible to a clearly psychotic Krampus declaring he's got cookies and I'm sitting next to a saint in a hospital gown.

Krampus is wearing a suit, pinstriped and black, with a crisp white shirt and a red shiny tie. He's tall and toned, possibly in his late thirties, with a well-coiffed mullet and a clearly trimmed goatee.

Nice touch.

His face is long, his hair colour too dark to be natural. Shoes are polished, his teeth the brightest of whites. I can't help but wonder if he has a fork-shaped tongue. He wears a thick gold chain around his neck. Some – possibly middle-aged women who like receiving dick pics online from strangers – could find him attractive, but I'd question their taste in men.

How did he get in? How is this even possible? I mouth and St Nick points at the ceiling.

The higher powers? Why? I mouth and St Nick shrugs his shoulders. I've no idea what's going on. Are the higher powers off their heads? Why would letting Krampus in here be a good idea?

'I know you live here, *Santa Claus*. I followed you home after one of your little trips to that coffee shop,' he says. I glare at St Nick.

'I will rescue you, Theodora Quirke,' Krampus says and I laugh. What is it with men thinking I need to be rescued? So far, it seems to be me doing all the fucking rescuing and holding together of the Christmas World. 'I'm your knight in shining armour. I drive a BMW and it's white.' He flexes his muscles and appears to lunge. 'I'm going to be the new King of the Christmas World.'

I shake my head and mouth, *What the fuck?* at St Nick.

'I've got the tabloids on speed dial. We'll be rich, little girl,' he says and I hear St Nick tut. 'I'll be your manager. We'll sell your story to the highest bidder. We can tell everyone that you were a naughty girl. That I kidnapped you for a year. We'll be famous. The world will know about Krampus Night. Money'll never be a concern for you again.'

I watch Krampus spinning on the spot, then ducking down as if he's peering under something. He's up, then down, then twisting right, then turning left. What the actual fuck? It's like he can't see us or the sofas or even all the other furniture in the room. He stays in the exact same spot too, like his feet are glued to the carpet but he's not yet realised.

'I know you're in here, *Santa*,' he shouts. 'Santa and Satan, they're the same person. Come out, come out, you evil pile of shit.' He pauses, his eyes darting around the room. 'My job's on the line; I need to deliver you to your public. Spitfire's invested millions in the search for you and I'm not going to give up until I get my fingers around your fat neck.'

'Well that escalated fast,' I whisper and St Nick giggles.

He heard that. He spins on the spot. 'Where are you?' Krampus shouts. 'I can hear you whispering. Is this all some big game to you? It is, isn't it?' He's punching the air in front of him, then spinning and punching at the side and behind him.

'It's time the world knew my name, brother,' he says. 'I've been in your shadow for far too long. December 7th and your reign is officially over. It's time for a reinstating of Krampus Night, of Krampus Day, of Krampus' reign. Come out, you bastard.'

'Why's he doing that?' I whisper. I point at the squirming, punching, ducking Krampus.

'Christmas magic,' St Nick whispers.

'I know you're in here,' Krampus shouts. 'I will find you

and I'll whip you in public. I'll have you hung, drawn and quartered. I'll—'

I hear St Nick laugh and it's taking all of my willpower not to burst into a fit of giggles.

'You think you're so fucking clever, don't you?' Krampus says and St Nick nods his head. Clearly Krampus can't see us, but still I watch his lip curl into a sneer. 'I am your hunter, *Santa Claus*.' He snarls. 'And I will catch you. And when I do, I'll skin you alive and then I'll feed that skin to Rudolph the fucking reindeer.'

'His plan is flawed,' St Nick whispers. 'Rudolph doesn't exist!' That's when I can't help but laugh. A loud, belly laugh. I snort too.

'You think this is funny, you Peter the Paedophile, you Cannibal the Lecter, you Vlad the vampire—'

'Oh for crying out loud, can't you make him stop?' St Nick shouts to the ceiling, and that's when it starts raining.

It rains from the ceiling. At first Krampus looks shocked. He holds his palm up, letting the raindrops bounce off his skin. He looks around the room and after a few seconds we see it dawn on him; that the rain's only above him. That's when there's thunder, then the rain changes to hail the size of Ping-Pong balls. I watch as Krampus looks up at the ceiling, clearly confused, and the hail bounces off his forehead.

'You fucker.' He rubs his head and backs out of the room. The hail follows him. He can see that it remains above him, that it's nowhere else in the room. Thunder rumbles again.

'Watch out for the lightning,' St Nick shouts.

'I will hunt you down, *Santa* fucking *Claus*. Now I know you're here, I'm going let the world know where to find you,' he says, as he runs out of the flat.

'I think we need to talk about security,' St Nick shouts. He gives the ceiling the finger. 'This is not acceptable. I'll be talking to my union rep.' He lifts his umbrella, stands and leaves the room.

SPITFIRE SAINT NICHOLAS UMBRELLA COLLECTIVE ☑

COMMUNITY

Hello friends! Mr Belsnickel, executive director of Spitfire, here.

I have hunted him out. I HAVE FOUND SAINT NICHOLAS.

I can confirm that the reports are true. He is holding Theodora Quirke captive and has barricaded himself into a flat above the new bookshop on Bold Street.

That's **96 Bold St, Liverpool L1 4HY**

I propose we all meet there, today, and flush Saint Nicholas out from his hiding place.

Act now. It's time to rescue Theodora Quirke.

If you'd like to find out more about details of the miracles that Krampus has performed, go to www. SpitfireSNUC.com/bemoreKrampus

THEO (THEODORA QUIRKE)

And, of course, Krampus did tell everyone. They're downstairs. The numbers grow each day. They bang on the outside door. They shout and scream to be let in. They want to kill St Nick. They want to save me. I want the noise to stop.

St Nick's promised the door's protected; the higher powers *'apologised profusely'* to him for their previous security failure. The angry mob won't get past the Christmas magic, but the banging doesn't stop.

Day: Bang. Bang. Bang.

Night: Bang. Bang. Bang.

We're trapped. They want in. There's no way out. I can't go outside; those angry people are camped at the entrance to the flat and I've got no magic to protect me. The police, the fire brigade, landlords, locksmiths; they've all tried and failed to enter. Christmas magic at its finest, but I'm going stir crazy. Somehow food's getting delivered, and the usual mail and newspapers, but people can't figure out how to get in. It's like the magic confuses their brains and they can't find a solution.

How the fuck can this end any way other than St Nick being either killed or captured? I don't understand why we're not time travelling away. Why are the higher powers keeping us here?

St Nick spends his time in his room: sleeping, crying, sulking. I hear his sobbing through his locked bedroom door. There's no conversation between us; there's no reasoning with him. He's sticking to his decision. He's resigned and, apparently, the Christmas World can go and 'fuck itself up the arse'. Which is nice.

I'm scared though. Scared he'll disappear without saying goodbye. Without me knowing how or where to contact him. I can feel his continued spiral; the lack of hope floats around the flat. And I hate that it's sticking to me too. I don't know what I'll do if I lose St Nick. Maybe I'm cursed. Everyone I love leaves me. December 6th's nearly here, four days remain, and it's down to me to decide on five of the final six possible candidates. I mean, is it even worth it? I don't think they'll even get their miracles now that St Nick's resigned.

Yesterday, I was emailed a report about SpitfireSNUC. It now has weekly meetings. None of the original members are involved. The group's been taken over entirely by Krampus and Spitfire. Krampus has suggested a change of date for St Nicholas Day to the night of December 5th. Said it'd make more sense to celebrate before the saint's actual day. More *sense*?

December 5th is Krampus Night. It's a tradition and festivity that's not really known by many in the UK. I can't believe others aren't figuring this out. He's destroyed St Nick and, in tiny and clever steps, is reinstating his own importance, ready for when he takes over on December 7th. He's a clever man. It won't be long before he reveals his true identity and the public embrace him like *he's* the fucking hero of the hour. The report concluded saying that SpitfireSNUC were talking about needing a larger venue for the next meeting. Someone suggested Wembley Stadium. It's out of control.

New letters still arrive from SpitfireSNUC daily. I don't know how they get here, they just appear in a red sack outside my bedroom. I take a handful and go into my bedroom, opening a few of the letters, even though they're addressed to St Nick. I wish I hadn't.

The words are all demands, lists and pleas for how worthy their families are. One letter, from a Holly Arnold, makes me sob. A mum of three, married for twenty years, she claims her family are going to lose their home if the mortgage isn't paid off by Christmas. She says she's just found out she has breast cancer, her eldest daughter's self-harming, her youngest son's got depression, that she goes without food so her '*babies*' can eat. By all accounts, her life's falling apart.

I open up my files on the six potentials for a Christmas miracle. Is there anyone I can move to next year? I chew on my fingernail, trying to figure out how I can help Holly. I think I might be able to arrange something. Maybe. I open a new tab and type '*Holly Arnold*' into the Christmas World search engine.

Fuck.

Turns out Holly Arnold's just booked an all-inclusive holiday to Tenerife next July, for all her family, and is having cybersex with her best friend's brother (who's also married). She's in serious debt but that's not stopping her spending. In the previous week alone, she's spent fifteen pounds on sunbeds, forty pounds on her eyebrows and nails, and two hundred and seven pounds (credit card) on an online designer brand's sale. Bargains, yes, but hardly the behaviour of someone starving and desperately worried about losing everyone she loves.

I type a new search of '*breast cancer*' into her file and watch a smiling Santa Claus rotate on the screen as the search happens. A few moments later and the words '*no results*' flash across the screen. What the fuck? I repeat the search this time adding '*Holly Arnold*' in case I've somehow screwed up. The '*no results*' is quicker this time. What a nobhead. There's no trail or record of Holly Arnold having breast cancer. She's lying to get money from St Nick.

I knock on St Nick's door. I need to tell him what I've discovered. I need him to help me make sense of it all.

'Their entitlement is killing me.' That's all St Nick says. He refuses to unlock his door so I hear those words being shouted and then the sound of his bed creaking as he rolls over. I walk back to my bedroom, sticking up my middle finger to the ceiling. The higher powers are to blame for all of this.

The constant banging on the downstairs' door is doing my head in. I've got no one to turn to and no one to talk to about what I should do next. I'm drowning in the bullshit claims of people who should know better. I want out of this fucking flat. I need the higher powers to intervene. We're basically sitting here and waiting to be captured.

Maybe they've all fucked off because St Nick's resigned and Krampus is waiting for his moment. I don't know how this works. But I do know that if the angry folk banging on the door get in, the best outcome is that they'll throw St Nick in jail. Then there'll be a public trial where no one will believe his true identity. And I'll be called as a witness, but will have had my memory erased and won't know what fucking day it is.

It's an anti-Christmas film waiting to be made.

THEO (THEODORA QUIRKE)

I think it's the day after the Holly Arnold catfishing thing. Days blend into each other now. St Nick walks into the front room to find me lying on the sofa with pillows pushed against my ears. He's back in his silver thong; he sprawls on his sofa and stares at the ceiling. The Christmas tree's still uprooted. It's dying on the carpet. Sometimes I think I hear it crying.

'I want to be a Christmas angel right now,' I shout over the drilling and banging on the front door. Locksmith again, I reckon. 'The sooner I make the transformation, the sooner we can get away from Liverpool,' I say.

Maybe if we're away from Liverpool, then St Nick won't resign and the Christmas miracles can still happen. I know I've got to stop Krampus from getting in power, but I don't know how. I can't be responsible for that evil fucker kidnapping kids each year.

'Not your decision. You've not been offered the job,' St Nick shouts, his eyes fixed on the ceiling. 'I'm not even sure you're suitable. I think I made a mistake—'

Bang. Bang. Bang.

'That's not your problem anymore. You resigned,' I shout.

'I'm still in charge until December 7th. *This* is not your decision,' he shouts.

'I can't bear the thought of ending up like you...' I pause. I shouldn't have said that. St Nick doesn't respond. Maybe he didn't hear. 'I just want to become a Christmas angel. I'll live in the now and then I'll make myself forget about Gabe. It's the best way. We can leave Liverpool. You won't have to resign. You can get away from Alice—'

St Nick growls. The sound's raw. Our eyes lock.

Bang. Bang. Bang.

'You selfish child.'

'What about all that shit you said? All that crap about how life might feel *too arduous* but that moments pass? What about all that shit about *strokes on a canvas*, about *layers and depth* and—'

'Yet another adult spouting bollocks at you, *darling* Theodora Quirke,' he says. He walks towards me.

Bang. Bang. Bang.

'You're being a constant nobhead,' I scream. I stand up. Trying to figure out the best way to the doorway. His anger terrifies me. I don't recognise him. 'Help me.'

'This isn't about you. GO.' He points out of the room but I'm already leaving.

I slam my bedroom door; my only act of defiance. I open St Nick's laptop. It's been in my room since he resigned and he's clearly not missed it.

This is all so fucked up. The Christmas World's falling apart. St Nick's doing nothing and, somehow, it feels like the burden's on me to make this better. I look at the date – December 3rd. We've no time for this shit.

Do I want to be a Christmas angel? I've asked myself this question so many times over the last few days. The answer's always the same: no, not really, not even slightly. But I want all this shit to end. I need to get St Nick out of Liverpool. Back to Verona. I need him not to resign. I don't want this fucking responsibility anymore. I want the banging to stop. I want St Nick to be happy again. And, more than all of that, I want there to be hope in the world again.

Bang. Bang. Bang.

I type an email to John Smith. I ask him to let me know

if I've done enough to become a Christmas angel. I tell him how St Nick's in danger and about the banging and drilling for over a week. I tell him about Krampus' plan and how St Nick resigning fits in with that. Someone needs to intervene and save St Nick, and me, and the Christmas miracles. Someone needs to stop Krampus. Liverpool isn't helping St Nick. It's destroying him. And St Nick's only in Liverpool because of me. He answered a call to save me. He felt duty bound because of my mum. He felt a responsibility for her death. He felt I was too fragile to be alone. John Smith needs to know all of that.

And I need St Nick to know that his duty's been paid in full. He's not indebted to me anymore. It's time he looked after himself. He no longer wants to be St Nick, but that might only be because he's here. Maybe all he needs is a little holiday, a change, medication, therapy, to regenerate, or whatever the fuck happens in the Christmas World when people have breakdowns. Anything but Krampus gaining power.

Bang. Bang. Bang.

I type, '*I'd like to be assigned a different guide,*' and that, '*St Nick's no longer capable of helping me understand my role.*' I type that, '*it's entirely my fault.*' That, '*St Nick is blameless.*' I type that, '*St Nick's resigned.*' A little reminder that there's no longer a St Nick. I mean – no St Nick and St Nick's Day is fast approaching. A little reminder that when St Nick fails to deliver, then his next in line automatically steps in. And that that's Krampus. I mean, how can anyone think giving Krampus power will be a good thing? Why the fuck aren't they doing anything?

I type that, '*I fear Christmas miracles will cease forever if intervention's not made.*' I type about Alice too. I type that, '*the higher powers have been nobheads,*' and that, '*they need to accept responsibility for their role in St Nick's downfall.*' I lie and tell John Smith that I'm ready to '*start my transformation into earthbound immortality*' and that I'll '*forget all about Gabriel*'; I tell him everything I think he wants to hear and possibly much that he doesn't. The email's all over the place and I don't read through to check my spelling.

Bang. Bang. Bang.

I press send. I hope that I've done enough to convince someone to help save St Nick.

THEO (THEODORA QUIRKE)

Two hours later, two more hours of banging on the door, and I'm lying on my bed with St Nick's laptop still open, when John Smith emails back.

Dear Ms Quirke,

Thank you for your email and for highlighting Krampus' plans. We will consider what action is required, with immediate effect.

The official line is that the role of the higher powers is to serve the reigning Principal of the Christmas World. They are a neutral entity.

The higher powers have been very impressed with your work and, as a consequence of St Nick's resignation, they are taking the decision-making about your employment out of St Nick's hands. With that in mind, an offer of employment will be made on December 6th. The offer will include the higher powers giving you all that you require to become a Christmas angel…

He goes on to explain that it's a done deal, and even says that he's very much looking forward to meeting me. Turns out he'll be responsible for taking my wing span measurements; his last Christmas angel fitting before he retires later in December. He also adds that he '*appreciates my honesty regarding St Nick,*' and that he'd '*no idea how dire the situation had become.*' Even apologises for not contacting me sooner.

Bang. Bang. Fucking bang on the front door.

I reckon that he's lying about not knowing how bad St Nick's become. The higher powers have been watching and messing with St Nick for months now. Apparently the other Christmas angels had been concerned about the '*lack of support*' from St Nick, this close to December 6th. They've all been waiting since November to give St Nick their chosen candidates for the Christmas miracles. He asks me to keep in contact, as '*counter procedures and plans might be needed this year.*' Whatever that means.

Bang. Bang. Fucking bang.

I close St Nick's laptop. I've no idea what it all really means or if it's all lies, but I'm grateful to John Smith for replying. No further details, no new contact, no additional support, but I'm hoping they'll make St Nick their priority.

I also now know that on the Feast of St Nicholas, in three days, I'll complete my transformation into a Christmas angel. I'll be immortal. Forever.

'I'm going to be a Christmas angel. I'll be immortal. Earthbound. I'll forget about Gabriel.'

I say the words aloud, mainly because I want to give them weight and for them to have life. I should feel happy. I should be bouncing around the room. But I'm not. Instead, I'm sweaty with a swirling in my belly and a pain that's working its way around my eyes like one of the masks they all wear in *The Incredibles*.

Bang. Bang. Fucking bang.

I'm lost. Again. I'm alone. Again. I'm going to be alone. Forever. Like, actually, for forever.

Francesca. Her name, then her face, then a memory of her holding me while I cried because I didn't have a mum and I wished she could be my mum. It'd been during a happy moment – she'd surprised me with a pair of Converse trainers – and I'd been overwhelmed by her kindness.

I miss her so fucking much.

I think about Gabriel, about my mum, about Alice, about St Nick. Everything's too fragile. Life changes too quickly. I can't keep up. People I love leave me too easily.

Bang. Bang. Fucking bang.

I've no idea if the final chosen five for the Christmas miracles will be the right five. I've no idea how to gather all the required information for the deliveries. St Nick won't step back into his role. Could I stand in for him? Would that stop Krampus? I don't even know how the deliveries into shoes are made.

I mean a small gift into every child in the world's shoe. How the fuck would I do that? Is that even possible? Where would I get the coins and small toys from? Then there's the miracles. How would I decide on the content of the miracle? Where would I even start with that? Is there a budget? With St Nick refusing to help, could the responsibility fall on the Christmas angels? Is that even allowed? Would that keep Krampus away? Is there even a sleigh? Do I need magic flying dust?

Too many thoughts.

Bang. Bang. Fucking bang.

It's a fucking, shitty, twatty mess.

St Nick brought me here, he fast-forwarded my life, but for what? To trap me in a massive pile of shit? I want to punch him in the face. I thought he was my friend. I want to hate him.

What if I end up like him? Bitter. Lost. Empty.

What's the point in staying alive if that's to be my final destination? Earthbound and enduring life while my pain makes me rotten inside.

Bang. Bang. Fucking bang.

A life serving others and destroying myself in the process.

A life without love.

Bang. Bang. Fucking bang.

A life forcing myself to forget Gabriel.

A life of secret craving. Too scared to say Gabriel's name aloud.

Bang. Bang. Fucking bang.

People in the Christmas World have no escape from their thoughts. No escape from Earth. St Nick's resigned. Can he die? Can he kill himself? Will Krampus murder him?

I can't stop the thoughts. I don't mean to think about killing myself. It goes against everything that a Christmas angel represents. If I become immortal, I'll never be able to kill myself. This'll be it – no getaway from pain. But I can't find hope anymore.

Bang. Bang. Fucking bang.

I open St Nick's laptop. I read the email again, and again. I search for clues. I search for a solution. I search for hope. But my mind's already locked on a thought. An escape.

Bang. Bang. Fucking bang.

And I'm not strong enough to live alone on Earth forever.

Bang. Bang. Fucking bang.

I need to act before it's too late.

Bang. Bang. Fucking bang.

A new internet search. I type, '*best way to kill yourself.*' I'm sure that's against Christmas World rules but I'm past caring. I find a website that outlines the easiest, quickest and most painful ways to die; it says to wait three days after deciding on method and before doing the deed. I don't have three days to spare. I either have to somehow deliver the Christmas miracles and become a Christmas angel or end my life and escape all of this shit.

Bang. Bang. Fucking bang.

I sit, I stare at the open webpage. A photo of a girl hanging herself stares back at me.

Bang. Bang. Fucking bang.

I have no one. I have nothing. I can't carry on living.

THEO (THEODORA QUIRKE)

I'm still sitting on my bed; hours have passed into a new day. Hours of banging. I'm exhausted, I'm scared but I've not taken any steps to end my life. St Nick's laptop's still open and the photo of that girl hanging herself still stares back at me. I've spent at least an hour wondering if the hanging was staged for the photo. It looks pretty real though. I zoom in closer, and there's definite marks around—

'What are you doing?' a voice booms into the room.

What the fuck? I jump back from the zooming in. My eyes ping to the closed bedroom door and expect St Nick to be standing there, hands on his naked hips and all glares. He's not there.

'What the actual fuck?' I whisper minutes later, when my breathing finally calms. I lean into St Nick's laptop again. Maybe I've clicked on a random pop-up. I mute the volume and move to zoom into the hanging girl again.

'But you have a role now,' the voice booms. It's coming from the ceiling.

'What the fuck?' I shout. I slam the laptop shut and jump up from the bed. I spin on the spot and appear to be shaking my fist at the ceiling.

'I'm so sorry, Ms Quirke. I had no idea. It's all going wrong, isn't it? I had to act before—'

'Who are you?' I shout. I lower my fist, concerned I look a little insane, and mainly because I'm shaking. I don't want whoever's watching to know that I'm terrified.

What if they banish me up into space and away from the

Christmas World forever? What if they decide to punish me for wanting to die? I mean, they won't know that I changed my mind.

'I received an email from a friend who was participating in volunteering work in the realm where those who take their own lives are healed. Your name was mentioned in a meeting that talked about guests to expect in the realm, and how best to cater for their needs,' the voice explains. He sounds calm, kind even.

'But I wasn't. The banging. But I've not—' I whisper.

'I can't let you end your life by your own hand,' he interrupts. 'There will be no more banging.'

'You won't *let* me?' I'm shouting now. Shouting at a ceiling.

'This is my only chance to save you.' There's sadness in the voice.

I'm hit with the fact that people want to save me. It punches into my belly. How many people, all through my life, have stepped in to my rescue? My mum, St Nick, Gabriel, Francesca, St Nick again, and now the higher powers. And where's my gratitude? How am I repaying them? When will they all finally give up on me?

'Who the fuck do you think—' I start to shout. It sounds angry, but really I'm embarrassed. I'm frustrated with myself. I'm annoyed that I gave up on hope.

'Can you stop spinning around the room? You're making me somewhat dizzy.'

I climb back onto my bed, and I sit crossed-legged, staring up at the ceiling. I'm all huffs and puffs. I'm acting like a spoilt teenager. I'm throwing a paddy because someone I don't even know has been kind enough to show concern over my mental state. I mean, get a fucking grip, Theo! There's silence, there's no banging. I know it's just because he's waiting for me to calm down. Minutes pass.

I wave both my hands at the ceiling. 'Can you see me?' I try to force myself to smile, to show that I'm ready to listen, but it probably looks more like a grimace.

'We see everything,' he says. Did he just giggle?

'That's fucking terrifying,' I whisper, staring down at my crossed legs.

'I don't have long. Please don't let this entire communication be about you sulking,' he says. I'm desperately trying to calm my breaths. 'I need you to listen carefully. Are you listening?' he asks.

I nod.

'I need you not to give up,' he says. I like his confidence. Like him saying those few words would be enough to stop someone who's decided to take their own life. I've already decided not to kill myself but perhaps it's best I let him think he's convinced me.

'But who are you?' I ask. I'm almost hoping it's God and this is a poncey divine moment that'll change my life forever.

'My name's John Smith. You've emailed me—'

'The trade union guy,' I say, a statement of fact. For a moment I'm disappointed, but then I ask, 'What are you doing in the ceiling?'

He sighs. 'Look, Ms Quirke, I'm breaking every rule possible here to offer you simple instruction. Do not take your own life. Distract yourself, focus on your new role helping St Nicholas. We need you to save the Christmas miracles. We need to stop Krampus. Lives depend on you. You have the power to change—'

'I thought the higher powers couldn't get involved?' I say.

'This isn't about them. This is about helping St Nick. He's been good to me. I'm risking a lot here,' he says.

'I can't do this on my own. I'm going to screw it up. Like I screw everything up. There are loads of people camped outside the flat. I can't even figure out how to leave. I can't—' I'm crying now.

'You can do this and you will. You have so much to give. Your life is precious. We all believe in you, Ms Quirke. Gabriel, Bess and I spend hours talking about you—' he says.

I jump up from the bed again, almost tripping as my legs don't unravel quite quickly enough.

'Gabe? You know my Gabe? Has he met someone else? Bess? Oh fuck, he has, hasn't he? I saw him with her—'

'Of course he hasn't, but it's complicated and I don't have time to explain. Now listen, I've got a plan to get Krampus out of the picture. You'll require paper and a pen.'

'But I can't—' I start to say.

'You can do this, Ms Quirke. This will be your purpose. You'll be the girl who saves the Christmas World. It's what you were born to achieve.'

I nod. I sniff.

'Tell me what I need to do,' I say.

SPITFIRE SAINT NICHOLAS UMBRELLA COLLECTIVE ☑

COMMUNITY

Hello friends! Mr Belsnickel, executive director of Spitfire, here.

I know many of you have commented, suggesting that the wrong address was given, but I can assure you that it wasn't.

Saint Nicholas is holding Theodora Quirke captive and is using Christmas magic to keep us all out of his flat above the bookshop on Bold Street.

That's **96 Bold St, Liverpool L1 4HY**

Think about this for a moment – what reasons can you offer as to why the fire brigade, locksmiths and police cannot break down a single door?

Let's all meet there today. More of us. All of us. They can't keep us out forever. Theodora Quirke needs us. We must save her.

If you'd like to find out more about details of the Christmas miracles that Krampus has performed, go to www.SpitfireSNUC.com/bemoreKrampus

THEO (THEODORA QUIRKE)

Time's running out. I've waited until the last possible moment. It's December 5th. It's now or never. I've got to attempt John Smith's plan.

St Nick's back lying on the sofa, wearing what looks like children's Speedos. The sight is practically obscene. The fucking weirdo's got a pair of orange goggles on his forehead.

'You off swimming?' I ask and St Nick grunts something that I can't quite distinguish.

'Listen, John Smith's come up with a plan. All you need to do is act like a weird drunk and pretend to be Santa Claus. You'll have no magic on you and you don't even need to get dressed,' I say, but St Nick doesn't move. 'Please. Can you just do this one last thing for the Christmas miracles? Then you'll be officially resigned and can wallow in your pit. Krampus will be the king and free to kidnap all the kids in the world. And, I promise, I'll leave you alone forever if you do this one last thing.' He doesn't move. 'After this you'll be free to go your own way. They'll probably still give you a reference...'

At first I don't think he's going to react or respond, but then he shuffles from the sofa. No words spoken, he picks a black, fake fur jacket from the coat rack. It's huge, makes him look like a wounded grizzly bear. Then he moves to his room and returns wearing red wellies. He looks both suitably inappropriate and amazing.

'Here,' I say. I hand him a half-full bottle of vodka. He looks at my outstretched hand and then takes the bottle.

'Umbrella,' he says.

'Thought it was a parasol?' I say, as I shake my head. He glares at me. 'You don't need it, it's not rain—' I start to say but then St Nick growls.

'All you've got to do is face the crowd, deny all knowledge of me and say you're Santa Claus.'

St Nick growls at that too, but moves towards the door and pulls his goggles over his eyes.

'Can you do that, St Nick?' I say. He doesn't respond and instead keeps shuffling forward. I've no idea if he can see properly with them on. I grab his umbrella from the tree trunk stand and rush out of the flat. I look over my shoulder as the door closes behind me.

For a moment my stomach flips at the thought of this all going wrong. St Nick could get arrested, I'll end up homeless and alone. I need to focus on the task ahead. Everything rides on a broken St Nick being able to convince the screaming public that he's a fraud. I clutch the umbrella and hope, with all that I can hope, that the magic still works with me holding it.

Please let me remain invisible.

St Nick's at the bottom of the stairs. The main door opens without me or St Nick doing anything. Christmas magic is here. Although I'm still hurrying down our stairs, I hear screams and chants. As I step outside, I see three policemen holding back the crowd. I'm faced with a stream of phones being held up to capture the moment. I turn and watch him.

St Nick ignores the gathered crowd and stumbles his way down Bold Street. Of course, the crowd rushes after him. Phones out, shouts of 'Oi, St Nick,' and, 'Pedo,' following him. No one turns to look at me. I keep wiggling the umbrella and hope the magic continues to work as I follow the crowd.

'St Nicholas,' one person shouts.

'Oi, St Nick, where's Theodora Quirke?' another shouts.

'You eaten the girl?' another shouts, and I hear laughter.

St Nick ignores them all and drinks from his bottle.

'Pedo,' one screams, rushing forward but a policeman is quick to act.

'Fat bastard,' another shouts.

'How the hell is *he* Santa?' another says and at that St Nick stops.

He turns, lifts his orange goggles back onto his forehead, and then he lets his tiny eyes travel across the mob of people. He doesn't focus on anyone in particular. To be honest, he looks like he's struggling to stay upright. Then he moves to the front of a shop and lets his backside squeak down the window to the floor. The window behind him displays a rotating nativity scene. Three plastic camels, two plastic dinosaurs, a plastic goat, two plastic cows and a sheep dog sit in an electric train as it loops around baby Jesus in his crib. An LED sign flashes 'JESUS LIVES' and a number of religious books are displayed. St Nick's fake fur coat falls open and his super tight Speedos are on display. His belly bulges out. It's covered in a rainbow of streaks from food he's eaten over the last week. All of this is being captured on the mob's numerous phones; it'll be all over social media within an instant.

'That's Santa?' someone shouts and that starts the crowd arguing. 'That fucker's supposed to be a mastermind who can make miracles happen?'

'He's not loaded,' someone says.

'Where's all his money?' a different someone says.

'Who wants to sit on my knee and tell me what they want for Chrimbo?' St Nick says. He's slurred his words and taps the vodka bottle on his legs. He's got a scouse accent?

'Fucking pedo,' someone shouts, rushing forward. 'He's killed the girl.'

'I ain't killed no one,' St Nick slurs.

'What's your name?' one of the policemen say.

'Santa bastard Claus,' St Nick says. 'I'm Kris buggering Kringle. Ho. Ho. Fucking ho.'

'Why's he wearing goggles on his head?' someone shouts.

'How's he going to give us money?' a different someone shouts.

St Nick puts his hand in his coat pocket and then pulls it back out. Palm up, there's a few coins on it. A couple of pennies, a five pence there too. He's a convincing drunk. I don't know if he's acting a part or if this is who he has become.

'Spare some change?' he asks the crowd. 'I'll sing you a song and then you can fuck off.' He bursts into a slurred version of *Santa Claus is Coming to Town*. Half the crowd laugh, the other turn to shout at one person. The ringleader. I recognise him instantly. A goatee in a suit; pinstriped, navy, with a crisp white shirt and a pale blue tie. Krampus. I watch the crowd. I look at that ringleader. The badge on his lapel identifies him as belonging to Spitfire, the clipboard he carries is branded with their logo. His smug face is looking decidedly less smug. He's underestimated his brother. He's entirely out of his depth.

'What the hell is this?' one of them shouts at Krampus.

'He's acting,' Krampus says, pointing at St Nick. I watch as the crowd takes a moment to consider if St Nick is in fact acting.

'Bullshit. He's off his head and stinks like he's not washed for a month,' one of the crowd shouts.

'Like bugger is he Santa Claus,' another says.

'Fucking waste of time this is,' another shouts.

'Definitely not Santa fucking Claus,' one says.

'Reckon Spitfire've been making mugs of us all,' someone says.

'Them getting loads of publicity and making us camp outside some drunk's house,' another says.

'Picking on an innocent bloke,' another says.

'Corporate wankers hounding an innocent out of his house,' another yells.

'He doesn't even look like the bloke outside Dante House with that girl,' someone shouts, and all the time St Nick's holding out one hand, taking swigs of vodka from the bottle with his other and singing out of tune in-between those swigs. It's about then that St Nick sinks nearer to his back. He's practically lying on the floor, too-tight Speedos fully exposed, and the vodka bottle clangs on the pavement.

'Poor bloke. We've been harassing the bugger for weeks,' someone says.

'I've just been in his flat. Ain't nowt but a mattress and empty vodie bottles in there,' another says, rushing to be in front of St Nick. 'There ain't been no girl in that flat.'

'Get him a cuppa and a sausage roll from Greggs,' another shouts, and that's when the crowd starts to disperse.

Of course someone, a woman, punches Krampus in the face and calls him a bastard. He crumples to the ground crying and cupping his bloody nose. All I can do is stand and watch from the shadows.

My society made St Nick this way.

THEO (THEODORA QUIRKE)

I walk over to Krampus. I poke his arm with the tip of St Nick's umbrella. He jumps on the spot, his hands still cupping his bloody nose.

'What the—' He looks over to St Nick, and then in my direction. He can't see me. 'Theodora Quirke?' he says.

I place the umbrella on his shoulder. He can see me now.

'A hairy devil appears on the streets. Seems like it really is Krampus Night,' I say.

'That's quite the performance from my brother.'

I take a few steps nearer to him, bending down to his ear. 'Why though?' I ask. 'Why do you hate the Christmas World so much?'

He smiles. He takes a handkerchief from the inside pocket of his suit jacket and holds it to his nose.

'Hate it?' he says. 'You've got me entirely wrong, Theodora. I love the Christmas World. It's my everything. My purpose…' A pause. 'All I wanted was what was rightfully mine.'

'Rightfully?' I ask, kneeling on the pavement beside him.

'I'm the older twin. I was born first. Krampus Night is the day before St Nicholas Day for a reason. But the higher powers selected my brother to reign, with me as the spare.'

I shake my head. 'All of this…' I point at the crowd still surrounding St Nick. 'Because you're jealous of your brother?'

'Jealous,' he says. He laughs. It's not a convincing laugh. 'I lived in *his* shadow for too long,' he says. 'Always the bad guy. The threat for children to behave, then my brother swoops in with gifts and joy. I was feared, he was anticipated.'

'This is so fucked up,' I say. 'I'm not going to give you any sympathy.'

'Used to be that if children misbehaved, then jolly old St Nick would send Krampus to punish them. I was his dark partner. He never actually expected me to turn up at the homes and punish kids, it was more about the threat of me. Leaving bundles of sticks outside their doors was the original idea.'

'But that wasn't enough for you?'

'He,' he nods in his brother's direction, 'made me this way. I decided to spice things up a bit and give the people what they feared. Whipping with horsehair—'

'What the fuck?' I say, but that seems to spur him on.

'Beating with birch sticks, kidnapping the little buggers in a giant sack. I even put the really bad kids in my lair for a year. I was on a roll and it was working. Society was in a better place. People lived in communities, people cared about each other. A bit of fear works. People needed to be saved from themselves… Until my darling brother and everyone in his precious Christmas World intervened.'

'Can you really not see why you had to be stopped?' I stand up, the umbrella's tip still resting on his shoulder.

'I was banned, Theodora. Mention of my name was actually banned. Someone from the Christmas World, disguised as a do-gooding freak, warned that parents would scar their children if they mentioned me. They made up research, said threatening kids with a visit from me was as psychologically damaging for a child as being robbed was for an adult. PC bollocks.'

I shake my head. 'So, this,' I point the umbrella at the mob, 'is your revenge?'

'Hello?' he says.

The umbrella. I place the tip back on his shoulder.

'Yes,' he says. 'A flawless plan to bring down my beloved

twin. He fails tonight and the next in line steps up. You know, some towns in Europe actually prefer Krampus to St Nick. They keep gold painted birch bundles around all year as a reminder for children to behave. A wave of a birch bundle and the kids are whispering my name and behaving like cherubs. I'm practically worshipped like a god.'

'Well, maybe you should have focused your attention on those European towns,' I say and Krampus shakes his head.

'I want what *he* has. It's rightfully mine. I can fix your society, Theodora. I've got more balls than that brother of mine.'

'You underestimated your brother, me and the Christmas World.'

I turn to walk away from the chaos and noise.

'Theodora?' Theodora?' Krampus shouts. He's on his feet. He's spinning on the spot, his arms stretched out. He thinks I'm still near him. 'I reckon I'm still close to winning. What have you done, Theodora Quirke?' He's punching out in front of him, to the side, spinning behind him. 'I will hunt you down, little girl.'

I shake my head. He looks like an absolute nobhead. The plan's worked though. No matter what he thinks, Krampus isn't winning anymore. I hope St Nick finds his way back to the flat, when it's safe to do so. I can't intervene anymore; I need to trust that he'll return to me and to the Christmas World when he can.

'Consumer wankers ruining Christmas,' St Nick shouts. I turn to look back at him. He's on his feet, shaking his bottle in the air and slurring his words. 'I want to be Santa Fucking Claus. Stop them commercial wankers. I believe in me,' he slurs.

'We believe in you too, Santa. Let's get you sober and

clean,' someone says, guiding St Nick down Bold Street.

There's kindness and apology surrounding St Nick now. I watch them walking away, the Christmas lights twinkling over them. Lights arranged into the shape of bells, of holly, and of Santa Claus's smiling face. Christmas songs blast out as shop doors open. People rush about, their focus on ticking presents from their Christmas shopping list. They're counting down to Christmas Eve. All are oblivious of the Patron Saint of Liverpool. The man who embodies the true spirit of gift giving at Christmas walks drunkenly amongst them. I don't know if he'll ever be fixed again. I wish, with all my heart, that I could make him better.

'Shame on you, Spitfire,' someone shouts. I notice Krampus shuffling away. His head's down. Not so bold and full of shit now. He's not making eye contact with any of the angry folk.

'Hounding the poor man,' someone else says, chasing after Krampus, who picks up pace and then sprints away. I smile at that.

I hurry back to the flat. There's no one outside, just discarded newspapers and a whole load of litter; no one's interested in where St Nick was supposed to have lived anymore.

I hurry inside. Slam the flat's door shut. Everything's as it was when I left. Christmas magic at its finest. I throw the umbrella into its trunk, and rush into the spare room. Of course I'm opening Facebook and refreshing the SpitfireSNUC as I sit down. I scan their Facebook wall for new posts.

There's an update, a post with a video of St Nick, with the caption: 'SO THIS IS THE BLOKE TO MAKE ALL YOUR CHRISTMAS WISHES COME TRUE? FUCK OFF SPITFIRE.'

I click down, over twenty thousand likes already and over five hundred comments on that one post. I scroll. Some are full of sympathy for St Nick, but the majority are questioning Spitfire; saying they've made up the whole St Nicholas thing. People are demanding refunds of their membership money, others are threatening legal action and talking about '*fraud claims*' and '*compensation*'. I read them all. I can't help but smile. The more I read, the more the comments keep appearing.

'*Employing actors.*'

'*Thieving bastards.*'

'*Boycott Spitfire.*'

'So proud of you, Ms Quirke,' John Smith booms from the ceiling. I think about Gabriel. I wonder if John Smith will tell him about today. My stomach flips. It's a physical ache. A pull to be with Gabriel.

'Thank you,' I whisper. 'Now, I just need to be St Nicholas tonight and make sure that these Christmas miracles happen. I need to give society hope again.'

There's a knock on the front door. I ignore it. What if it's Krampus again? What if he wants to whip me with a birch bundle? I don't know if the door's still protected by Christmas magic. Am I unprotected, now that St Nick isn't here?

Another knock; I jump. I don't know what to do. And then there's a voice. I tiptoe to the door. I'm holding my breath, so as not to be heard.

A sheet of paper is pushed under the door. I bend down and pick it up. It's a poster and there's a photograph of me on it. It's a picture of me and Gabriel, taken on my eighteenth. I'm holding a glass of champagne up to the camera. Smiling. Francesca took it. She took several until I liked one enough to make it my new profile photo on Instagram. The word 'MISSING' is in black, bold letters. There's a ten thousand pound reward being offered. There's a contact phone number and an email address. The contact name is Francesca.

What the fuck? She's willing to pay ten thousand pounds to find me?

I can't move. I don't know how long I've been crying. I'm being missed. Francesca is missing me. Gabriel's mum misses me.

'Theo,' a female voice says. 'I saw you outside. With Saint Nicholas when he came out of the flat. I was the one who punched Mr Belsnickel,' she says. 'I'm not after no reward. My name's Dottie Smith. I founded that Facebook group, the Saint Nicholas Umbrella Collective.' She pauses and I wonder if she's going to go away. 'I'm not involved with Spitfire no more; I made a mistake.' She pauses again. 'A pretty big mistake.' I nod; you reckon? I think she's waiting for me to respond.

'Theo, I'm here on my own. I want to help with the Christmas miracles.'

I open the front door.

THEO (THEODORA QUIRKE)

She's got wild black hair, olive skin and the deepest brown eyes I've ever seen. I stare at her. Look her up then down. She does the same to me.

She's round in shape. Her face is slightly lop-sided. Her front tooth chipped when she smiles, but there's something refreshingly honest about that smile. She looks all prim and proper in a buttoned up to the neck cardigan, with a little lace collar showing, and a long velvet skirt that trails along the floor. The rounded tips of ballet pumps poke out from under her skirt, and she's carrying a bright purple tote bag. I can't help but wonder why she isn't wearing a coat. I think she might be younger than the way she dresses. She's probably about the same age as Francesca. I know straight away that I want her to be my friend.

I direct her into the living room.

'Would you like to sit down?' I say.

She balances on the edge of my squishy sofa. She's not comfortable. She rubs the tops of her arms furiously, like she might be cold. The Christmas tree is back up, with new – terrifying – Santa Claus face baubles, and new multi-coloured tinsel wrapped around. The tree sprouts up in the corner of the room again and its twinkling lights reflect a rainbow over the white sofa. I'm still clutching the poster.

'They're up all around town,' she says. 'Didn't you see them?'

I shake my head and place the poster on the coffee table.

'Can I get you a drink?' I say. 'Tea? Coffee?' She's my first ever guest at the flat. She shakes her head.

248

'Theo,' she says. 'I need to say I'm sorry.' Her voice is like marbles in a tin. I don't want her to cry. 'I never meant for any of this...'

'I wasn't his prisoner,' I say and she nods. She knows that already. She's on my side. 'He showed me joy and hope,' I say. 'He gave me one of his miracles back when I was eleven.'

'I had one of them too,' she says. 'Here.' She bends to the floor and rummages round in her tote bag. 'I want you to read this,' she says. She hands me a notebook. I open it. A title 'MY STORY – BY DOTTIE SMITH' and then there are pages and pages of handwriting.

'I started writing it when I broke all ties with Spitfire. I was going to give it to the press. Not for money. Just to get my side of the story out there,' she says. 'But now I've found you, I want you to have it instead.'

'You could still give it to—'

'It's more important to me that you *get* why I did what I did,' she says.

And that's when and why I start reading her story. I read about the deaths of her children and husband. I read about how she kept on living and about the Christmas miracle that St Nick gave her. I read about how Krampus, although she doesn't call him that, got involved with her little group and how quickly it all got out of control. She's ridiculously honest about her motivation, greed and about the insecurities she has about people not liking her. I look up every time I reach the bottom of a page, but she's never looking back at me. Pages and pages, me reading in silence and her sitting opposite, all tense on the edge of the sofa.

'It was Christmas Eve when I met St Nick,' I say, when I've finished her story. 'Not December 6th.' I pause. She nods. 'Thank you for sharing this with me.'

'When Noah, Betty and Neil died, I had nothing. Everything I loved and owned was lost in that fire,' she says. She's looked down at the carpet all the time I was reading. Did she worry that she'd see hatred when she looked at me? She wouldn't have; we're on the same side.

'I can't even begin—' I start to say.

'And nor should you,' she says. She looks up then and she smiles. 'Life became 'bout simply surviving each day. Self-loathing, wild bursts of anger and tears, guilt—'

She stands and comes over to sit next to me on St Nick's sofa. I reach out and touch her hand. It's ice cold. I dread to think how long she'd been outside waiting for me and St Nick to leave the flat.

'But I kept going,' she says. 'I woke up each morning, and I tried to do one small task each day. That soon got to me doing more and more tasks. I asked for help from my doctor and I ended up with a therapist, who asked the right questions. I talked and talked. If the thoughts get trapped in your head,' she taps the side of her head with two fingers, 'you believe they're your friend.'

I smile at that. 'You're so brave,' I say and she shakes her head.

'I'm honestly not. We're both survivors, we just got here via different routes.'

'Survivors,' I say. It's an echo. I stand. 'You're freezing. Let me make you a hot drink,' I say. 'Oh… and then I'll tell you all about how Belsnickel is Krampus.'

'Shut the fuck up,' she says.

THEO (THEODORA QUIRKE)

I told her about Krampus. She didn't speak for a good three minutes, then she said, 'Let's not tell the public 'bout him.'

At first I was a little confused, but her reasoning was right. If we told the public, it'd only give Krampus more attention and that's what he craves more than anything else. Dottie also reckoned he'd get loads of supporters too. That the UK wasn't always good at making the right decisions. I love that Dottie's as devoted as me to not letting Krampus take control of the Christmas World.

Now we're in the kitchen and I'm piling St Nick's dirty bowls into the sink. I've never washed a dish the entire time I've been living here. I've no idea if that was Christmas magic, St Nick or the higher powers sending a daily cleaner. I hate that I never asked; I took too much for granted. Today though, I'm the last one standing and the kitchen's a mess. It's another hint that much of the Christmas magic left the flat with St Nick.

'Sorry about all this,' I say. I point at the dried-up teabags, breadcrumbs and crusts, at the Coco Pops that have escaped St Nick's bowl and at what looks like grated cheese that's scattered across the countertop. I turn on the taps and rinse the bowls. I stack them, ready for when I wash up later.

'Hope is a choice,' Dottie says. I turn back and I nod. I wipe my hands dry on my T-shirt. 'My mum used to always say that to me when I was little. I was adopted you see.'

'Adopted,' I echo. The word causes a tiny flicker in my memories. Francesca appears in my head again. I shake my head. I can't think about her.

'I was chosen...' Dottie says.

'And she gave you the name Hope,' I say. It's a statement, not a question.

'Dottie Hope,' she says. She moves next to me. She reaches out her hand for me to shake it. She's introducing herself. Her touch is ice and I place both my damp hands around hers. I hate that she's so cold because of me.

'Directly after Noah, Betty and Neil died, people used to tell me that I had so much to live for, and I'd want to punch them in the face,' she says. 'I had nothing to live for. Everything I loved was gone and it wasn't temporary. It wasn't something that a few tablets could fix.'

I open and close cupboard doors. I'm looking for teabags and a teapot. 'What the fuck?'

There are fully decorated, tiny yet very real, Christmas trees in all the cupboards. Their lights twinkle like they're winking. Each of them seems to be growing out of the wood in the cupboard.

'Theo?' Dottie Hope says, and I point to the tiny, very perfect trees.

'Christmas magic,' she says. She laughs. I nod and look up at the ceiling. I guess the higher powers are happy that Dottie Hope's here.

'But you kept living,' I say.

'Because the right person asked, "How can I help?" and that got me talking. It gave me more hope. 'Cause it were right and normal to feel all them emotions I'd been experiencing. I was reacting to devastation and I thought life would only be getting worse,' she says.

'I don't know how you kept going,' I say as I fill the kettle with water.

'After Saint Nicholas' miracle, everything went wrong. I

was at my lowest. I was ready to give up, but then he became my obsession.'

'Like sexually?' I ask. I screw my face up at the thought of it. Thankfully I've got my back to Dottie. I don't want to offend her and her weird sex tastes.

She laughs. 'God no,' she says. 'Although I did have dreams where he was—'

'No,' I say. I whip around and laugh as I hold up my palm to stop her from sharing any more of that dream. She laughs too. It's a proper laugh. She holds her belly as her whole body jiggles with the sound.

'He made me feel special, though. I guess, like I were worth something.' She pauses. 'You know, even now, sometimes I envy people who die.'

'I was jealous of Gabe for dying,' I say.

'And now?' she asks. I shake my head.

I reach into the cupboard for two cups. There's one with a Santa Claus face on it. St Nick never found it funny and I never tired of making him a cup of tea in it.

'Have you not taken a moment to look at how far you've already travelled?' she says and I shake my head. 'Bloody hell, Theo, you really need to be a bit kinder to you.'

She steps towards me and we hug. I like her.

'Letting go and accepting life unfolding,' she says pulling out of the hug. 'It all sounds bollocks when I'm saying it out loud. But somewhere in here,' she points at her belly, 'I believed life would get better.'

'And belief is enough?' I ask.

'I didn't have no fear of the future,' she says. 'Despite the worst things happening in my life, I still had hope. I can't explain how or why, but I did and I still do.'

'St Nick said it was 'cause your heart's pure,' I say.

I pop two teabags in the teapot and search for a clean spoon. I pull open the cutlery drawer. It's one of those drawers with an embedded plastic tray. It's got three compartments that normally contain spoons, knives and forks, but instead of utensils I find the drawer's been filled with mini-Christmas crackers.

I look up at Dottie and she's clearly confused. I shrug and grab a cracker at random. I pull both ends. There's a crack and a fork spills out, bouncing to the floor. I pick up the fork and place it on the counter. I grab another cracker and pull. Another fork. I take a third cracker. I grasp one end and offer the other to Dottie. She smiles and pulls. A crack and a spoon clatters to the floor. We both laugh. I pick up the spoon, washing it under the tap.

'That Saint Nicholas is a right joker,' Dottie says.

'Actually, he's a miserable bastard. Most of the time. These are a present from his… *bosses*.' I smile. I glance up at the ceiling.

'I think I wanted her to miss me,' I say, pouring water into cups.

'Her?'

'Gabe's mum,' I say. 'Death forces people to miss you, doesn't it? It makes people think about you and to notice all the good qualities you'd wanted them to notice when you were alive,' I say. She nods for me to continue. 'It would make her realise that I was worth something.' I pause. 'She always loved Christmas. September the first and out came her Cath Kidston Christmas planner. She was all about making the festivities last as long as possible,' I say.

'Why not give her another chance, Theo?' she says. 'She put up every one of them posters and I've read her blog posts. She's never given up hope.'

'She blogs?'

'She calls you her daughter. Her saving grace,' she says. I gulp over the lump in my throat and my nose twitches as I try not to cry. 'Phone her.'

'I'll think about it,' I say, pushing away any thoughts of Francesca. I can't think about that now. 'First of all, I have to save the Christmas World.'

'And that's why I'm here,' Dottie Hope says. 'I want to help you.'

'But how did you—'

'An email from John Smith,' she says. 'It said, *"Save Theo – Spitfire and oral"*. And gave me your address.'

'Oh, you're a few months too late. I don't need saving,' I say. 'And fuck knows what "oral" they're talking about. There's been none of that. St Nick got the same message last year and—'

'It were yesterday,' Dottie Hope says. 'I got the email yesterday.'

And that's when *Grown-Up Christmas List* starts playing into the flat.

THE SAINT NICHOLAS UMBRELLA COLLECTIVE ☑

COMMUNITY

Hello my dear friends. DOTTIE SMITH, actual founder of both the SpitfireSNUC and The Saint Nicholas Umbrella Collective, here for one last post.

Mr Belsnickel lied to you; I haven't been on holiday. The truth is that I no longer wanted to be associated with Spitfire and their hunting of Saint Nicholas, so I refused to work for Mr Belsnickel anymore.

I need you all to know that I remain a firm believer in all of the genuine acts, miracles and donations that Saint Nicholas has made, all over the world, on and around December 6th. He is the purest and best man you'd ever have the privilege of knowing.

It is my belief that Mr Belsnickel's intention was always to discredit Saint Nicholas and to gain free publicity for his company, Spitfire. Please break that connection between our Saint Nicholas and Spitfire's desire to exploit us all.

In light of recent developments and legal claims, I have removed my association with Spitfire and, as I created this page, I will be deleting it over the next week.

As one last bid from me though, and offered to you all from my sincere and grateful heart, remember to check inside your children's shoes on the morning of December 6th. And, when you find a little something there, be sure you share that truth with everyone you know. #IbelieveinStNick

For details on how to receive a full refund of your membership fee from SpitfireSNUC, go to www.SpitfireSNUC.com/refund

THEO (THEODORA QUIRKE)

We're sitting at the kitchen table. I've got St Nick's laptop open and I'm showing Dottie Hope the five people I've selected. She knows about Christmas miracles and the people who have been chosen previously. I'm one of them. She's one of them. Some of her best friends are others. Her heart's pure and having her agree with my choices is increasing my confidence. *Let it Snow*'s playing from the ceiling – the higher powers clearly support this new direction – and Dottie Hope's singing along. Her voice is angelic.

'And this is the final one,' I say. 'Her name's Elsie.'

'Did she join SpitfireSNUC?' Dottie Hope asks.

It's been the same question five times now. I shake my head and she smiles. None of my chosen five had engaged with SpitfireSNUC; they'd all been too busy surviving life. None of them had thirty pounds to spare. But more than that, as far as I can tell, none of them even visited the SpitfireSNUC Facebook page or website.

'A dinner lady from Preston. She delivers food to homeless people every night,' I say. 'But more than that, she does it without anyone else knowing. She pays for the food, prepares it all and delivers it. She asks for nothing in return.'

'Sounds like a good soul,' Dottie Hope says.

'There's more,' I say. 'Her husband's lost his job and they're set to be homeless themselves just before Christmas. Eviction notice is being served next week.'

'What do you propose for her miracle?' Dottie Hope asks, but I know she's already thinking the same as me.

'Paying off her mortgage and all her debts, maybe even a little extra that I know she'll put to good use helping others. They'll keep their home and have a fresh start,' I say.

'Perfect,' Dottie says. I hear *Rudolph the Red Nosed Reindeer* playing from somewhere else in the flat. Dottie's humming along and not questioning where the music's come from.

'Do you have any idea how this all comes together tonight?' I ask Dottie Hope and she shakes her head. 'St Nick'd resigned before he taught me the ins and outs of it all. I don't have a clue—'

'Is there no one you can ask?' she says.

'There's one man I trust…'

I find the last email from John Smith and I type a message. I thank him for sending me Dottie Hope and explain how we're all set to step in to deliver the Christmas miracles and a tiny present to every child in the world. If we can pull this off, the Christmas World will have a year to fix St Nick and we'll keep Krampus unemployed.

John Smith emails back within a few minutes, saying how the higher powers are '*thrilled*' and how much they're all looking forward to meeting me '*in the near future*'. I skim the email and realise that no details have been given on how we actually deliver all the gifts.

'Ask him for more particulars,' Dottie Hope says. She's so close that our shoulders touch. 'Time to be direct, Theo. Shy folk get nowt.'

'Okay,' I say and I type, '*How do the gifts and miracles get delivered?*'

His reply is instant: '*By you.*'

Dottie Hope laughs. The sound comes from deep within her belly. I laugh at her laugh, which makes Dottie laugh even more.

'A joker,' she says. 'Maybe all us Smiths are hilarious. I like him.' She's loving this and her excitement's contagious. 'Quick, type,' she says, pointing at the laptop.

'*But I can't deliver it all in one night,*' I type.

'*Has Saint Nicholas taught you nothing?*' is his reply and then, '*You stop time.*'

'Stop time,' Dottie Hope shouts. 'We get to stop time!'

She jumps up and starts twerking to the music. The dance and how Dottie Hope's dressed clash; the sight's full of joy. I can't help but laugh. A deep, true, no holding back kind of laugh.

'Type Theo, type,' she says. She's bent over, and it's taking her a minute to catch her breath.

'*How do I stop time?*' I type.

'*Look in the microwave. There's a gadget called a Walkman. Inside is a cassette tape full of festive pop songs. As long as the Walkman is playing, time will stand still, you can travel and your festive team will remain invisible.*'

'Well that sounds simple,' Dottie Hope says.

Her tone's full of sarcasm and we're both laughing again. She rushes over to the microwave and pings open the door. Inside, on the glass plate, there's a red Sony Walkman cassette player. Dottie Hope holds the Walkman up to the ceiling *Lion King*-style and does wobbling lunges back to the table.

'There are no headphones,' she says.

'Press play. See if it works.'

She sits down next to me at the table and she presses play. *Baby It's Cold Outside* blasts out. The air changes. We both feel the shift. Dottie Hope shouts, 'Bloody hell,' and presses the stop button. The music ends mid-lyric.

'My festive team? What do you think that means?' I ask her. She sits down next to me, placing the Walkman on the table carefully. That thing's full of magic that we don't understand. 'How do we travel around?'

'Ask him,' Dottie Hope says, pointing at the screen.

I type the question and John Smith's response is instant, '*You can have any method of transport you desire. Reindeer and sleigh, unicorn, giant hamster…*' I laugh when I read giant hamster aloud, but, also, it gives me the best idea.

'He's genuinely funny,' Dottie Hope says. 'We've got to be related.'

'Any method of transport,' I say, mainly to myself. I know what I want. I type my response, with Dottie Hope reading over my shoulder.

'What the actual—' she starts to say, but I've already pressed send. 'A girl could go insane hanging out with you,' she says, but she's laughing. She's as excited about this as I am.

'What 'bout how we actually deliver the gifts?' Dottie Hope says.

'Like if there's some kind of magic Christmas dust?' I say and she nods. I formulate the question and press send. I keep refreshing my inbox. I'm impatient and full of excitement. The email pings.

'*Choices available at such short notice are magic key, down a chimney or magic dust,*' I say. 'Seriously? That's so clichéd.'

'Can we just use a magic key? Keep it simple,' Dottie Hope says. 'What with your unusual method of transport…'

I type the response and press send. 'I think that's it,' I say, but then the email pings again. 'What weather would we like?' I say.

'Weather?' Dottie Hope echoes.

'Snow?' I ask and Dottie Hope says, 'Don't see why not.'

'How do we know where to go?' Dottie Hope asks.

'Good question,' I say as I type the query to John Smith.

'*Christmas magic will guide you,*' Dottie Hope reads aloud and I shrug my shoulders.

'Trust, I guess,' I say.

I email our thanks to John Smith and then he responds telling us that our transport will be outside at one minute before midnight. He warns us not to be late and to remember to stop time.

'Looks like we're all set to go,' Dottie Hope says.

'I might leave a note and St Nick's email address for each of the chosen five, just in case I do something wrong or they have any queries,' I say and Dottie Hope nods.

'With all the press of late, what if they sell your note to a tabloid?' Dottie Hope says, but then quickly adds, 'They're all pure of heart. They won't.' I nod. I trust and believe that my five Christmas miracle candidates will keep the secret. Dottie Hope hands me some paper and a pen.

'My spelling's rubbish,' I say.

'Just write from your heart,' Dottie Hope says, as I nod and pick up the pen.

THEO (THEODORA QUIRKE)

Notes written and mince pies eaten, we sit in silence at the table for a good five minutes. The enormity of the task finally sinks into my belly. I'm full of nerves. I can't help but wonder if Dottie Hope is too.

'We can't miss anyone,' I say. 'Not one child. We need to make sure Krampus doesn't get to reign.'

'Right, we'd best get wrapped up,' she says, breaking the silence, 'what with you choosing snow for the weather.'

I look at the time; we've only got fifteen minutes to spare. I hurry into my bedroom, Dottie Hope close behind.

'I'm sure we'll find something for us—' I stop. Two piles of clothes are folded on the bed.

'Santa suits,' I say. 'For fuck's sake.' I pick up the fluffy red jacket and matching trousers. I let my fingers dance along the fabric of the whopping red coat and think about when I met St Nick for the first time. I miss him. The material's all fluffy and soft. Carmine, I remember.

'Someone's having a laugh.' I look up at the ceiling, knowing John Smith is watching. I shake my head but I'm smiling too. I pull the Santa Claus outfit over my clothes. Dottie Hope removes her floaty skirt, then does the same.

'We look like giant red strawberries,' she says, and then we're headed for the front door.

I grab the Walkman from the kitchen table and I press play. The air alters and there's a gush of icy wind. The Beach Boys' *Little Saint Nick* blasts out and I can't help but giggle. It's a nervous sound. There's magic and excitement in the air. Dottie

Hope does a wiggling dance on the spot. I'm so glad that she's here to help and to share this experience with me. She's as eager as I am.

This is it. This is the start of my new career as a Christmas angel. I grab the umbrella from its stand. Dottie Hope holds the front door open, her face the perfect picture of happiness.

I already feel sweaty in my armpits. 'St Nick said these suits were hot as fuck,' I say, mainly to myself. 'You ready?'

'I were born for this moment,' she says, and we rush down the stairs giggling. We open the outside door.

And then it's there.

A huge green brontosaurus is waiting for us as we step out onto Bold Street. It has a plastic sheen. It towers above the buildings. It's the life-size replica of little Theodora's plastic toy. I'm crying; the emotion of the evening's already caught up with me. I wipe my eyes on the fluffy cuff of my Santa Claus jacket.

'How the hell can't others see this?' Dottie Hope asks.

Her neck's bent back and she's smiling up at the dinosaur. I look around and see others frozen to the spot next to and around the dinosaur: some mid chat to friends, most have their eyes fixed on their phones, some stare ahead, some are drunk and mid stagger towards the taxi rank. Not one of the passers-by has looked up and seen my dinosaur.

'Christmas magic,' I whisper, as I walk around the magnificent creature. There are no wrinkles in the towering, forty feet tall, green, plastic Brontosaurus. I asked to transport the Christmas miracles on the back of my old dinosaur toy; they really did deliver exactly what I wanted. Sacks hang from the dinosaur saddle. They'll be full of coins, sweets and small toys.

'You couldn't have gone traditional with a reindeer and

sleigh, could you?' Dottie Hope says. She's laughing from her belly. 'Or perhaps one of them fancy Rolls Royces to go all *Chitty Chitty Bang Bang* flying on me?'

'Where's your sense of adventure?' I say, as the green dinosaur bends its head down to say hello. I stroke her nose – there are bite indentations from a toddler's nibbles – and that's when flakes of snow begin to fall.

'How the hell do we get in that saddle?' Dottie Hope asks.

We hear a clatter. We hurry to the side of the dinosaur and see a tall wooden ladder resting against it.

'After you,' I say and Dottie Hope squeals.

'This might be the best day of my life.'

I nod. I think it might be the best day of mine too.

THEO (THEODORA QUIRKE)

It's done. We're back on Bold Street. I switch off the Walkman. *All I Want For Christmas Is You* stops mid-song and a gush of icy air vibrates off me. I shake off the flakes of snow from my Santa Claus suit and undo the jacket's buttons. My T-shirt's soaked with sweat underneath. It's so hot; I can't wait to take the suit off. I look at my watch. One minute past midnight.

'Happy St Nicholas Day,' I say, to myself. 'Not one child missed.'

Dottie Hope needed to clear her head, so she's gone off for a little walk. I'm going back into the flat. Five Christmas miracles have been delivered successfully. Toys, coins, sweets, all dropped into a shoe of every child. I also heard, via a voice through the Walkman, that all of the other Christmas angels had also been successful with their deliveries of Christmas miracles. I'd not even considered all the worldwide work that needed to be covered thanks to St Nick's resignation. John Smith's been quite the hero organiser. I'm shattered, I'm happy, but above all else I feel proud of myself. Lives have been changed tonight, because me and Dottie Hope didn't give up on ourselves or on St Nick's legacy. I'm in awe of the magic key too.

'St Nick,' I shout as I walk in and slump down on my swishy white sofa. I wish he was here. I want to tell him all about my adventures; I hope that he's proud of me.

I spot a red box on the coffee table and shuffle off the sofa to grab it. Inside there's a letter and a bottle of red liquid. Hanging from the bottle is a small luggage label with the word 'DRINK' written on it. I unfold the letter.

Dear Ms Quirke,

Congratulations! You have passed your probationary work period with flying (dinosaur) colours! We, the higher powers, are incredibly happy with both you and your commitment to our cause. It is, therefore, an honour to offer you the role of Christmas angel within our organisation. You will be the first female ever appointed in the role.

The next stage is simple and pain free, but must be entered into by yourself and without external coaxing. To become a fully-fledged, immortal Christmas angel, simply drink the liquid provided and go to sleep.

We look forward to welcoming you into our world.

The Higher Powers.

I roll the bottle between my two palms. I hold the bottle to the light. The liquid is dense. It looks like blood. All I have to do is drink the liquid and then I can escape from Liverpool. I'll forget all about Gabriel, not have to face contacting Francesca, stop being me, live in the now, push aside thoughts of Gabriel with a new girlfriend, and devote my life to Christmas miracles.

And that feeling, the one I had when I came back to the flat – that feeling of contentment and purpose – I can have it all the time. I need a purpose in my life. I need a place where I belong. I won't have to fear love or loving or being alone again, because my expectations will be realistic; I'll have a role and I'll live in the now. I can make a difference. I'll be the first ever female Christmas angel. Such an honour.

I can sacrifice myself. I can. I must.

I don't have a choice. I've nothing else to live for and nothing to die for. I look at the Christmas tree sprouting up from the corner. Fuelled by Christmas magic, it twinkles and glimmers. My mind flicks to the missing posters. What did she write on her blog about me? Dottie said that Francesca had called me her daughter, her saving grace.

I chase away the thoughts. Not now. I can't think about her. I give the bottle a little shake.

It's time.

I unscrew the bottle and I lift it to my lips, when the door slams open and all I hear is, 'NO.'

THEO (THEODORA QUIRKE)

I drop the bottle. The red liquid spills onto the swishy sofa and then disappears or evaporates or something. I look up. Two people rush into the room.

A man, a tall man. Over six foot. He's lean and he's handsome. A long nose, stubble, long eyelashes, chocolate coloured eyes. His mouth is wide; his lips are full. His teeth are perfectly straight and dazzling white. He's smiling at me in a way that seems familiar. Then there's Dottie Hope. She's grinning like she's the happiest person in the world.

The tall man sees the empty bottle. 'Did you drink it?' he asks. He slides to the floor and crouches in front of me. I can't move. I want this to make more sense than it does. 'Theodora Quirke. Theo,' he says. His accent is exotic; I don't recognise it.

'Who the hell are you?' I ask, before turning to Dottie Hope and saying, 'What the fuck is this?'

But before Dottie Hope can answer, the man has moved from the floor. He sits next to me and places an umbrella between us. I look at the umbrella. I look at the handle; I think it might be ivory, I think it might be worth something. And that's when I look up and that's when I realise.

I see who is sitting next to me. I reach up to touch his face. 'You're so beautiful,' I say.

St Nick laughs. He hugs me; the hug is brief but full of love. He pulls back and holds both of my hands in his. 'I was in Nieuwveen, in the Netherlands,' he says.

'And this...' I nod at his beauty, 'is a reflection of their society?'

'Embracing the Dutch way of life might be the next

UK publishing phenomenon,' he says and I look confused. 'Togetherness, relaxation, indulging, being present, having comfort. They're all about seeking out what gives them a better quality of life, and it's never consumerism.' He pauses. 'My new face is a reflection of that.'

'But you're back here?' I say.

'There's hope for your society. There's a spark. Can you feel it?'

I nod. I can.

'The chaos that my brother and his Spitfire caused has made people pause and look at their Christmas priorities and traditions,' St Nick says.

'Krampus said he'll hunt me down,' I say.

'We'll deal with Krampus,' St Nick says. 'What matters is that people are talking about me, about St Nicholas again. The true meaning of gift giving at Christmas is being rediscovered right this very moment, all over the world. That's all thanks to you and Dottie Smith.'

'Do you still want to resign?' I ask.

St Nick shakes his head. 'No. I don't think so. They've suggested I need a break instead. Rest and recuperation. They're lessening my workload for a few months. Everything's starting to come together.'

'How?' I ask.

'People will notice the coins, sweets and small toys that you left tonight. They'll want to believe. They'll want magic and simplicity in their lives again. And if you combine all of those little shifts with the right person guiding them on all things St Nicholas.' He nods at me, a hint that he's talking about me being that person.

I nod. I know he's right. I felt the shift in the air tonight. I don't mean just because of that Walkman.

'They've let me come back to see you, and for you to see this.' He points at his new face. He smiles. 'Who'd have thought that resigning would get the outcome I wanted,' he says. 'I'm sorry for being such a rubbish role model for you, Theodora Quirke.'

I lean over to the coffee table and pick up his locket. I hold it on my open palm and he takes it. He's still smiling. 'Them bringing Alice back to me when I looked the way I did—' He sighs— 'Well that was the final straw for me. I was going to stop being St Nick... I really was. I was going to let that brother of mine take control of the Christmas World. I didn't think getting a new face and rebuilding my reputation were options.'

'Did John Smith help you?' I ask and St Nick nods. All the time I'm focusing my eyes on St Nick and absorbing his new face, but Dottie Hope is still there. I don't think she's taken her eyes from me.

'His last defiant act before he retires. Although how smoothly the Christmas miracles ran without me is a little disturbing,' St Nick says. 'Not one child missed.'

He's proud of me. He's not saying directly but I've perfected reading the truth behind what adults actually say. He's smiling and there's nothing crooked or yellow about his new teeth.

'They're letting me see if I can win Alice's heart,' St Nick says.

'You want to try?' I ask.

'I have to. I've waited too many lifetimes to meet her again,' he says. 'Time for us both to face our demons and stop fearing loss.'

'You're worried about Alice—' I start to say.

'This isn't about me and Alice, this is about you,' St Nick says. 'I made a mistake. A big mistake. Tell me you didn't drink it?' He nods towards the empty bottle.

'No,' I say. I've failed him.

'Thank fuck for that,' he says. I hear Dottie Hope laughing but St Nick has more to say. 'Remember how I was never convinced about you being the first female Christmas angel?'

'And how I thought you were sexist,' I say. St Nick laughs.

'Oh, my defiant Theodora, I was almost right. You were never destined to be a Christmas angel. The message from Gabriel was all confused. It got all jumbled during its travel through the realms. Then I jumped to the wrong conclusions, and—' he says.

'Message. From Gabe,' I say. An echo while my brain catches up.

'Remember: "*Save Theo – Spitfire and Oral*",' he says and I nod. 'It was all jumbled. That was never his message,' St Nick says. 'It seems it was Dottie Smith who was always destined to be a Christmas angel.'

'Dottie Hope,' I say. 'How?'

I look at her and she gives me a double thumbs up.

'That's amazing,' I say. I mean it. The relief sweeps over me. I'm smiling. 'You're going to be the first ever female Christmas angel.'

'This is what I was born to do, Theo,' Dottie Hope says. 'The gift of giving and living my life with purpose. It's an honour to be chosen.'

'I've enlightened the higher powers,' St Nick says. 'They're still happy for you to work for them—'

'Do I have to be immortal?' I ask.

'No,' St Nick says. 'You just have to live the best life you can. Just keep being you, Theo.'

'Has Gabe stopped loving me?' I whisper.

'Never,' St Nick says.

'Who is she?' I whisper.

'Who?' St Nick says.

Dottie Hope steps forward and crouches down beside us. 'She's Bess, Gabriel's guardian in the other realm. She's been guiding him and looking after him,' she says.

'I thought he'd moved on,' I whisper.

'No offence to Bess…' She smiles. 'But she's old enough to be his grandma and very much married.'

'What do I do now?' I ask.

'You let Gabriel go. You live your life with purpose and gratitude,' Dottie Hope says. 'Live in the moment, Theo. Live the best life. Be the best you.'

'But Gabe—' I start to say.

'Wants you to live in this now. The future will unravel as it's supposed to unravel. Grab your life, Theo, grab it with both hands and be bloody brilliant,' Dottie Hope says.

'Learn from my mistakes, Theodora Quirke, don't endure life. Don't reject friendship and love out of fear of loss and pain,' St Nick says.

'But the message from Gabe?' I say. 'That was all for Dottie to be an angel?' I'm so confused.

St Nick shakes his head and hands me a piece of paper. 'Seems the letters were right but the words were wrong…'

~~SAVE THEO–SPITFIRE AND ORAL~~

THEODORA VISIT FRAN–PLEASE

I can't help but laugh.

'You fucking idiot,' I say, looking at St Nick. He shrugs his shoulders.

'I can't be held responsible for faulty communication,' he says. He shakes his fist at the ceiling. Fake fury.

'Thank fuck I didn't pursue "oral",' I say.

I can't help but be overwhelmed and confused, yet somehow I'm also the happiest I've been all year. I have hope,

I have purpose, I have a million questions to ask.

'Francesca's been looking for you,' St Nick says.

'Dottie Hope showed me a poster,' I say. I look over at the coffee table. It's still there. I'm crying again. 'Francesca didn't give up on me.'

'Promise me you'll call her,' St Nick says, and I nod. 'It's what Gabriel wants. He's been busting a gut to get the message to you. He loves you both so much. She's your family. You need each other,' he says.

He pulls me into him and I sob into his chest. This isn't from despair, it's a release of all that's bad, of all that won't ever be, yet suddenly my future offers so much more.

'I've missed Gabe every single day for twenty-two months,' I say.

'Who the fuck dies from sneezing?' St Nick says and I can't help but laugh.

'Are you going to leave me too?' I ask St Nick.

'Not until you're back with Francesca,' he says and I nod. 'But I'll visit and I'll never give up on you. I'm indebted to you, Theodora Quirke,' St Nick says.

'And I'm grateful for you both,' Dottie Hope says. She strokes my hair and hums the sweetest of tunes.

CHRISTMAS EVE

THEO (THEODORA QUIRKE)

I'm clutching a mug of hot chocolate – with cream and marshmallows threatening to melt down the mug – and the Christmas tree twinkles in the corner. It's decorated with multi-coloured tinsel and those scary Santa Claus face baubles from St Nick's flat. But I don't live there anymore.

It's dark outside. The curtains are closed. I'm wearing new pyjamas even though it's only four o'clock. They're fluffy, they're red, they've got smiling santas all over them. My feet are up on the coffee table; slipper socks with reindeers on them. Francesca's next to me. We match; her pyjamas and socks are the same as mine. My lovelock's lying on the coffee table next to our feet. It's the one that has GABE + THEO written on it in red sharpie. It's the one that was left next to Gabe when me and St Nick time travelled. My key to Francesca's house is attached to it. She was going to give me that key at Gabriel's funeral, but then everything got fucked up until Gabe (eventually) sorted us out.

How is it that something so complicated and impossible makes perfect sense?

Elf's on the TV. I'm warm, safe and loved. This is my home now. There's an open tub of Roses next to me. The purple hazelnut whirls are my favourite. I dip one of Sally's – my old neighbour from Dante House – cookies into the cream.

'I still can't believe that Sally remembered me,' I say. She called around yesterday with a Tupperware box of cinnamon cookies and to check I was really alive. We've even arranged to go for a drink next week.

'You're not that easy to forget,' Francesca says, mince pie crumbs escaping as she talks. She says it's the first mince pie she's eaten this season and there was a hefty dollop of brandy butter alongside it.

On top of the mantle there's a Yule candle that we'll burn tomorrow on Christmas Day. It'll burn all day, for the memory of Mum, of Gabriel and of Dottie Hope's loved ones too. I blow on my hot chocolate, budging the cream away from the liquid, before taking a sip.

There's one gift under the tree. It's from St Nick. It looks umbrella shaped. I keep looking at its red wrapping paper, covered in fat, smiling santas. His choice of wrap perfect. I gave him a new jumper last week. It had a huge Santa's arse heading down the chimney on the front. A Primark special and he loved it. He's different now. All of his anger has gone and I think it might be a reflection of the changes in our society too. Spitfire did that. Krampus' plan backfired big time.

On December 6th, there were photos of the coins and small gifts they discovered in their shoes posted all over social media. People were ecstatic. Christmas magic travelled through space and it was the most amazing thing to watch. #IbelieveinStNick trended, went viral, became the most requested tattoo during the following week. The greed and commercialism that so many had chased was pulled into a fuck off massive spotlight. It made people look at St Nicholas' story. Really look. Really take time to want to understand. There are already Facebook groups all over the world promising to celebrate St Nicholas Day next year. There's talk of parades, public holidays, street parties, and so much more.

Because, thanks to St Nick, people seem to want to become better versions of themselves. Since December 6th, people have been inspired to do good. A record smashing number of donations to foodbanks, countless reports of charitable acts, numerous stories about people volunteering or people inviting others into their lives and homes for Christmas. People are being kinder, strangers are hugging each other and communities, all over the UK, are opening their doors, are getting to know their neighbours, are talking to each other. St Nick did this. All of this. St Nick has moved and stirred and motivated us all to be better humans.

'Make a wish,' I say, as Francesca finishes her last mouthful of mince pie.

'A wish?' she replies.

I nod. 'Tradition,' I say.

She closes her eyes for a few seconds.

St Nick and Dottie Hope stayed with me for the days after St Nicholas Day. I talked and talked, they listened and never judged, and then they both held my hand as I made that call to Francesca.

She sobbed when she heard my voice. She made me promise not to hang up, as she collected her keys and ran for her car. She was terrified I'd disappear again. Kept me talking as she drove her battered Ford Fiesta into the city centre. Even parked on double yellows on Bold Street. She turned up at our flat with no shoes on, entirely out of breath and her mascara had streaked all down her cheeks. I've never felt as loved as I did when she held me, sobbing with joy.

She stayed in the flat with us, all day and that night, while we talked her through everything. I think, at first, she mainly said, 'Bullshit,' and her first instinct was definitely to punch St Nick in the face for keeping me hidden. Thankfully there was proof to show her. It's fair to say the story was a *little bit* farfetched without that proof.

But then she listened and she held my hand when I told her

about how I was after Gabriel died, about the séance and stuff, and then about wanting to live forever so I could forget him. I told her about the time travelling, about seeing Mum and little me, about that Christmas miracle of meeting Gabriel, and all about that green plastic dinosaur too. She laughed when I told her how we'd actually delivered the Christmas gifts and miracles.

'Only you would pick a dinosaur,' she said.

I could feel Gabriel watching and smiling. I just knew he was close. And he'd been right – I needed Francesca and she needed me. She listened, she accepted. I told her all about the Christmas angels on Earth. I explained how Dottie Hope was going to be the first ever female Christmas angel and all about her pure heart. Francesca was pretty excited about it all. I think it's given us both hope and focus. Knowing that Gabriel's safe, that he's surrounded by love and that he can watch if he wants to, well all of that helps too. We know that we're lucky to have been given permission to move forward in our lives. More than that really, as Gabe's pushed us back together.

Then, of course and because we couldn't help but interfere and it seems I'm now the person who wants everyone to have a happily ever after, we went into Bold Street Coffee with St Nick and his new face. Alice was working. The recognition was there again, but this time there was an instant attraction too. They exchanged numbers and St Nick's hanging around in Liverpool for now. The higher powers are even considering eventually altering a rule about St Nick's future wife – or is she a queen? – becoming an earthbound immortal too, but that's a long way off.

Krampus has gone into hiding. There are rumours that he's branching into Christmas miracles of his own, somewhere in Europe, but that's yet to be confirmed. The higher powers are monitoring the situation. Whatever the fuck that means.

And I've had a few emails off Elsie, the dinner lady from Preston. Seems she'd heard a noise in her house; was armed with a spray can of deodorant and ready to pounce when she saw me leaving. Then she'd found my note and her miracle. Couldn't get her head around it all. She thought I'd given her my own money and was worried sick about taking so much cash from someone who looked *'homeless and underfed'*. I had to email and explain how St Nick's Christmas miracles worked, and still she wanted to pay me back monthly. Seems she was oblivious to the Spitfire Saint Nicholas Umbrella Collective. I like her even more because she was.

Then Dottie Hope was fast-tracked through the Christmas angel process, what with her already having been part of delivering the Christmas miracles. She's set to become the first ever female Christmas angel in a couple of weeks and has already been measured for her wings. She's given me all of the money she earned from Spitfire. Every single penny of it. Of course I protested, but she insisted. It's being invested for my future.

And I start my new job next week. John Smith retired today and they wanted someone who had a knowledge of the Christmas World, but was impartial, to be head of the Christmas angels' trade union. St Nick and the higher powers decided that person would be me.

I've already had my induction and have met all of the Christmas angels now from all over the world; their identities no longer need to be protected from me. They're the best people. I'm also going to run a website all about St Nicholas Day. It's even going to be endorsed by the higher powers. Francesca's keen to help too. My work is all paid, but, thanks to Dottie Hope, I don't need the money. Francesca and me have been thinking about this a lot. We're going to set up a charity in Gabriel's honour, and all of my wages will go straight to his charity. Money doesn't bring happiness, but it can help with our quality of life and the quality of life of others too. That's what I've learned from Dottie Hope.

'Do you think Dottie Hope wants us to contact Jack Warner for her?' I ask. It's the only loose end left.

'He gave up on her,' Francesca says and I nod. I'll not contact him.

When I moved in here with Francesca, she sorted everything out in terms of legal matters and the fact that I'd been a missing person for a year. Of course there was press interest in me – I told the journalist from *The Sun* to fuck off. She printed a weird story about me claiming I'd been abducted by aliens, which was nice.

I exist again now though – on lots of levels. Francesca's my family. I'm her family. I read all of her blog, mainly in tears, and that showed me her deepest thoughts and worries. Stuff we'd never have said to each other. She wrote about not being able to describe how she felt when Gabriel died. She wrote that her language was insufficient. How no one was able to quieten her ache, and about how the condolences of strangers pissed her off. How some fuckers were even frightened that they'd catch her pain or that by showing empathy they'd somehow make bad things happen to their family too. She wrote about how she missed me. The one person who could understand.

I'm the daughter she always wanted. I was never 'just' Gabriel's girlfriend; I see that now. Gabriel connected us, and now me and his mum are the same but different. We always were family, but now that I've accepted that I deserve her love and that I want her love, well I've no desire to run or to hide. We have work to do together. Exciting work.

We don't really understand what happens after death, but I like that there's more than *just* this life. That's enough, for now. I take another sip of hot chocolate. It's sweet and it tastes of Christmas. Later, we'll attend midnight mass. It was Francesca's suggestion; I think both of our religious outlooks have widened over the last year and we both love Christmas carols. I'll be singing loudly; not caring that I'll be out of tune and not worrying if strangers laugh or judge me.

'What time are you getting up tomorrow?' Francesca asks and I must look confused. 'Christmas Day, to see if he's been,' she says. 'Gabriel always had me up at five.'

I can't help but laugh as I say, 'Can you imagine St Nick's face if, after all this, I told him I believed in Santa Claus?'

It's a struggle accepting that it's okay to have our own Christmas traditions, and that that doesn't mean we're rejecting St Nicholas in any way. Christmas is a national holiday, it's part of our culture and we're keen to enjoy the festivities, just without consumerism.

'I've got something for you,' Francesca says. She rummages behind the cushion.

'It's not Christmas yet,' I say.

'I wanted you to…' She pauses and I smile. 'It's not even for Christmas.'

She holds out her palm and on it rests a gift. It's a small, square box, the wrapping paper covered in robins and there's a red ribbon tied around it. It's familiar. I pull the ribbon apart, and gently undo the Sellotape that secures the robins in place. I open the box and stare at the silver name necklace.

'It's so beautiful,' I say.

This time there are two names that interrupt the chain. One will rest on my left collarbone, Theo, the other will rest on my right collarbone, Gabe. It's perfect. I run my fingers over the letters.

'John Smith emailed me earlier,' Francesca says. The change in topic makes me hold my breath.

'What did he say?' I ask. I exhale.

'That it's taken a couple of weeks, but the higher powers have finally forgiven him,' she says. 'And that I should be very proud of my son.' There's pride in her voice.

'I miss him still,' I whisper, but there are no tears and no snot to wipe away.

'Merry Christmas Eve,' Francesca says, as she places the necklace around my neck and connects it. I love her so much.

'The trifle should be set soon,' Francesca says. 'All ready for tomorrow. Plus there's stinky cheese, a variety of creams, turkey, pigs in blankets, sprouts...' She's tapping her fingers as she recites her list. Mainly the fridge smells of sherry. I think she used a litre bottle in one trifle.

'And the dining table looks awesome,' I say. I smile thinking about the tablecloth that's covered in Santa Claus faces, not forgetting the matching napkins, the Santa Claus shaped salt and pepper shakers and the wine glasses that have hand painted Santa Claus faces on them.

'And wait until he goes for a pee in the downstairs toilet and sees that Santa Claus toilet seat cover,' Francesca says and I laugh.

'I can't wait to see St Nick's face,' I say. 'Especially as he can't yet say anything in front of Alice.'

Tomorrow we're expecting St Nick, Alice and Dottie Hope for lunch. I'm hoping they'll stay the night. I want to celebrate the good things in life with good people around me. I'm desperate to play charades and hunt the thimble. Francesca laughed when I told her. She's bought Twister and Pie Face.

I know we'll play them all. I emailed John Smith to say he was welcome, but I received an email saying that he no longer worked for the trade union and that all further enquiries should be directed to Theo Quirke. To me! I take another sip of my hot chocolate and I watch Buddy the Elf's excitement at seeing Santa.

I smile, remembering when I first met St Nick. It's been quite a year.

'I believe in St Nicholas,' I say.

'And St Nick believes in you, Theo Quirke,' Francesca says. 'You're practically his Rudolph the Red-Nosed Fucking Reindeer.'

THANKING

So many supported me as I wrote this festive story, but none more than my daughter, Poppy, who is already wiser, more creative and kinder than I'll ever be. This book could only ever be dedicated to you, qalbi.

The Unwrapping of Theodora Quirke was written as I came to terms with personal grief and loss. I hate that Jaka isn't here to read this one. I can't imagine a day when I won't miss her laughter, wisdom and hearing her voice. Ramon – I love you so much; I'm forever thankful that we're family.

I am indebted to my publisher and friend, Clare Christian. Discovering me online back in 2006 and being the first person to ever truly listen to my story, your generous and continued belief in my writing (and in me) means everything.

I owe a huge thank you to the fabulously enthusiastic team at RedDoor Press – to Clare, Heather, Lizzie and Anna – who have all been so very supportive and wonderful. I'm beyond thrilled that I've been able to work with Clare and Heather again.

And here's a declaration of continued admiration and appreciation of Luke Cutforth; that we'll be eternally bonded by Arthur Braxton makes me so very happy. I'm delighted that you found your Delphina.

And all the thanks to St Nick, Kat Nokes, Lauren Black, Bernie Pardue, Keith Rice, Alex Brown, Anne Taft, Lynne Machray, Birgitte Calvert, Wendi Surtees-Smith, Sarah Maclennan, Cathy Cole, Robert Graham, Rachael Lucas, Keris Stainton, Amanda Brooke, Sarah Hughes, Paula Groves,

Richard Wells and Margaret Coombs, for your advice, encouragement, arse kicking, reassurance and friendship.

And, lastly, my heart and affection are forever with Gary, Jacob, Ben and Poppy. You accept my too frequent doubts and my countless fears, and love me despite them. Your support and love make everything better.

ABOUT THE AUTHOR

CAROLINE SMAILES worked as a lecturer for several years before turning her hand to fiction in 2005. *The Unwrapping of Theodora Quirke* is her seventh novel. She lives in Liverpool with her husband and their children. She can be found at:

www.carolinesmailes.co.uk
and
twitter.com/Caroline_S

#theodoraquirke

BY THE SAME AUTHOR

In Search of Adam
Black Boxes
Like Bees to Honey
99 Reasons Why
The Drowning of Arthur Braxton

As Caroline Wallace

The Finding of Martha Lost

With Nik Perring and Darren Craske

Freaks!

Find out more about RedDoor Press and sign up to our newsletter to hear about our **latest releases, author events,** exciting **competitions** and more at

reddoorpress.co.uk

YOU CAN ALSO FOLLOW US:

 @RedDoorBooks

 Facebook.com/RedDoorPress

 @RedDoorBooks